TWO IF BY SEA

To Sherry,
Best wishes +
Good health

TWO IF BY SEA

RICHARD MCCANN

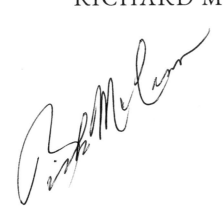

Commonwealth Books Inc.

A Commonwealth Publications Trade
TWO IF BY SEA
This edition published 2021
by Commonwealth Books
All rights reserved

Library of Congress Control Number: 2021947765

ISBN: 978-1-892986-33-7 (Trade)
ISBN: 978-1-892986-34-4 (E-PUB)

First Commonwealth Books Hardback Edition: September 2021
PUBLISHED BY COMMONWEALTH BOOKS, INC.,
www.commonwealthbooks@aol.com
www.commonwealthbooksinc.com

Manufactured in the United States of America

ACKNOWLEDGEMENTS

I could not have accomplished writing this book without much help and encouragement from many people, more than I can name here, who rescued me when I sought information about the various specialties and aspects of this book. I would be remiss if I named only one or two of those who helped me, so, you know who you are. Even if you gave me only a word I was searching for, your help was gratefully appreciated.

There are two very special people in my life. First is my wife, Peggy. Without her belief that I could accomplish this goal, it wouldn't have grown from a thought into a published work. Second is our good friend, Wendy, whose youthful exuberance for the book kept me focused on the ultimate goal.

A heartfelt thanks for all of you.

I would like to dedicate this book to all the men and women who have gone to sea, are at sea, or will go to sea to ensure the world is supplied with the goods that make life livable. Some went to sea and never returned. Others returned only to chance life and limb by leaving port to challenge the sea repeatedly. May merchant mariners be forever respected and honored for their dedication to duty and commitment to a way of life that so few can endure. May your seas be calm and your winds fair. Godspeed.

ABBREVIATIONS

AIS   Automatic Identification System

ASAP   As soon as possible

C&D   Canal Chesapeake and Delaware Canal

De'd   Pronounced Dead Reckoning, a projected course line on a chart without wind and current factored into the equation; a very basic form of navigation

DEA   Drug Enforcement Agency

DHS   Department of Homeland Security

EDT   Eastern Daylight Time

EOT   Engine Order Telegraph

ETA   Estimated Time of Arrival

F.V.   Fishing Vessel

FBI   Federal Bureau of Investigation

1. J. Joey James

Lic   Lamar in charge

M.V.   Motor Vessel

MO   Modus Operandi

PD   Police Department

Penn D.O.C. Pennsylvania Department of Corrections

PPC   Palm Petroleum Corporation

S.V.   Sailing Vessel

SAT   Scholastic Aptitude Test

SCUBA   Self-Contained Underwater Breathing Apparatus

SUNY   State University of New York

True (T)   True degrees in relation to True North

ULCC   Ultra Large Crude Carrier

VHF   Very High Frequency

PREFACE

August 7, 2002
Delaware Bay
Underway aboard the ferry *M.V. Twin Capes*

"Skipper, did you watch the terrorist attacks on 9/11, and was the ferry running or shut down, being that New York's right up the road?" Bubba, the helmsman, asked.

Bubba stood six-feet-eight-inches tall, a behemoth of a man who started working for the Cape May Lewes ferry in June, 2002. Before then he worked on tugboats and was on his way to Puerto Rico towing a container barge the day the world stopped. Out of TV range, they received information only secondhand, depending on the tug's satcom (satellite communication system), along with the chatter on the VHF radio from other ships and tugs in the area, for information regarding the attacks.

"Well, Bubba," Larry, the captain, replied, "I was on my way home from a little sleepover, if you know what I mean."

Bubba laughed. "I guess the swordsman stories I hear about you are true, eh?"

Captain Larry just smiled. "I wouldn't believe everything you hear, Bubba. I was all smiles heading home and listening to an oldies station on the radio when the announcer broke in to say, 'A plane just collided with the World Trade Center's Twin Towers.' That made me rush the rest of the way home to turn on the TV and see what was happening.

"I just made coffee and sat down to watch from my easy chair when I saw a plane enter the picture frame and smack right into the other tower. I knew it was a terrorist attack, but I couldn't believe it was for real. The announcers kept trying to downplay the fact that two large, modern jumbo jets didn't hit buildings within minutes of each other on a beautiful sunny day without it being on purpose.

"Rumors about hijackings and other planes headed for DC started airing on TV. The Pentagon was hit next, then we heard stories about passengers calling home to tell their loved ones they were on another hijacked plane. We heard about that one going down in Pennsylvania.

"Was that ever a screwed-up day. I didn't have a clue if we would continue to run or not, so I got ready at the normal time and came to work. By then, all flights were grounded, which was eerie. The sky overhead is always busy, with contrails during the day and flashing beacon lights at night. That afternoon, it felt as if the entire world stopped.

"We didn't carry much traffic, and there weren't any other ships or tugs out. The only thing moving on the way to Delaware was us, until I noticed a thirty-footer shadowing us across the bay. That was pretty spooky, and we didn't take our eyes off him.

"We were ready to call the Coast Guard if the boat came any closer than half a mile. We were on the way back home when a rubber dingy zoomed toward us and started playing chicken with us. I called Bridges, the cop, to go down on the fantail and stand guard. He later said all the passengers on the stern hollered for him to shoot them, like the crowds in the Bible hollered for Jesus to be sacrificed.

"I'm glad he didn't. We called the Coast Guard, and they caught the guys in the canal down by the West Cape May Bridge. They didn't know what happened that day. They borrowed their father's boat early that morning. They were in enough trouble without ol' Corporal 'Deadeye' Bridges blowing them out of the water with his nine mil.

"9/11 is a day I'll remember as being one of the most-bizarre days I ever had."

"Wow," Bubba said. "I'm glad I was out to sea, and all we got were bits and pieces. It got a little weird out there, too. After a while, the radios were quiet, and there wasn't anyone else on the radar. It seemed like we were the only ones left. I never want to feel that way again.

"We need a new Paul Revere to say, 'One if by land, two if by sea,' and now we need 'three if by air.' What's next? 'Four if by space?'"

"Yeah," Captain Larry said. "What's next?"

CHAPTER 1

The gentle breeze blew through the blonde tufts of neck hair that didn't quite reach the bun holding the rest of her long, blonde hair. At work, she always wore her hair in a tight bun, not only to allow her the freedom to do her job without interference but to make her look professional and efficient, something she worked very hard and tirelessly to convey, because her job wasn't one often held by women. It had to be done better than most of the men who held the same position just to ensure she was seen as being on par with her peers. She accomplished that, and, along the way, she earned from her bosses and the men and women working for her, past and present, their respect and admiration.

From day one, there were two distinct paths that led to advancement for women in her line of work, each well-worn by women who preceded her. Karen Ann Murphy chose the only path her very Roman Catholic conscience could consider—she studied, learned, and put into practice everything her chosen profession offered. She worked side-by-side with the people she led, and she always accepted sound advice when it was offered or when she asked, from the seasoned hands around her. That earned her their affection and respect.

Her hard work and study brought her to a very successful career. She soon reached the pinnacle of her chosen profession. Her United States Merchant Marine License read, *Master of Steam or Motor Vessels of Any Gross Tonnage on Any Waters.*

Her mind wasn't on her job at the moment. She watched one of the most-beautiful sunsets she ever saw on a job where she saw the

1

sun set almost every day unless the horizon was overcast, hiding the sun from view. The sky around that brilliant red ball held some of the deepest oranges that melded into the finest yellows until there was a hint of light green leading to the palest blue of clear sky, then on into the ever-deepening color in the east, where violets and deep purples met the beginning of the night sky's blackness.

Enjoying the cool breeze, she watched God wink at her as if saying good night, as Bo Arden, a grizzled and tattooed old salt once said when he worked for her when she was just a junior Third Mate. She couldn't help thinking she just witnessed the best sunset ever seen anywhere in the world, and she'd seen practically all of the world in her twenty-five years at sea.

Knowing she had the most-spectacular viewing platform for those fabulous sunsets made her smile even more. She stood on the bridge wing of one of the largest, most-sophisticated ships mankind ever put to sea. The funny thing was, the sunset that transfixed her happened where it all began, at least for her—right there on Delaware Bay.

Delaware Bay is a relatively small body of water separating the states of New Jersey and Delaware at the mouth of the Delaware River. General George Washington made that location famous by crossing it one cold winter morning with his troops to catch the British and Hessian troops off guard, turning a failing American Revolution from a rout to a victory.

The bay is the entry point for ships leaving the Atlantic Ocean heading to Philadelphia, Pennsylvania, Wilmington, Delaware, and even Baltimore, Maryland via the Chesapeake and Delaware (C&D) Canal. The bay is twenty-eight-miles wide at its widest and thirty miles long where it leads into the Delaware River.

In the little coastal community of North Cape May, New Jersey, Karen Ann, at the age of eleven, would go to the shore of the bay and walked the beach. She called those walks "parent breaks." Whenever her parents and she were at the point of getting on each other's nerves, she went to the beach to cool off and clear her mind. That was where she fell in love with the water and the ships she spied on the horizon, making their way up the bay to offload cargo at the wharves in the big cities. They then came back down the bay and headed into the Atlantic Ocean to unknown destinations, but she fantasized about them a lot during her parent breaks and at night when she fell asleep.

When she turned sixteen on April 1, 1976, she went to the Cape May Lewes ("Louis") Ferry to look for a job. It was a passenger and vehicle ferry operating out of the Cape May Canal, crossing the mouth of Delaware Bay to arrive in Lewes. That portion of the seaway connected U.S. Route 1 and U.S. Route 9. Route 1, with Follow the Gull as its moniker, was the original way for East Coasters to go to Florida from the northern states. It was a slow, scenic route for people who took as much fun and pleasure in the journey as in the destination, taking travelers through all the coastal cities and towns on the east coast. After the completion of I-95, Route 1 was all but forgotten.

Karen Ann found she could work only in the Steward Department, which was leased to an outside vendor, and she would be a glorified short-order cook and cashier. None of that mattered. She wanted to see the big ships up close, and her dream of working on one would finally come true.

She was given a letter of intent to hire to present to the U.S. Coast Guard Examination Center in Philadelphia and an application for her Seaman's Document. She would also need her parents' permission, because she was a minor. She knew she would get it, because she'd been hounding them for years, saying she wanted to work on the "big white ships," as she called them, even though they were only 320 feet long and weren't deep-sea vessels having a shallow draft of only seven feet.

Karen Ann didn't care. They would take her out to see the *really* big ships she watched from the beach during her parent breaks. She didn't know it at the time, but she was hooked, and the only way through her life would be going to sea.

While working weekends, holidays, and summers on the "boats," as the crews called them, she showed a genuine interest in the sea, the ships plying it, and everything about the men and women who sailed them. Even at the age of sixteen, she was more a woman than a child, and not just in her body but also in her mind.

She quickly learned how to deal with the opposite sex and their advances. Even though any sailor who crewed a boat she worked on would step in if she were hit on by a customer who refused to back off, Karen Ann was able to fend for herself and send him off. The crews, considering her a baby sister or daughter, refused to let anything happen to her. She didn't mind their over-protectiveness, because she understood they respected her for who she was and how she handled any situation that came her way.

She was five-feet-six-inches tall and weighed 105 pounds, making some think of her as a young Ann Margaret. The first crewman who told her that was a sixty-year-old crewman named Bob, someone she regarded as a grandfather figure. She didn't know who Ann Margaret was and stared in bewilderment.

Bob laughed. "You need to watch the old Elvis movie *Viva Las Vegas*. Then you'll know what I'm talking about."

Karen Ann Murphy was very pleasant on the eyes besides being a joy to have around and talk to. She wasn't like most of the other kids who were hired for the food concession and were there only for the money.

During breaks, Karen Ann hung out with the other crewmen and asked them everything she could think of about the maritime world. She was totally captivated by any story told by one of the "Old Salts," men at the twilight of their careers.

When high-school graduation loomed for Karen Ann, the crewmen started to ask her where she intended to go to college and what her major would be. To their dismay, she said, "I don't want to go to college. I want to work the ferry full-time and get on deck with you."

All replied she was being silly. She had to go to college to learn something constructive that would take her out of Cape May County and see the world. Working the ferry for a young person was a dead-end job. She had to make something of herself. Fighting back tears, she returned to work in the galley.

Though all were well-meaning, they unintentionally almost crushed her soul.

Then a twenty-six-year-old seaman named Larry "Bull" Halsey, who took his nickname from a famous admiral in World War Two, and who gave up going deep sea to raise a family, approached Karen Ann, as she gazed over the aft rail. She stared at the horizon, looking for the ships she dreamed of as a way to ease her troubled mind.

He came up quietly and startled her when he asked, "So, Karen Ann, what do your parents think about your plan not to attend college and just work at the ferry?"

Something broke inside, and she started crying. Sobbing, she threw her arms around him. "Nobody's on my side! They're all taking my parents' side in this. I thought they'd support me. I don't understand why everyone insists that college is so damn important. None of them have college educations, and they're doing OK for themselves."

She cried against his shoulder. "My parents demand I go to college and forget working on the water with all those seamen, as if that was a dirty word."

He patted her back and stroked her long, blonde hair. Eventually, her sobbing eased, and he said, "Look at me." He wanted to have her full attention when he spoke next.

"I have a proposition for you to think over if you really want to make working on the water your life."

Confused, she looked up at him, her eyes as trusting as those of a dog regarding its master, its head cocked to one side and one ear raised when it wasn't sure what command had been used and didn't know what to do.

"Larry," she said finally, "doesn't anyone listen? Of course that's what I want! I want to work on the water with you guys."

"I'm not talking about working just on the ferry. I'm talking about the possibility of working as a seaman on deep-sea ships, too."

"I'd love that, but I don't see how I could. My parents don't want me to work here, let alone out there." She pointed across the stern toward the Atlantic.

"I need a little time to gather some information about an idea I have," he replied. "Maybe, I can help you reach for your dream and make it come true. I'll get back to you as soon as I can."

She looked at him as if he were the Messiah, then she grabbed his face and said, "I love you, Larry!" She gave him a big kiss, much to the surprise and condemning looks from the passengers who were aft with them on the promenade deck.

"Whoa, there, Karen Ann." It took him a moment to get his lips apart from hers. She was surprisingly strong. "I haven't done anything yet. I don't know if you or your parents will like my proposal."

She jumped back in shock. "My parents?"

"Yes, your parents. I'll need to meet with them and you when I'm ready."

"Oh. All right." She spun and ran back to the galley to finish her shift, knowing Larry would make everything all right.

Later that week, Larry told her what she had to do for her part of the proposal, so her parents would consider letting her pursue a career at sea. She had to study for her SATs and make an appointment to take them.

"You need a good score to make sure all the avenues and options will be available to you."

She could hardly control herself. "I will! I will! You know I'm a good student and get good grades."

She reached up to kiss his cheek. "I'll do anything I can to keep working on the water, either here or out there." She pointed to the ocean, then went back to work.

One month later, Larry announced he had everything ready to meet her parents. The next day, Karen Ann got back to him.

"My parents said you can come over Tuesday night around seven," she said. "I have a date to take my SATs in two weeks from Saturday."

"Great. Keep studying hard, and things will work out for the best."

"You know, Mom and Dad have really eased up on me since I started studying so hard. I think I get what you're saying. I just hope they'll go for the idea."

"I can't promise that anything will change. All I can say is I'll try to get you and your parents to see things from a different perspective. Hopefully, everyone will win in the end."

The rest of the weekend, Monday, and Tuesday, dragged for Karen Ann. She couldn't concentrate on school. The only thing she thought about was Larry coming over on Tuesday night, hopefully bringing her salvation.

He arrived promptly at seven. A personable fellow, Larry quickly made her parents feel comfortable with him, creating a feeling of trust. Hopefully, that trust would soon be validated, and he would help them find a win-win situation.

He wanted them to understand that the classification of seaman was the same as that of accountant, construction worker, doctor, or scientist.

"There are good and bad people in all professions," he said, "except for maybe politicians, what with everything making the news in the last few years, like Watergate and stories about JFK and Marilyn Monroe coming out."

They shared a good laugh.

"Most seamen are good people trying to make a living like everyone else. Sure, there are heavy drinkers and carousers, but you have those in all the professions. It's just that you can't make exciting stories out of everyday folks who just want to make a living."

Once everyone felt more relaxed, he was ready to explain his proposal. With luck, it would offer Karen Ann and her parents what they both wanted, although each side would have to give a little to get a lot if it was going to work.

"I agree with your parents that it's important to have a college education in this world," he began. "Without one, it's almost impossible to get a well-paying job. I'm twenty-six with only a high-school education and a trade-school certificate. I have a new wife and a baby on the way, and I have to do manual labor onboard ship in an unlicensed position, trying to support my family on six dollars an hour. I constantly look for overtime to increase our standard of living, which almost defeats my purpose of not going to sea to stay back and help raise my family."

His approach to the topic made Karen Ann sink into her seat, shooting daggers at him with her eyes. Unfazed, he continued expounding the virtues and advantages of a college education and graduating with any kind of a degree, because it opened doors to a world that kept expanding and in need of more educated personnel in the workforce.

She was ready to assume Larry had betrayed her, especially when she saw her parents eating up his words.

"You see, Karen Ann?" her father asked. "Larry knows how the world works. Pretty soon, you'll need a college degree to dig ditches or pick produce on a farm."

"Oh, Daddy," she said, near tears, in her most-disgusted voice.

"That might be a bit extreme, Karen Ann," Larry said. "He's exaggerating to make a point."

Then he changed gears and laid out the brochures he received in the mail from all the Merchant Marine academies he could reach in the previous month. As he spread them out on the table for Mr. and Mrs. Murphy, he told Karen Ann to join them on the couch, so she could see them, too.

He had brochures from Kings Point, the U.S. Merchant Marine Academy; one from Fort Schuyler, the State University of New York (SUNY); and one from the Maine Maritime Academy, part of the University of Maine.

"There are more schools that offer the same programs," Larry explained, "like Massachusetts Maritime, the University of California Maritime, Texas A&M University, and Great Lakes Maritime."

The family was speechless.

"You see, Mr. and Mrs. Murphy, Karen Ann says she wants to go to sea, not to college. You demand she attend college and forget going to sea, which, at this point in her life, is what she believes she wants to do. What I offer you is a win-win situation for all. She can attend any of these schools and get a degree in any of these subjects."

He picked up a brochure and opened it to the degree programs. "She would graduate with a Third Mate's Unlimited Tonnage Oceans License or a Third Assistant Engineer Unlimited Horsepower License, depending on her choice of career path, assuming she passes the license testing. That would allow her to sail as an officer on ships, or she could use the degree to open other doors shore side and land a good job if she changes her mind about wanting to go to sea.

"All these schools have fine reputations and are well-respected for turning out well-rounded, disciplined, well-trained individuals. That's because they have a military-style boot camp atmosphere, which includes standing watches, doing drills, marching, and even inspections. The students have very little time to get into mischief."

"Well, now, Larry," her father said, "this is all fine and dandy, except aren't these schools strictly for men? If you haven't already noticed, Karen Ann's a girl, and we can't afford a high-priced lawyer to break the gender barrier like they've done at other schools. I won't subject my little girl to that kind of thing, anyway."

"Mr. Murphy," Larry replied, "all these schools were all male until recently. Women attend all of them now. Just to confirm that I'm not blind, I noticed your little girl has become an intelligent, young woman who's the spitting image of her beautiful mother."

Mrs. Murphy, blushing, thanked him.

"With that out of the way," Larry said, "I'd like to offer a compromise that I think you three could live with. First, Karen Ann, you promise your parents you'll go to college at whichever school you three agree on. You'll study hard to keep your grades up, so you can graduate with a degree all of you can be proud of.

"For you, Mr. and Mrs. Murphy, you need to assure her that when she graduates with her degree and license, you'll support her and not protest if she decides to go to sea, assuming she still wants to become a seaman.

"How about it? Is this something all three of you can be happy about and feel like you're all winners?"

Her parents looked at each other silently. Karen Ann stared at them, praying they would be OK with Larry's proposal.

Finally, Mr. Murphy broke the silence after one last look at his wife. "Well, we want her to attend college, and we know if we force her against her wishes, we're throwing good money away even if she graduates. If she's willing to persevere and do all the extra things these schools require, then I guess her mother and I can live with the idea she might really want to go to sea."

He looked at his wife again to see if she expressed an adverse reaction, while Karen Ann felt ready to explode. She jumped into her father's lap and took her mother's hand, saying, "Thank you, Mom and Dad! Thank you!"

They held each other tightly in a group hug. Karen Ann kept thanking them and saying how she loved them and would make them proud of her.

Once the family calmed down, Larry explained the details of how to apply for the three schools. When he finally stood to leave, it was well past ten o'clock.

The Murphy's escorted him to the door. Mr. Murphy shook Larry's hand and looked into his eyes. "How come you're so intelligent at such a young age, yet you never went to college yourself?"

Larry gave him a steady look. "I only knew about the military academies and Kings Point. I wanted to fly fighters for the Navy, but my eyesight wasn't good enough, so I was really disappointed.

"My grades weren't spectacular to begin with, and they fell off when the Navy turned me down as a pilot. That knocked me out of qualifying for Kings Point. I enlisted in the regular Navy and figured I'd do it the hard way.

"I found a niche where I was happy. I went into the submarine force and had some great times, but the Navy didn't have what I wanted out of life, so I decided to quit when my enlistment was over. Once I was discharged, I started sailing deep sea on merchant ships as an ordinary seaman. I didn't know anything about these other schools until I talked to the officers aboard ship. By then, it was too late for me.

"Finally, I met my wife and knew I wanted to watch my kids grow up, so I applied for a job with the ferry. At least I'd be home every night with my family. I've got a lot of 'I wish I knew that' in my life. I didn't want anyone else to have the same, trying to do things the hard way without knowing what was available."

Mr. Murphy glanced at his wife and daughter. "Larry, all I can say is thank you for your help with my family. Your family is lucky to have you and your wisdom to guide them through the world."

Karen Ann stepped forward to kiss Larry's cheek. "I'll never forget you or what you've done for me."

He looked at her and smiled. "Do the best you can, and be the best you can be no matter what you decide to do with life in the future. Just make sure you stay in school and get that piece of sheepskin. That's the key to opening whatever doors you choose later.

"Good night, now. The next time I see you, I expect a full report on your progress with all this, OK?"

He turned and walked toward his car.

CHAPTER 2

He stood on the dock, wondering how he got into this mess. It wasn't the money, as it usually was for a criminal. It was the ego-soaring feeling of outsmarting the opposition, though the money hadn't hurt, at least at first. Now it was building his offshore bank account.

The power he felt when he outsmarted the system was the drug he became addicted to, and he couldn't get enough. Power, control, and money were an aphrodisiac to him. The more he got, the more he wanted. First it was just grass, then coke and heroin. He always took bigger risks for bigger money and the feeling of being smarter than everyone else.

How could he complain? He was no longer a punk kid standing on a West Philadelphia street corner, dodging city cops to feed the junkies who wanted his goods.

Lamar Westin was a well-respected member of his little community on the Misipillion River in central Delaware. His brains were the reason he escaped the city without being carried out in a body bag or wearing a one-size-fits-all pair of silver bracelets and an orange jumpsuit with *Penn DOC* on the back, sharing a room with permanent blinds on the windows like 98% of the people he knew back on the Philly streets.

Lamar Weston, the successful financial advisor and local businessman to his Milford, Delaware, neighbors, wife of ten years, Wendy Lee, two kids, and the family's Sheltie Collie named Butch, was an upstanding and well-liked addition to the community. Where he grew up in the hood, all the brothers and his business contacts knew him as Lic, Lamar in Charge.

He received the moniker by always being the leader, even from his youngest days. He wasn't the biggest or toughest fighter. He used his phenomenal brain to get the others out of trouble and lead successful deals. Lic never carried or used a weapon, relying on his quick thinking and resourcefulness to carry him through every situation he encountered—until now.

Now he wasn't so sure. He wasn't in charge of anything anymore, least of all his life expectancy.

He always enjoyed studying history, especially the 20th century that explained how man got so cock-sure of himself as the ruler of earth without bothering to learn from history. Man created weapons of mass destruction strong enough to annihilate the entire population. The weapons were programmed to lift off and bombard an already-useless, uninhabited world.

He learned from his studies and didn't want to repeat history, using his knowledge the best he could when dealing with others. He created plans to use his knowledge to his best advantage.

His fabulously useful talent finally led him to standing on a dock, waiting to help an enemy use his own ideas against his own country, and he couldn't see any way out that would enable him and his family to keep on breathing. He wasn't in charge of this one. Somewhere, somehow, things were going terribly wrong.

He dealt with ruthless people before, but no one was as bad or controlling as Ali Mohammed Modula, not even the far-reaching, all-knowing Colombian cartel he dealt with for the past eleven years. Lamar had plenty of plans to escape the cartel if the situation ever went downhill, but it seemed even they feared Modula and his ability to inflict harsh revenge.

Modula could infiltrate any group he wished, and he did. The Colombians found that out too late, which was how Lamar found himself in his present situation. The cartel introduced Lic to Modula's men with the intention of having him pay off their debt to Modula.

It would end the cartel's most-successful drug-smuggling operation the world had ever seen, which would lead to regret from many drug addicts.

The smuggling operation was Lic's brainchild, and he ran it for the entire East Coast. The eventual disclosure of the operation would cost the cartel hundreds of millions of dollars and thousands of kilos of product when they were forced to return to their old smuggling methods.

Lic conceived of the operation's supply line while attending West Philadelphia High. He had trouble keeping his regular customers supplied, because the DEA and Customs were getting more vigilant at cracking down on drugs entering the country. He decided to devise a more-reliable transportation method of smuggling merchandise into the country.

It took time to gain the cartel's trust, but, by the time he finished college, they had faith in his operation. He attended Villanova on a full academic scholarship, so the money he made distributing drugs to his dealers in Philly helped his mom and little brother leave the city for a nice, not-too-flashy suburb, where Lic could keep his brother safe from the pitfalls of the gang life he hated that was so self-defeating for a Black man.

Lamar brought in more money than his mother needed, so he began his own business after graduating Summa Cum Laude with a Bachelor's in Business and Finance. His start in the business world was slow, but he soon gained a reputation that brought in highly placed, respected businesspeople with their portfolios to manage through the up-and-down maze of Wall Street.

He could have left the dangerous world of drug smuggling and distribution, but he couldn't bring himself to do it. He was addicted to the thrill of the danger, being a master of deception. Of course, there was always the money. He was as hooked on the money as a drug addict to his daily dose.

After ten years of keeping drugs flowing freely into the inner cities of the U.S., keeping his MBNA account respectfully full, his cover business solvent, and paying taxes on the money he earned legally, his life was suddenly turned upside-down.

His offshore accounts would soon reach ten figures if he could pull off this last operation and live long enough to share it with his family. The money was alluring, and the challenge of the operation was the driving force and aphrodisiac that made him a not-so-willing but trusted member of the endeavor.

For the first time in his life, Lamar was scared that if he failed, his family would suffer. They would be killed or maimed, or they would have to deal with the stigma of knowing their loving husband and father was a criminal and traitor to his country. The feeling of being a traitor nagged at his soul and affected his judgment. He couldn't brush off his feelings of guilt. No matter what, he was still an American.

His drug line worked flawlessly, and his greatest accomplishment would be used by some ragheads to fight a war. It wasn't even a real war in the honorable meaning of the word, if there was such a thing. It was a sneaky, subversive, cowardly type of war.

Damn, even the Japs were more honorable, he thought, *than what these monsters will be. When the Japs attacked Pearl Harbor in World War Two, at least they tried to send a Declaration of War before they bombed us.*

If he was to have any chance to live, he had to do his part in the operation, keeping it all in as sterile a view as he could while controlling his emotions. The conscience he never thought he had was stirring to life, which really bothered him.

Lamar, shaking his head, walked down the dock to the commercial charter fishing boat he owned and his very uncertain future.

CHAPTER 3

The Motor Vessel *Palm Princess* sat at anchor in the Big Stone Anchorage, an oil tanker lightering area. The large overdraft ships, which sat too deep in the water to sail up the relatively shallow river, stopped at the anchorage, and tugs brought empty oil barges alongside. The ships pumped off enough cargo to allow them to rise in the water and make the upriver transit safely without fear of running aground in their prescribed channel.

Most of the supertankers had to perform some kind of lightering operation to enter most of the harbors and rivers they used to deliver cargo. The MV *Palm Princess* was the newest and largest tanker in the Palm Petroleum Corporation's fleet of fifteen tankers. Her length overall (LOA) was 1,300 feet, and her beam was 300 feet wide. Her fully loaded draft reached 100 feet into the sea.

She was one of the biggest ships ever built to sail the high seas. The largest tanker ever built was the MV *Jahre Viking*, built in 1979, at a length of 1,503 feet and a beam of 226, holding 4.2 million barrels of oil. When fully loaded the MV *Palm Princess* carried four million barrels of oil, each barrel holding about thirty-seven U.S. gallons.

The MV *Jahre Viking* began a new classification of ships called ULCC, Ultra Large Crude Carrier, which the MV *Palm Princess* received when she was launched. When the *Palm Princess* sailed on her maiden voyage, the Palm Petroleum Corporation immediately retired five of their oldest and smallest tankers in their fleet, which made the Marine Department downsize and lay off several dozen seamen. That resulted in some very angry, very spiteful, very unemployed seamen.

Joey James was one of them. He also said he was the great-grandson of Frank James, Jesse James' brother from the old west outlaw gang, the James Gang. Joey always said Frank was the smarter of the two, because he wasn't shot in the back like his dumb-ass brother. So JJ, as his shipmates called him, always fancied himself as part outlaw and part superstar.

After the downsizing, JJ frequented the local sailor bars around Houston, Texas, the city where Palm Petroleum had its head-quarters. When the seamen were called in and given notice of the down-sizing and their severance pay, they also received a plane ticket home with a note that basically said, *Don't call us. We'll call you if we need your services again. Good-bye.*

Joey was in the Pilot House Bar, a seamen's hangout, spouting off about how bad PPC was to work for, and how they were the worst to be canned from. He vowed he would repay them someday for their high-and-mighty attitude and horrible treatment.

The regulars mostly ignored him. JJ was a common sight when he was in port, and they were somewhat grateful that PPC canned him. They hoped he would leave town and not bother them in their bar any more.

A man sat at the bar, sipping beer, listening to Joey ramble. Soon, Joey had to visit the restroom, much to the relief of the other patrons. Once Joey left, the man at the bar got up and followed him.

Inside the restroom, he checked to make sure he and Joey were alone, then approached Joey.

"Is what you're saying about PPC true?"

Joey looked at him. "If it isn't God's honest truth, then let the Big Guy come and strike me right here in the can."

"You really want to avenge your being fired? I can help you with that, if you aren't just blowing smoke up everyone's ass trying to look cool."

Joey regarded the man through blurred vision. "You give me the chance, and you'll see what kind of stock came from ol' Frank James' loins."

"Meet me across the street five minutes after I leave here. That is, if you're serious. Five minutes, and not a minute longer. Keep an eye on the clock. If you don't show up, this opportunity will be gone for good."

He walked out.

Joey splashed water on his face and looked at his reflection in the dirty, cracked mirror above the sink. He tried to comprehend what just happened and whether he should take up with the strange, slightly scary man.

He left the restroom and sat at the bar, a little subdued, which the other patrons were glad to see. He glanced once at the stranger sitting at the end of the bar, then at the ship's wheel clock over the bar. He wasn't sure if he heard the man right. It sounded like something from a movie script.

The man paid his tab and stood to go. Joey saw the clock read 8:10. At exactly 8:14, Joey paid his tab, and, much to the bartender's delight, left a hefty tip before walking out the door.

"See you later, JJ," the bartender called, as the door closed.

CHAPTER 4

Captain Karen Ann Murphy walked off the bridge wing into the bridge of the MV *Palm Princess* to meet the Watch officer and find out how the second lightering operation in the last four days was going.

The first lightering took place fifty miles off Cap May, New Jersey, in the open Atlantic. The massive operation took eight super-barges two days to raise her ship thirty feet in the water, which meant Karen Ann could then safely but gingerly sail into Delaware Bay with a seventy-foot draft to reach Big Stone Anchorage, then go through lightering again.

That time, it was much safer and a lot less stressful on everyone. The big ship was at anchor, and the barges nestled alongside in relatively calm water compared to being underway on the open ocean.

The Watch officer looked up, as Captain Murphy entered the chart room behind the bridge and knew what she wanted. Hoping to impress her that he was on the ball, he rattled off the necessary information.

"The *Princess* is two feet lighter, and we expect the next barge alongside in two hours to begin off-loading cargo to port."

With a barge on both sides of the *Princess,* and crude being pumped at the amazing rate of 70,000 gallons per hour, the *Princess* would rise to the draft the captain wanted, so she could proceed with her orders from the company.

"With this good weather and no hold-ups with the barges, I expect we're slightly ahead of our expected underway time."

"Very well, Mr. Simon. Remember we don't tolerate safety being compromised for expedience or showmanship."

"Aye, aye, Captain." He felt slightly deflated.

Karen Ann left the bridge and went below to her master's cabin to sleep and recharge. She would be up again in a few more hours to make her rounds and check on the ship and crew.

Lightering continued throughout the night and day in all but the most-inclement weather. Work onboard a ship never stopped. Men and women stood watch twenty-four hours a day, seven days a week.

Lamar saw the huge ship lit up like a small city from miles away. He saw it when he cleared Misipillion Inlet. He hadn't been on one of his runs in years. His hands were usually clean, or as clean as they could get in the illegal drug-import business, but not that night.

He wasn't just risking possible jail time. He could be shot as a traitor to his country in a time of war. Ever since 9/11, they'd been at war, and the government was ready to threaten, if not fulfill the threat, of any citizen who contemplated treason. The normal fate of a traitor during wartime was death from a firing squad.

When Lic informed his regular pickup men that the night's mission had some changes to the normal routine, they were very inquisitive, and he had to tell them he couldn't offer any details, although they were allowed to refuse the mission.

The boys, immediately nervous, both said, "Hell, no," to the mission.

"That's OK. That means our time together is over, and I appreciate what you've done for me and my business." He gave each of them $1,000 and added, "Forget you ever knew me and what we've been doing these past few years."

His instructions from his Bogota contact were to inform him if anything changed in the plan even in the slightest way. Lamar, as a very careful man, immediately called his contact and informed him that the two men quit, not realizing he just signed the death certificates of two of his closest childhood friends.

Two days later, the Delaware State Police found the bodies of two African-American males floating in the Chesapeake and Delaware Canal with gunshot wounds to the backs of their heads and their hands duct taped behind their backs. The State Police ran their prints through the system and had two positive hits belonging to Willie DeLong and Leroy Preston. Both rap sheets had the usual information that small-time city criminals possessed, including a few aliases and their arrest records for break-ins and assaults, with a smattering of drug charges. A note in each file indicated both men had disappeared from the local Philly Police Department for a while, but both were suspected of dealing drugs.

The investigating officers weren't surprised after reading the rap sheets. They gave each other a look of understanding, having worked together for many years. It was a dead-end case, but they had to go through the motions to satisfy the bigwigs. They knew that finding leads to solve the hit of small-time drug dealers was virtually impossible.

They'd been through it before. The case would go into the cold-case files until someone with a big mouth let slip something while trying to impress a girl or make himself look like a bigshot to another loser at a local bar. An informant would overhear the conversation and think he would make a quick buck selling it to the cops.

The detectives prepared for several boring days going through the motions until a more-pressing case was handed to them from their bosses.

That was how Lamar found himself as the delivery boy for the special package he had onboard the FV *Hammerhead*. He also received word from his Colombian contact that he would have to make all the other deliveries where he had companies up and down the East and Gulf Coasts. That was because they took care of his other employees like they did Willie and Leroy. They didn't want to risk someone talking before the operation was finished, and the monies were transferred into their Swiss bank accounts.

Lamar felt so many tangled emotions, he lost track and couldn't concentrate on anything longer than a few minutes. His wife saw something was bothering him, and he was more nervous than even the Colombians had made him. He hoped his wife of seven years wouldn't figure out what he was doing. He had a good cover story for his recent trips, but Wendy Lee Westin was no one's dummy.

They met in college. At first, she didn't want to have anything to do with a city boy who hadn't been anywhere or seen anything except the city and a college campus. Once Lamar set his mind to something, though, he usually won. He finally won over the sassy little Army brat, as he called her when she first rejected his advances.

He hoped he could keep the truth from her. She might not leave him if he was involved with illegal drugs, but her military upbringing wouldn't allow her to do anything but leave him if he was a traitor to their country. Her father, the General, would make sure he was shot.

"God help me," Lamar whispered, as the small shark fishing charter boat headed out to the Big Stone Anchorage.

Lamar invented and brought to fruition the most-daring, successful, and profitable drug-smuggling operation the Bogota cartel or anyone else ever attempted. It was almost too simple, which was why the cartel rejected his idea initially.

The cartel moved a large shipment of drugs throughout South America with impunity due to their bought-and-bribed government officials, border guards, and police. The shipment went from Colombia to Caracas, Venezuela, the oil export port, where large tankers loaded up with Venezuelan light crude oil and brought it to the oil refineries in the Gulf of Mexico or up the East Coast of the U.S. to ports like Philadelphia, Norfolk, and Wilmington.

There were also clean oil ships, carrying refined oil products, and barges carrying gasoline and heating oil to other ports for distribution to various companies that sold them, in turn, to smaller companies until they reached individual users.

Lamar figured that since smuggling drugs into the country and distributing product to major cities was the riskiest and costliest part of the operation, he would have someone else do it for him who already had a functioning distribution system, with an invisible, regular, dependable schedule but who wasn't on the payroll. It would be the safest, most-profitable delivery system ever attempted. His stroke of genius was what he called his "limpet mine."

He created a waterproof container with powerful magnets that could be attached to the hull of the ship in Venezuela. Other divers would remove it at the destination port in the U.S. Once there, the goods would be divided and placed in new containers on the clean oil ships and barges that kept the drugs moving to their final cities without ever coming near a major highway. That meant an ignorant mule would never be stopped for speeding, and the cops would never uncover the drugs, meaning a lost shipment and profits.

He got the idea after watching old movies on the History Channel about World War Two and how British frogmen went on secret missions to plant magnetic mines on certain enemy ships that would either blow them up in port or later when they were at sea at a specific location or time. The hardest part was devising a magnet that could hold to the ship while it was underway and in stormy conditions but still be easy to release by the retrieval crew in the U.S.

He spent two years developing his final functioning magnet and container, which could hold 1,000 kilos of drugs in transit through any kind of weather against a ship's hull. It was an ingenious work of art and mechanical simplicity.

The container was shaped like an Italian loaf of bread cut in half, with the flat side against the hull. The flat side held the magnet, while the rounded, slender body was the case for the drugs. He studied ship stability to decide how much weight he could safely place on the hull without making the ship show any sign of list, which would trigger an alarm to the crew or the ship's computers that assisted in loading and off-loading cargo.

He couldn't depend on exact placement on the hull, so the load had to be small enough that placement could be compensated for without suspicion. Those were minor concerns. The retrieval of his limpet mine was the hard part, and his solution was equally remarkable.

The magnet had to be strong enough to hold onto the hull without being too strong for a diver to pull off. Lamar's solution was to attach several magnets together to form one large, powerful magnet that would do the job. When the diver came to retrieve the container, he used a nonmagnetic wrench to release each magnet, then he carried the entire container to shore and prepared to install it on another ship. The pods were used in both directions, bringing drugs into the country and sending money out. The Cartel was very pleased with his innovation.

The final part of the operation required setting up several small charter fishing companies in each port city or anchorage area. Each business was handled by two trusted employees Lamar recruited from his gang and college days of supplying campuses with drugs for the students. The operations were designed to blend into the local area to avoid calling attention to themselves, and they had to show a profit, so the IRS wouldn't come snooping around. The first company he set up was the shark-fishing charter boat out of the Misipillion River.

That was a natural choice, because Delaware Bay was one of the biggest shark nurseries on the East Coast. Every few months, he set up another cover company in another city where the Colombians had a street network in place to handle a large, steady influx of drugs. All the boats had hidden diver-accessible compartments, called "moon pools," to allow divers to enter the water unseen by even the most-curious observer.

Lamar made sure his employees were trained as expert scuba divers to avoid any accidents that might require a government investigation. The U.S. government even helped pay for the training and original equipment purchase through the Small Business and Minority Program. His operation was a complete success, and the Cartel raised his income several times, as it was being set up.

It came as a complete surprise when the Cartel notified him that the operation would be shut down. They couldn't say if or when it might reopen. What really shocked him was when he was told to undertake a new operation, and he had no choice. If he didn't cooperate, he would be eliminated.

Lamar knew that meant his death, not just having someone replace him as the head of the stateside operation. The only thing that eased his fear was the knowledge that the income he would receive from that one mission would allow him to retire anywhere in the world and be able to buy anything he or his family might need. The Cartel mentioned the first names of all his family members, although he never told them he even had a family. He recognized a warning when he heard one.

His suspicions were confirmed when he asked, "What will become of our local distributors and their clients?"

"Fuck the distributors and their clients. They can fight for what's left on the street and kill each other for all we care."

Lamar thought long and hard about the cover story he needed to tell the only woman he ever loved. Wendy was the only person he would even consider going straight for and give up the rush he felt knowing his operation was successful. He felt like a kid who was never caught dipping into the candy jar.

Wendy was five-feet-four-inches tall with wavy brown hair, cocoa-colored skin with a creamy feel, cow-brown eyes, and the prettiest lips he ever saw. Her firm, full, A-cup breasts that she called, "Perky if not large," gave her a shape most women her age only dreamed about, especially after having two kids and living the life Lamar provided for her. She was his refuge when life took a toll on him.

He always kept his illegal income separate from his business interests. He funneled his drug profits through dummy businesses to a very secure, numbered account in Grand Cayman. Wendy didn't know she was part of the 15% most-wealthy people in America.

Soon, if he pulled off the operation, and the Cartel came through with their promises, they would be in the top 5% of the richest people in America, although he doubted they could keep living in the country. Wendy's good life came from Lamar's career as a financial advisor. He had a knack for handling money and making it grow for his clients and himself, but that rush wasn't enough no matter how good he was. His reputation as a whiz kid was well-earned. He could make money when few others could, which made it easy to keep Wendy in the good life she deserved and in the dark about his clandestine actions.

The MV *Palm Princess* grew larger, and the night grew a little chillier, as Lamar stood at the helm of the FV *Hammerhead,* trying to concentrate on the business at hand.

CHAPTER 5

Joey James, walking across the street, caught up to the stranger from the bar. "Buddy, you'd better not be one of those bastards at PPC."

The stranger turned and put a .38 revolved in Joey's face. "Do I look like I'm from the PPC?"

"Whoa, now. Hold on there. I just wanted to make sure. That's all, Man."

The stranger led him to a parked car around the corner and told him to get in and wait. Soon, the door opened, and a Hispanic-looking man sat beside JJ.

"I hear you want to get back at the PPC."

"Yeah, that's right. Who are you, and why do you care?"

The man slid closer and said quietly, "You need to be more respectful and not be so inquisitive, Young Man." He put an arm around Joey's shoulder and let a switchblade snap open beside his throat.

The swiftness of the move caught Joey's attention. He stammered, "Don't hurt me."

"I just want you to know I don't accept insolence and disrespect from my employees." He had a slight but noticeable Spanish accent.

Releasing Joey he slid back across the seat. "Let's get down to business. First, my name doesn't matter. All I want from you is information. For this, I will pay handsomely."

It sounded like an easy way to make a buck and get back at the PPC simultaneously, so Joey nodded.

"I need information about their ships, their future schedule, and any change in that schedule. Can you provide me with that information?"

"Sure. I still have connections on the inside."

"Fine, fine. When you provide me with that information, you'll receive four times this amount for your troubles." Handing Joey a sealed envelope, he gave him his final instructions.

When Joey got out of the car, the first of the strangers got behind the wheel and drove away.

The shock of the strange encounter left him completely sober. Touching the envelope in his breast pocket, he slowly walked to the rundown rooming house he registered in when he arrived in Houston to receive his separation notice.

He walked into his room and sat at his battered desk, turning on the table lamp. As he reached for the envelope, his hand shook. He didn't know what the information would be used for, and his Southern Baptist upbringing tried to wake up his conscience, but he fought that off with thoughts of how PPC handled his discharge.

Joey opened the envelope and stared at fifty $100 bills. His mind raced, wondering what his relatively minor information could be used for and why it would be so valuable to the Hispanic man.

He counted the money repeatedly, then he realized the man promised him four times that amount when he delivered the necessary information. He couldn't believe someone would pay him $20,000 for not doing squat but handing over some schedules and probably not much else. PPC was a well-oiled machine that rarely faced an emergency schedule change.

Joey's heart raced. *Wow. Twenty-five Gs. That's half my yearly salary, and it's tax free. I better not fuck this up. I can't lose out on a gig this easy. I always knew I was special.*

He couldn't sleep that night, thinking about the change in his fortune and how the guys hiring him had to be idiots. Most of what they wanted could be easily found on the PPC website, and whatever wasn't listed probably didn't matter. How could such information be so valuable?

Finally, he slept with dollar signs dancing in his head and a fool-proof plan that couldn't fail.

The following morning, he still couldn't believe his good fortune. He dressed for success—at least in his own eyes—and walked out of his room. As he reached the street, he patted the prepaid disposable cell phone in his pants pocket the man gave him, saying he could use the programmed number only to give reports to anyone who answered.

Twenty grand for a couple phone calls? he wondered. *What could be easier?*

He walked toward PPC's headquarters and the little redhead he'd been flirting with in dispatch the last few times he was in port before the downsizing. She was his ticket to easy money. No chick could resist his charm when he turned it on.

He reached the skyscraper that was PPC's headquarters, where the company occupied the top four floors. Looking up at the building, he laughed softly. *Who has the last laugh now, Suckers?* he wondered.

He found Linda, his redheaded connection, in her cubical on the 58th floor of the sixty-story office building called the Palm Tower. He thought it was pretty pretentious of the company to place itself in the same league as the Twin Towers of the World Trade Center. They deserved whatever the Hispanic man did with the information he wanted.

"Hi, Linda. Remember me? JJ at your service."

"Of course I do. Don't be silly, Joey. They only laid you off a couple weeks ago. I'm surprised to see you. I thought you'd go home to Missouri."

"Babe, I couldn't leave without seeing you and saying goodbye, could I?"

She blushed, "Why, Sugar," she said in her sexiest Southern drawl, "I thought you'd want to be as far away as you could. I heard how you took getting laid off and all."

JJ tried to match her drawl with his reply. "Come on now. Y'all know I'm pretty sweet on you. How could I leave when I have all this free time, and we ain't even been on a date?"

They shared a laugh so loud that her coworkers came over to ask what was so damn funny.

JJ grabbed Linda's hand and said, "It's coffee break time." The two of them walked down the corridor.

Two weeks later, JJ made his last phone call to the preprogrammed number in the disposable phone. His final piece of information was that the *Palm Princess* was headed to Venezuela for a load of crude. The man told him his services were no longer needed.

"Be at the same bar where you were first contacted for the final payment tonight at nine o'clock sharp. Don't be late."

Joey arrived early and took a ribbing from the regulars. They usually expected to see him every day. When he didn't show up, they assumed he'd gone back home after being humiliated by PPC.

He smiled and ordered a beer. *Suckers,* he thought. "Well, Guys, I'm going home soon but not with my tail between my legs. I've been busy. The way I see it, I gave back to them what they did to me. I'm going home with my head high. Great-grandad Frank James would be proud of his bloodline. The James Gang rides again."

The clock above the bar showed it was nine o'clock. *I'm here,* he thought. *Where are they?*

He glanced down the bar and saw the man who first approached him. The man flashed a "let's go" sign and walked toward the door.

JJ got up, said good-bye, and followed the man out. The same car sat across the street and down the block. Joey walked toward it.

"Good work," the Hispanic man said, as Joey got into the car. "Let me have the cell phone."

JJ handed it over and asked, "Where's my money?"

A silenced gunshot to the head prevented him from complaining.

"Get him out of here and have my car cleaned," the Hispanic man told his driver, as he got out to wait for a second car that pulled up.

Two days later, Joey James' body was found floating in Galveston Bay.

CHAPTER 6

It was a warm, humid August morning on the Delaware River waterfront at the PPC Delaware City Refinery, one of two PPC had on the Delaware River. Although it was only nine o'clock, Captain Murphy felt the heat and yearned for the air-conditioned comfort of the bridge on the *Palm Princess*. She had to finish the rounds of her ship she always completed before departure. She trusted her well-trained officers and crew, but it gave her a sense of inner peace to make the final inspection round herself while allowing her to see some of the crew she normally didn't meet for days at a time, like the engineers and most of the stewards.

Karen Ann made it a point to know the names of all her crew, male or female. The Maritime industry didn't bother with politically correct language most other lines of work adopted recently. She felt honored to be a crewman, because the term had a long history and tradition that couldn't be dishonored by changing a title whenever someone complained.

For almost as long as men went to sea, women went, too, although not as many. One of the most-famous female captains of all time was Ann Bonney, a pirate who sailed the Caribbean in the 1700s, along with another pirate named Mary Read. In World War Two, a Soviet woman captain, along with other women from her country, sailed the Murmansk convoy runs and helped their country survive by bringing in supplies to fight the Nazis.

Karen Ann felt a sense of pride at being called a crewman or seaman, and she passed that pride along to any woman who mentioned that the Maritime world needed to catch up to modern language.

All seemed shipshape and ready for sea, as she exited the elevator and walked to the bridge to make final preparation for departure to Venezuela for another load of crude to fill the empty tanks. However, the ship wasn't as empty as she thought. Aside from the ballast water they brought on to help stabilize the ship at sea, she carried something very sinister and destructive attached to the hull, courtesy of Lamar Weston.

Lic placed the package he picked up at one of his drug drop-off points and followed the instructions not to open it or look into it, although it seemed extraordinarily heavy. He placed it in his limpet mine canister three days earlier.

As he swam under the big ship, he sadly made peace with the thought that his greatest underworld accomplishment was ending. He returned home and delivered the bad news to Wendy that he had to make a business trip, and he would miss their little girl's first swim meet. He had to finish all the last jobs himself and put his businesses up for sale. The operation would be totally shut down soon. He knew his former employees came to the same end as Willie and Leroy, but he couldn't protest and show that he cared without putting his family even more at risk than they were.

Wendy, upset that Lamar would miss the swim meet, argued with him to postpone his trip. They had their first fight in three years. Lamar left with his clothes packed into a duffle bag, announcing he would sleep at the office and would leave on his trip the following morning. He promised to be back in three days.

Wendy fumed after he walked out without saying good-bye to the kids, then she cried herself to sleep. Lamar realized he hurt the only adult other than his mother and brother who he truly loved, but he had his orders, and he had to carry them out to the letter. It was his only hope of keeping his family alive.

The following morning, Lamar drove to the airport and his Piper Saratoga, a six-passenger, retractable landing gear, single-engine, private plane he used to fly to his job sites and stay as far under the radar of the authorities as possible.

He touched down at Norfolk, Virginia, and accomplished his mission. Upon returning to the dock, he informed the marina attendant he needed the boat hauled from the water and offered for sale. His company would not be renewing its contract.

"Why?" the attendant asked. "I haven't seen Byron and the other guy around for a while, either. I need to tell my boss about this."

"They moved on to greener pastures," Lamar said. "The company's fallen on hard times, and the bosses need to cut their losses. I'm just doing my job."

"Sorry to hear that. I'll get this taken care of for you."

"Deduct any outstanding debt and broker commission from the sale of the boat and mail the remainder to the address on the contract."

Lamar called a cab and rode to the airport, thinking about Byron and James and hoping someday their bodies would be found so they could have a proper burial.

He flew next to Charleston, South Carolina, and spent the night there before going through the same scenario. He repeated the process in Miami, New Orleans, and Houston before returning home to beg Wendy's forgiveness.

He finally left Houston and flew all night to get home, although he knew it wasn't safe to fly right after a dive. He didn't care if he got the bends and crashed the plane. He just wanted to be home and see the faces he loved. For the first leg of his flight, he stayed under 3,000 feet to reduce any chance of getting the bends brought on by the lower air pressure if he flew any higher.

He drove up his driveway and turned off the car, as Sally, followed by Lamar, Junior, ran out to greet him.

"Look what I won, Daddy!" she shouted, holding up a bronze third-place medal.

He opened the car door, and the kids piled on him to kiss him hello. He hugged them tightly and cried.

Captain Murphy welcomed two river pilots aboard. A ship that size always required two first-class pilots for transit up or down the river. Suddenly the radio operator approached with a dispatch he received from the company home office in Houston.

She accepted the dispatch and continued welcoming the two pilots aboard, exchanging vital statistics about the ship and ensuring their information about the ship was accurate.

After the preliminaries, she turned the con over to the docking pilot, who undocked the ship under its own power, with an assist from several tugboats to move the huge vessel away from the pier and headed downriver. Once the docking pilot finished the undocking evolution, he turned the ship over to the lead river pilot and went to the main deck to leave the ship via the pilot ladder to a waiting launch that would ferry him back to shore.

The river pilot guided the ship downriver, giving all navigational commands, although he wasn't the final authority even though his presence was required by law. The Master of the vessel was the responsible person onboard if anything happened to the ship or if damage was left in its wake.

Captain Murphy was comfortable with both river pilots, because they were two of the most-senior pilots in the Delaware River Pilots Association. Don and Bill Sounder, who she met years earlier, were brothers with parallel careers. She remembered when she'd been a third mate in charge of the boarding ladder crew to bring them on and off the ship.

There was one other connection between them. They were from the Cape May area, just like she was, and they talked about growing up there in the low-stress area of the transit up or down the river. Very few such pilots came from New Jersey. Even though New Jersey and Delaware shared the bay and the river, the Delaware boys kept a strong hold on the organization, saying, "After all, it's the Delaware Bay and River."

With the Sounder brothers aboard, she allowed herself the liberty of going to the chart room, located just aft of the wheelhouse but still part of the bridge deck, to read the dispatch she just received. It was a normal weather dispatch, although it contained something she would have to watch later in the week during her run down to Venezuela.

The ship glided past Brandywine Lighthouse at eighteen knots. The pilot called the engine room to alert them they would reduce speed soon. Karen Ann sat in her captain's chair on the starboard side of the wheelhouse behind one of the ship's radar units, which scanned twelve nautical miles ahead, and looked at the Cape of New Jersey, her childhood home, when she saw a blip on the radar screen that she instinctively recognized without having to look out the windows.

It was one of the ferries she worked on as a teenager. She allowed herself a moment of reflection about those good days and realized that most, if not all, of the people she once knew were retired or had passed on to the Big Fleet in the Sky. Sadness washed over her for a moment.

A voice called, sounding very real. With a small shake of her head, she realized the pilot had called the ferry to exchange crossing signals, a way to inform the other pilot what their ship was planning to do and how to stay out of each other's way.

To her surprise, she heard Larry's voice reply.

He's the one to whom I owe my entire career, she thought. *I wonder if he's still as cute as he was.*

She had a big crush on him as a teenager, which explained why she didn't accept dates from boys her own age. None of them compared to Larry. That secret she kept close and never told anyone, not even her most-trusted girlfriends.

She walked over to the pilot handling the radio communication with the ferry. When he finished, she asked, "Do I have time to call the ferry and go to a working channel?"

Captain Murphy spoke in her most-professional voice, and Larry replied with a slight change in tone as if asking, *What do you want now? We just finished exchanging signals.*

She smiled. He clearly didn't remember her voice. "Is this the captain speaking?"

"Affirmative. What can I do for you?"

"This is the captain of the MV *Palm Princess,* and I request you switch over to answer on one of your working frequencies. Please advise what channel."

He told her, then he changed channels to match. "*Palm Princess,* I'm standing by."

"Larry, is that really you?" she asked in an excited voice.

He was puzzled. The voice was definitely familiar, but he couldn't recall the name. "You have me. I know that voice, but who's attached to it?"

"Larry, don't you remember me? Think Ann Margaret."

That knocked the cobwebs from his mind and brought back a flood of good memories. "Don't tell me that's our galley girl Karen Ann, all grown up and playing in the big leagues?"

"It sure is. The one and only at your service, Larry, but I can't talk much longer. We have to drop off these pilots soon."

"I understand. I'll be busy shortly, too, but if you have a pencil and paper handy, I'll give you my cell number. If you get some time after you get that big girl on course and before you're out of cell range, give me a call. I'd love to talk some more."

After Larry gave her his number, he ended the communication and immediately faced questions from the others on the ferry bridge. There were plenty of questions about Ann Margaret and some snide remarks about Larry's secret life, with plenty of swordsman comments being bantered about.

"Just mind your own business," Larry said, "before I send you down to clean the bilges."

They laughed.

The bridge of the *Palm Princess* was more formal. The mate on watch and the helmsman shrugged at each other. They just witnessed a side of the captain they hadn't seen before.

Captain Murphy got the ship on course after clearing the entrance buoys. She turned the watch and con over to the mate on duty and reminded him of her standing night orders, then returned to her cabin with her cell phone and the scrap of paper she wrote Larry's number on. A whimsical grin came to her lips.

The mate looked at the helmsman. "What do you think? Who's this Larry?"

"Got me, Mr. Mate. A blast from the past, I'd have to say."

Karen Ann began dialing before she closed her cabin door. Larry answered immediately with a hearty hello. She asked questions about various crewmen she knew. Joe retired to Florida, while Bob was doing OK for a man eighty-five who had two ministrokes.

"How are your wife and kids?" she asked finally.

"Well," he said slowly, "Patty left with another guy fifteen years ago. I raised the kids until they went to college, and now it's just me and the dog."

"So no lucky lady has snapped you up yet?"

"Ah, come on, Captain Murphy. I thought this was a friendly call." He laughed.

They talked a little longer, then, as Larry was ending the call, he said, "Keep an eye on Peggy."

"Who?"

"Peggy the Hurricane. It just went from a tropical depression to a hurricane in five hours, and your course takes you right for it. It looks like it'll be a big girl."

"Oh, that's right. I got a notice this morning when we left the dock. Thanks for thinking of me. Next time I'm in port, I'll call. Let's try to get together for coffee or something."

CHAPTER 7

Delaware State Police Detective Warren Sharper and his partner, Detective Gavin Hobnobski, were busy with a case when they were called and told to return to the station.

"Don't they know we're busy?" Sharper asked, as he pulled around the corner to the trooper station.

"Yeah. You think they'd have more respect for us when they know it's lunchtime and how grumpy you get when you don't eat on time."

Inside the building, they were told to see the captain.

"He's got some Feds with him," the desk sergeant added.

"The Feds?" Hobnobski asked. "We haven't stepped on their toes in a while. What could they possibly want with us?"

They knocked on the captain's door and walked in.

"You wanted to see us, Captain?" Sharper asked.

"Not me," the captain replied. "This special agent from the FBI is here on Department of Homeland Security business, and he thinks you can help him."

Introductions were made, and Special Agent Max Gordon got down to business.

"I'd like to know what you can tell me about Willie De Long and Leroy Preston," Gordon said.

"Willie and Leroy?" Sharper laughed. "You think those two were involved in a national-security issue?"

"They were just small-time drug dealers who screwed with the wrong supplier and paid the price for doing bad business," Hobnobski added.

"We have some intel that says the Colombian Cartel has been approached by Al Qaeda. When you entered the killer's MO into the national database, it came up as Colombia Cartel except for a little detail that made it to our hot list watch and gave us a red flag."

"OK," Sharper said. "What was that detail? We probably screwed up when we entered it into the database and wasted your time. Those two couldn't be involved in anything like what you're after."

"You said their eyelids were superglued open. Is that correct?"

The two detectives looked at each other.

"Yeah," Sharper said slowly. "That did strike us as a bit weird for a bad drug deal killing."

"I need everything you've got on those two losers."

They took Agent Gordon to their desks and brought up the files.

"Here you go," Sharper said. "This is everything we have on those two. We even had Philly PD send everything they had to us, thinking it might shake something loose, but we didn't get anywhere and ran into dead ends. They fell off the radar about seven years ago."

"We don't have a current address for either of them," Hobnobski added. "The last address we had is seven years old, and when we checked it out, the building was torn down two years ago. It's a vacant lot now."

Gordon flipped through the files, listening to what the two men said. "Detective, who's this Lic guy? He keeps popping up in the files."

"He was their gang leader back in Philly," Sharper explained. "He fell out of sight even before they did. He must've been one lucky guy. He was never arrested, let alone had anything pinned on him or his gang. He disappeared, and the gang went bust. They all started going down."

"Yeah," Hobnobski said. "We couldn't even come up with a last name or a set of prints for that guy. They knew he was dirty as hell, but they couldn't ever prove it. They didn't even have a good enough reason to pick him up."

Agent Gordon looked up from the file. "I think this Lic character is the key. He disappeared first, then three years later, these guys fell off the map. It sounds like Lic set up something and recruited from his old gang to handle the grunt work in the new operation, whatever it was. Now these two are dead.

"Find Lic, and we find the connection. Sounds like a good place to start, don't you think? Thanks, Detectives."

He was halfway to the door to the squad room when Sharper asked, "Special Agent Gordon, if you find anything, can you keep us in the loop?"

He stopped and turned. "This will probably be a need-to-know case, but if I can let you in on anything, I will. Thanks again."

He walked through the door and vanished.

Sharper punched his partner's arm.

"What the hell was that for?" Hobnobski complained, rubbing his arm.

"That's for not picking up on that Lic thing. It could've been our break into the big leagues. I'm hungry. Let's get out of here." Sharper turned to leave.

CHAPTER 8

Karen Ann was just drifting off the sleep, thinking of more innocent days and secret loves, when her sound-powered phone to the bridge rang.

"Captain," she said promptly.

"Captain, this is the bridge. We just received a telex from Houston I thought you might like to be aware of before your next walk-around."

"OK, Mr. Hanratty. Go ahead and read it to me. I was just getting into bed."

"It says, 'Hurricane Peggy has intensified to a Category-Three hurricane and has increased its forward speed to eighteen knots. It's expected to cross your track in two days. Have ship's crew make all preparations for heavy weather ASAP.'

"It also gives coordinates, Captain, which I plotted on our hurricane plotting sheet."

"Very well. Pass the word to the chief mate, the bos'n, and the chief engineer to start preparing for heavy weather, Mr. Hanratty. I'll get some sleep, but have the messenger of the watch wake me before you are relieved. I want to go over this with you and the oncoming watch. Good night, and thank you."

She hung up and returned to her thoughts of the past. It was only 6:30 PM EDT, but she'd been up and on duty since midnight, preparing the ship to get underway.

The messenger knocked softly on the captain's door and said, "Captain, you asked to be awakened before the watch change. It's half an hour until the four-to-eight is relieved. There's fresh coffee on the bridge."

Karen Ann opened her eyes. "Thank you. Please let the mate know I'll be on deck soon and won't delay his being relieved much."

She'd been dreaming about getting back to port and calling Larry. She wanted to return to sleep and see how the dream ended, but she forced herself out of bed to throw water on her face to help her wake up.

She looked at her reflection in the mirror. *Wake up, Kiddo,* she told herself. *You have a hurricane coming and a $250 million ship with twenty-eight lives depending on you. Now is the wrong time to get wishy-washy about a guy. Shape up, Sailor.*

The *Palm Princess* was fifty miles off the coast of lower Maryland, making good time, and the seas were light and calm with variable winds. Mr. Simon, Mr. Hanratty's relief on the bridge, was getting the turnover of the watch when Karen Ann entered.

"Good evening, Skipper," Mr. Hanratty said. He could get away with the familiarity, because he'd been sailing with her for six years, and they became good friends during that time.

"It was until the messenger woke me," she said, chuckling. "OK. Let's get down to the business at hand, so Mr. Hanratty can get some sleep. It seems like we'll have a couple of very busy days ahead."

She went to the hurricane plot and added what she wanted done above and beyond the company's regular hurricane plan. She wanted the mate on watch to monitor the National Weather Service radio broadcast every hour and plot Peggy's position, as well as provide Karen Ann with an update every watch relief.

"Pass the word to the engineering and steward departments," she added. "I want to see the chief engineer and chief steward along with the chief mate in my cabin at 0900."

Once she went over everything she could think of with the storm two days away, she dismissed Hanratty to get some sleep. She ensured Mr. Simon had the situation under control before returning to her stateroom for a little more sleep.

Karen Ann rose at 0800 the following morning and prepared for the day by ordering breakfast in her cabin before the meeting with her top officers and department heads.

They arrived at 0900 sharp, and they sat down to work. She told engineering to prep all their spaces and secure all gear for heavy weather, as well as coordinating with the Chief Mate to ensure if he needed anything that might require an engineer's expertise, someone would be available at all times.

She turned to the Chief Steward. "I want you to make sure the crew can eat no matter the weather. Cook enough food that can be reheated in the microwave, or eaten cold, or made into sandwiches."

The three left to carry out their duties and start all personnel preparing for Hurricane Peggy.

She went to the bridge to check the path of the storm and listen to the latest update on NWS radio to hear the hurricane's projected path, so she could formalize her own plan.

Peggy grew to a Category Four by early afternoon, with no sign of letting up. Her plotted course was straight toward the Bahamas, then to Florida, making landfall near Cape Canaveral. Karen Ann felt she had a good sense of how the situation was shaping up. If the *Palm Princess* kept to her present course and speed, and Peggy did the same, they would end up sailing into Peggy's right forward quadrant, with the ship passing west of the Bahamas.

That area of a hurricane had the strongest winds and fiercest seas. She already received two inquiries from Houston about her proposed plan of action. She wanted to say she intended to sail due east for 500 miles, then turn southwest toward Venezuela, but she knew the managers would reject the plan, because it would ruin the intricate dance of arrivals and departures of vessels using a busy port like Caracas. Such a change would create disarray in everyone's schedule, from the pilots to the refineries to the corner gas station running out of gas, because the delivery was late.

She had a few options. She had another five knots of speed she could use to make up for her course change, or she could slow down, or use a combination of the two. Her dilemma, faced by every captain who had a major storm coming their way, was called "The Choice." She'd been through a few large storms in her career and always did well with her decisions, but it was never easy making The Choice, because many lives depended on it.

She sent a telex to Houston outlining her plan to skirt the storm to the east of the Bahamas and make up the time difference using her reserve speed. Changing course so as not to pass between the Bahamas and Florida bought its own problem. She would be trapped and forced to go right through the storm if it circled around and headed north-northeast. She couldn't head west toward the islands at that point, and turning any farther east would probably get her fired from her job. Plus, she wouldn't be able to outrun the storm, anyway. Such a situation would place her ship in very strong tropical-force winds and very high seas created by Peggy.

The Choice was always a compromise and a gamble. She had to bet that the forecasters were right, and she was making the correct decision on the available information, her experience, and her instincts. Either way, the result was the captain's fault if things went sideways and something bad happened.

By the time she received a reply from Houston and helped Second Mate Mr. Hanratty, the ship's navigator, chart their new course and speed that would enable them to still reach Venezuela on time, it was suppertime. When she looked up, she saw the lunch the steward brought to the bridge for her was still untouched.

She decided to take it to her cabin and store it in the minifridge to avoid hurting the steward's feelings. She wasn't very hungry for supper, either, but she had to eat to keep up her strength. It looked to be a long two days even if all went as planned.

As she left the bridge, the first high clouds were visible on the horizon, and the ship began moving to the swell that rose ahead of the hurricane. The entire crew knew they were in for a rough ride.

CHAPTER 9

Special Agent Gordon sat at his desk in the Washington, DC, FBI building in the area created for DHS-attached agents, going over the files for De Long and Preston, when the phone rang. Caller ID revealed it was Agent Ferrow of the DEA, whom he called earlier to ask about any leads they might have on Colombian Cartel associates known to be in the USA, especially in the northeast.

He lifted the receiver and said, "Hi, Tim. How'd you make out on the search?"

"I'm fine. How are you today, Max?"

"Sorry, Tim. I'm scratching my head on this one. I'm not getting anywhere, and it's frustrating."

"Cheer up. Your day just got a lot better. I found something that might be helpful for your search. Do you want to come over here and see, or should I visit you? It's not anything I can give you over the phone."

"That's great, Tim. If you could come over here, I'd really appreciate it."

"See you in thirty minutes." Ferrow hung up.

Gordon smiled for the first time in two days. He might get somewhere on the case after all. *If I can just figure out who Lic is and where he lives, I can blow this case wide open.*

"Hi, Max," Tim Ferrow said, as he was shown into Gordon's office. "It's been what? Two years since we actually saw each other?"

"Yeah, something like that. The Barnnett case, wasn't it?"

"That's the one. Let's get you started on this case, because we haven't been able to do much with these guys. They're model citizens while they're here in country."

They began discussing what Ferrow dug up on two guys who appeared to have taken over the northeast drug market.

"OK," Gordon said, "so this Martinez guy is the one who gets a lot of phone calls from those prepaid cell phones, right? He's the one I need to connect with the two dead guys fished out of the C and D Canal a few weeks ago.

"Have any of the numbers changed or stopped recently?" he asked.

"Let me go over these phone records that, thanks to you and your DHS connection, we were able to subpoena. How recently are you talking?"

"Go back about a month."

"That's twenty-five pages. I'll be here all day."

It was two days after Lamar's business trip, and Wendy was just beginning to act normally again when he was home. He tried very hard to pretend life was normal—so hard, it almost gave him an ulcer. He had to get Wendy and the kids out of harm's way, but he didn't know how or where to go. He didn't know how to convince her they needed a sudden vacation to get away from home just in case someone came looking for him. He knew they'd come for him to tie up any loose ends. Just like Willie, Leroy, Byron, James, and the rest of his crew, he was another loose end.

He decided to suggest an extended family vacation. Either that, or they could drop the kids off at Wendy's parents' house, and the two of them could have a second honeymoon.

She just might buy that, he thought. *We haven't had any alone time since Sally was born.*

"Max, look here," Tim said. "I think I have what you're looking for."

Max looked at the sheets. "That looks promising. It's a steady number that goes back awhile, then stops cold, while the other numbers keep calling."

"All right," Tim said. "Let's say that was our two dead guys. It seems to stop right about the time they decided to take a midnight swim in the C and D."

"Is there any indication that a new number picks up on the call schedule?" Max asked.

"There's a new number, but it doesn't seem to be on the schedule like all the others. Look how all these other ones drop off the grid like that first one, too." Tim frowned. "Max, this is weird. All the numbers from each location stop one after the other, then this number picks up and makes one or two calls from each location."

"That's pretty strange. Seems like many were reduced to one. Let's see if this is another throw-away phone and a dead end or not."

CHAPTER 10

The sharp ring of the sound-powered phone reverberated through the cabin's darkness, startling Karen Ann from her sleep. As she rolled to reach for the receiver, she felt the ship heave a lot more than the last watch's report from the bridge. She had a clinometer on the bulkhead beside her bunk, but she didn't want to turn on the light to read it and fully wake up, so she gave a mental estimate of fifteen degrees of roll, as she answered the phone.

"Captain here."

"Captain, this is the bridge with your requested report," Mr. Hanratty said.

"Yes, Mr. Hanratty. What do you have for me?"

"Skipper, she's getting bigger all the time. She's a Category Four with sustained winds of 140 miles per hour, and they don't think she's done growing. You can probably feel our girl rocking a bit more. We're taking steady fifteen-degree rolls, with a twenty-degree roll on occasion, but we haven't seen any really big winds yet according to the anemometer. It's roughly at a steady twenty-five knots, with an occasional gust up to thirty-five.

"The seas are eight- to ten-footers, with an occasional twelve to fourteen thrown in. One thing that might interest you is that Channel sixteen on the VHF radio is getting pretty active up and down the coast, from North Carolina to Florida. I can hear the Coast Guard on almost all the calls, but right now, I haven't caught many of the ones making the calls."

"Very well, Mr. Hanratty. I want you to ensure that the AIS is functioning properly and has all our proper information inserted correctly. When young Mr. Simon relieves you, I want you to make sure he has a good grasp of the situation and the severity of the weather we're approaching. This is his first big blow.

"One more thing. Let's have my reports come in twice a watch from now on."

"Aye, aye, Captain. Will do. Try to get back to sleep. I think you're going to need it. Good night."

Karen Ann hung up and realized it would be a long night and it would only get worse, but she had a well-built ship and good crew. She made a point of checking that everything was done right, with a well-trained crew of mixed ages, from youthful strength and vitality to knowledgeable, experienced older hands.

Knowing that allowed her to return to sleep despite the worsening weather.

"Good evening, Mike," Hanratty said, as Simon entered the bridge to relieve the watch.

"I guess so, Pat. What size rolls are we taking now?"

"She's only doing a steady eighteen degrees, with a twenty-five-degree one thrown in now and again to keep us sharp."

"It must've been one of those twenty-fives that almost threw me across my stateroom when I tried to get my pants on just now."

"I would've paid money to see that." Hanratty fought back laughter. "OK, Mike. Let's go to the chartroom and make sure you know where we are and what we're up against tonight."

As Hanratty turned toward the chartroom, he asked, "This is your first time east of the Bahamas, isn't it?"

Simon nodded, looking at the chart to see where they were in relationship to the 700 islands of the Bahamian Nation.

"We couldn't get a star fix earlier due to cloud cover, so our only fix is off the GPS. We need to make sure we're getting good satellite locks and low interference readings when we plot a fix. You know the captain likes all that recorded in the log when we have to rely on just one method of getting a fix."

"OK. No problem, Pat. Is the captain still getting updates once a watch?"

"No. She wants it twice a watch now."

"Fine. If that's everything, consider yourself relieved."

"On other thing. If you have any questions or aren't sure of something, call my stateroom before you call the captain's. She won't get much rest with our two-hour update calls."

"I'll be fine, but thanks for the offer. If I need you, I'll call."

Hanratty nodded and went below to his stateroom, and, he hoped, to sleep.

"The NWS just raised Peggy to a Category-Five hurricane and adjusted its projected track, Captain," Mr. Simon said into the phone. "The winds are sustained at 155 miles per hour, with gusts up to 170. They also said the seas in the front right quadrant are reaching seventy feet, and they expect a storm surge of twenty-five to thirty when she reaches shore. Her forward speed has slowed to twelve miles per hour in a northwesterly direction. So far, we seem to be going in the right direction to miss the main part of the storm.

"Our set and drift is more to the west than what was projected on our De'd Reckoning course, according to the last GPS fix I recorded. Do you want me to adjust course more to the east?"

"Very well, Mr. Simon. How far west of our course are we?"

"Right now, we're two miles west-northwest of our course line, and our speed made good was one knot slower than projected. The winds have increased to forty knots steady with gusts up to sixty. Seas are good twenty-footers with a thirty showing up now and again."

"Very well. You can alter course to get us back onto the projected course line. We'll remain at our present speed for now, but if we get into any bigger seas, I want you to reduce speed so we don't beat her up. Please call me when you reduce speed. Is that all you have for me at this time?"

"Yes, Ma'am. That's it for now."

"Good night, then." She hung up.

The phone rang, and she reached for it again, unable to believe it was two hours since she talked with Mr. Simon. "Captain here."

"Captain, this is the bridge," Simon said in a hurried voice.

Hearing his tone, she sat upright in bed. "Yes, Mr. Simon? What is it?"

"Captain, a Coast Guard C130 airplane is trying to raise us on Channel Sixteen. They're asking for our assistance in a rescue operation they're attempting. What do you want me to do?"

"First, calm down. Second, get all the information and tell them I'll be on the bridge directly to talk with them. I also want you to call Mr. Hanratty's stateroom and ask him to meet me on the bridge ASAP. I'll be there in three minutes. Good-bye."

Throwing on her uniform, she headed for the bridge. She arrived just before Mr. Hanratty, who came in looking disheveled and pulling on his right shoe.

"What's up, Skipper?" he asked.

"Well, Pat, it looks like the Coast Guard wants our help."

"Oh, really? Are they gonna give us a break on the next quarterly inspection?"

"Now isn't the time to be a wiseass, Pat. I need you to do some quick calculations and give me a course, speed, and ETA for these coordinates." Her tone was stern yet forgiving.

"Sure thing, Skipper. Give me two minutes, and I'll have everything you need. Who's in trouble out there?"

She had already picked up the receiver on the satellite phone to call Houston and inform them of the situation and that there would be, most likely, a delay in their expected arrival.

"Captain, I have this position as seventy-five miles northwest of our present position," Hanratty said a minute later. "If we can get up to twenty-five knots, we'll arrive in three hours. Our ETA would be

0145. We need a new course of 320 degrees true, using our present set and drift figures."

"Very well, Mr. Hanratty. Mr. Simon, come right to a new course of 320 degrees true. Make turns for twenty-five knots."

"Aye, aye, Captain." He gave the order to the helmsman and also rang up the revolutions on the Engine Order Telegraph, to make their new speed twenty-five knots.

The huge ship began its slow starboard turn, and her heeling increased, sending her right into the path of Hurricane Peggy.

CHAPTER 11

"Well, Tim, it's one of those disposable phones," Max said dejectedly.

"But it's one of the newer kind with the new embedded code. It can be traced to the store where it was purchased. I think we could still be OK on this one, because it's a Delaware tag. When Congress passed the regulation for the tag, Delaware passed a law that all security tapes need to be kept for six months. They were one of twenty states that took the suggestion from the DHS to make some sort of surveillance law with a time requirement for retaining the tapes."

"You're right. I forgot about that. I haven't had to use that law since it was passed. You're a lifesaver."

Wendy Weston was just coming home from the gym with Sally and Lamar, Jr., and was a block from her home when she saw a van with out-of-state plates parked across the street from her house. A moment later, she saw a man who seemed out of place leaving her backyard.

She drove past the house, accompanied by the children's laughter.

"You missed the house, Mommy!" Sally said, still laughing.

"I want to go to the store. I forgot, so we're going now."

A moment later, she told her voice-activated car phone to call Lamar's office, putting on the headphone so the kids wouldn't overhear.

"Lamar," she whispered into the microphone, "I just saw a stranger leaving our backyard and watched him get into a van with New York tags. I'm calling the police."

Lamar sprang upright in his chair behind his desk. "What did he look like?"

"I can't say for sure, but I think he was Hispanic, and we don't have any Hispanics living in our neighborhood."

Lamar knew immediately what the man was doing at their house, and he couldn't let Wendy call the police. "Honey, it was probably just someone looking for a friend's house or something. I wouldn't call the cops now. We'd be labeled as racists."

He chuckled and added, "Why not go somewhere, like to the supermarket, to be on the safe side. I'll go home and check it out. I'll call on your cell to let you know it's safe to come home."

His mind spun, but he managed to tell his secretary to cancel his appointments for the rest of the day, saying he wasn't feeling well.

"I hope you feel better Sir. Good-bye."

He walked out the door toward his Lincoln Navigator in the parking lot.

"Tim, I traced our burner phone to a Super Wawa on Route 1 around Dover, Delaware," Max said, returning to his desk.

Tim looked up from the list of calls the subject phone had made. "That's great, but I'm not sure it'll help us get this guy when we identify him from the surveillance tape, because it's really active for four days. It was all over the place according to the cell towers he connected to."

"What do you mean?"

"In four days, the guy went from Delaware to Texas and several places in between. Then the calls stopped as fast as they started. There hasn't been any activity from that phone for over a week."

"Well, I'll go to Delaware in the morning and track down that surveillance tape," Max said, feeling dejected. "Maybe we'll get lucky and get a good facial to run through the DMV database and come up with an ID. I hope, if we get a hit on this guy, he's still around. I have a bad feeling about this one, like we're running out of time."

Lamar came up with a plan on the way home. He would cruise the neighborhood before going to his house and would stay away from his usual route to see if anyone was following him. He didn't have a clue what he'd do if he found the van and driver. Should he run or fight? His family couldn't stay in the house any longer.

He was so engrossed in thought, he ran a stop sign. An oncoming car slammed on its brakes and skidded to a stop. The horn blared, and the driver gave Lamar the finger.

Lamar was so shook, he pulled off to the side of the road and tried to sort things out before driving any farther.

Max saw Tim to the elevator. "I can't tell you how much you've helped with this case. At least I have a place to start, which is a lot more than I had yesterday."

"Glad to be of assistance, Max," Tim replied. "I wish you the best of luck with this one. If you can, keep me in the loop, will you?"

"You bet."

The elevator door closed, hiding Tim from view.

CHAPTER 12

The *Palm Princess* was rolling a lot more now. The seas were between twenty and thirty feet, and the wind was steady at fifty-five knots, with gusts reaching hurricane force of over sixty-four knots. The last position from the NWS put the eye fifty miles east of the Bahamas, with hurricane-force winds just starting to reach the easternmost islands. Peggy's eye was only 110 miles from the *Palm Princess,* and Peggy was still growing.

The bridge was a busy place compared to its normal routine of one mate, a helmsman, and, in occasional bad weather, a lookout brought up from the bow.

Karen Ann woke the entire crew. Those who didn't have specific duties stood additional lookout posts everywhere there was shelter from the storm that gave a view of the sea. Seven people crowded the bridge, as the crew prepared to assist the Coast Guard's attempt to recuse two very frightened sailors from a forty-five-foot, two-masted schooner, the SV *Natural High,* caught in the stormy seas ahead of Peggy.

The hurricane surprised everyone when it picked up speed and grew to a Category Five, with winds of 145 knots, gusting to 160, in a very short time. The Bahamas were getting the storm almost thirty-six hours ahead of schedule when Peggy was first listed as a hurricane. Her track hadn't wavered like most hurricanes, which jogged up and down or meandered in the open ocean. Once formed, Peggy took off toward the Bahamas and the U.S. coast with a vengeance. The tourist industry in the Bahamas would take a beating due to Peggy's unusual speed. People didn't have time to evacuate, and thousands of tourists were caught in the storm's path.

Besides the watch standers and the captain, the second and chief mates, and an additional lookout were on the bridge, Mr. Hanratty took fixes and plotted their position every thirty minutes, passing on their updated ETA to Mr. Farber, the Senior Third Mate, who passed it to the Coast Guard.

The captain and chief mate went over all their options and the different scenarios the rescue attempt might throw at them. So far, the Coast Guard only asked them to provide a lee for the sailboat, so a helicopter could pick up the two sailors aboard. According to the Coast Guard's C130 airplane that was on the scene over the sailboat, waiting for the *Palm Princess* and the Coast Guard chopper to arrive, the weather was pretty bad. A standard rescue seemed less and less likely.

"We need to be ready for anything, Jim," Karen Ann said.

James Carbini, the chief mate for the past six months, sailed for over twenty years and never saw a storm this bad. For the past hour and fifteen minutes, he and the captain bounced ideas off each other, trying to have a ready solution for anything that might happen during the rescue attempt.

"Captain, I'm all out of ideas," Carbini said. "I know there have to be at least a thousand more things that could happen, but I'm fried."

"That's OK, Jim. We've covered enough scenarios that we can improvise off any of the plans we've got. Why don't you get the deck gang ready? We should be nearing that sailboat by now, and I need your guys prepped."

"Captain," Mr. Farber called, "the Coast Guard's on the horn. They want to talk to you."

"Very well, Mr. Farber. I'll be right there." She looked at Carbini again. "One last thing, Jim. Keep in mind, and make sure you pass it on to the rest of the crew, that I don't want anyone playing hero. We do this by the book with safety first. One hand for the ship and one for themselves."

"I don't think we have any heroes in the making, Captain, but I'll pass on the word."

"Captain," the C130 radio operator said when she answered the call, "we have your AIS showing you're one-zero miles from our location. The chopper should be there in three-zero minutes. This looks like it'll work out pretty well for coordination."

"You just tell us where you want us and how close to that schooner, and we'll give you whatever assistance we can, Sir."

"One potential problem is that the chopper's almost at its maximum fuel range. It won't have much time to spend on the scene. We need to do this in one take. It has to be perfect."

"We'll do our best to assist. Pass on to that pilot that we have a helicopter pad. If they run into trouble, we could be a last resort for them. We did drills bringing in Coast Guard helicopters four months ago on our shakedown cruise, but not in this kind of weather."

"I'll pass that information along, Ma'am. As soon as they get here, I'll have them contact you with their plan."

The call ended.

"Captain," Hanratty said, "I've got us at one mile from the last reported position of that sailboat."

"Very well, Mr. Hanratty. Mr. Farber, pass on to the rest of the crew that we're close to the rescue position. Everyone has to be on his toes."

Farber reached for the PA system mic. "Aye, aye, Captain."

"Vessel bearing two points off the starboard bow!" the starboard lookout shouted in excitement.

"Got it," Farber said, taking a look through his binoculars. "Oh, my God. Would you look at that? She's a floating wreck, Captain."

"Do you see that helicopter anywhere, Mr. Farber?" Karen Ann asked.

"Not yet, Captain." He swept the area with his binoculars. "Captain, I have two, repeat two, people onboard the sailboat, hunkered down in the cockpit with PFD's on."

"Very well, Mr. Farber. Let the C130 know we have them in view, and the occupants appear ready for evacuation."

"Will do, Captain."

Larry awoke with a start and sat bolt upright in bed, staring at his alarm clock, which read *1:40*. He had no idea what woke him, but he couldn't get Karen Ann out of his mind.

He reached for the TV remote and called up the Weather Channel. The broadcasters were in severe weather mode, and all they talked about was Hurricane Peggy.

"Man, I hope you make it through this thing, Kiddo," Larry muttered.

"So far, Hurricane Peggy hasn't really affected anyone yet," the newscaster said.

"Yeah," Larry replied. "You people never give a second thought to the poor bastards at sea who have to deal with these things. You sure like to drive your cars, listen to your stereos, and eat your fresh fruit and anything else that's brought to you by sea, Asshole."

He took one last look at the satellite view of Peggy getting ready to pulverize the Bahamas before turning off the TV and rolling over to sleep. Before he closed his eyes, he said a short prayer to all those in Peggy's path, including those at sea.

"The helicopter's calling us, Captain," Mr. Farber said.

"Very well, Mr. Farber." She went to the radio and picked up the mike. "This is the *Palm Princess* standing by for your instructions."

"Very good, Captain. Could you place your ship half a mile upwind of the *Natural High* and try to maintain that position while we attempt the rescue? Make sure you can vacate the area if you start to drift down on that vessel too fast. If your drift forces you to move, please give us a heads-up, so we can be ready. None of us will be looking your way."

"Can do. Proceeding to position." She turned toward the bridge windows and said, "The captain has the con.

"We need to do a Williamson turn, Mr. Farber," she added. "I want to maintain a half-mile distance directly upwind from the sailboat. I need you on the radar. Keep singing out ranges and hearings while Mr. Hanratty, you keep an eye on the anemometer, with direction and relative bearings and wind speed. I'm looking for any gusts or large direction changes."

"Aye, aye, Captain," both men said quickly.

"Hard left rudder," Karen Ann ordered.

The ship swung to the left.

"Helmsman, sing out when we pass 280 degrees, so I can set us up for a turn back to the reciprocal course of 140 degrees."

The twenty-one-year-old helmsman, a freshly documented Able Seaman on his first sailing in the AB position, was scared to death he would screw up and make a mistake with the helm change. He began muttering softly to himself, but it wasn't soft enough to keep Karen Ann from overhearing.

She moved a little closer and whispered, "You just relax now. All you have to do is follow my commands, and try to be as deliberate in your actions as you can. Everything will be fine. Take a deep breath and relax. Be loose for me, OK?"

"Uh, yes, Ma'am, Captain," he stammered.

A few seconds later, he said in a calmer voice, "Captain, passing 280 degrees."

"Very well. Be ready. When the course swings to 260, you'll start shifting the rudder."

"Aye, aye, Captain. Coming up to 260 degrees and preparing to shift the helm. Mark, 260 degrees. Shifting helm to hard right as ordered." He swung the little steering wheel on his helm command station.

"Very well," Karen Ann said. "Let me know when we pass 120 degrees.

She conned the ship to the exact position the Coast Guard asked for. Just as she stabilized the ship, a lookout reported, "The helicopter is making its approach to the sailboat, Captain."

The *Palm Princess* rolled dramatically once her speed was taken off and she sat broadside to the seas, but the plan was working. The seas passing toward the *Natural High* were noticeably smaller, and there wasn't as much direct wind on the chopper, making the pilot's job a little easier.

"Captain," the lookout called, "the chopper's dropping the basket. It looks like they're trying the easy way first."

"Let's pray it works," Karen Ann said.

In the background, she heard Mr. Farber calling out the bearing and range to the sailboat, while Mr. Hanratty gave wind speeds and direction between the radar bearings. She was proud of their professionalism and calm.

"One away, Captain," the lookout called.

"Very well," she said. *They'd better get a move on,* she thought. *We're starting to slide, and we need to get moving before we start bearing down on them.*

"Better hold on," the windward lookout said. "Here comes a big one, and it's a rogue."

Karen Ann swung around and saw the rogue wave heading toward them. "Full ahead on both! Mr. Hanratty, call the chopper and tell them we have to bug out. Warn them to watch for a rogue wave."

"On it, Skipper." He reached for the radio microphone.

The stern took the brunt of the wave and was heaved into the air, causing the props that just started spinning up to lunge halfway out of the water and send a nerve-wracking vibration throughout the ship.

"Captain, the chopper has its basket almost all the way back down," the lee side lookout called, holding on as best he could.

Karen Ann looked back at the rescue attempt just as Mr. Hanratty passed on her message to the chopper pilot. She saw the wave lift the sailboat and raise it toward the helicopter in the sky overhead.

The *Natural High* was on a collision course straight up with the Coast Guard helicopter. The pilot did everything in his power to evade the boat that came at him faster than he could bring up his aircraft to avoid the broken masts and windblown loose rigging. The lone sailor was left clinging precariously to the wreckage, with the seemingly distant helicopter suddenly growing so fast in his eyes that he saw the crew chief's fearful look, as he desperately raised the basket.

Finally, knowing he couldn't get the basket clear in time, the crew chief reached for the quick release lever and told the pilot what he did.

Once the basket was released, the chopper became a little more maneuverable, and the pilot got them out of the way of the rising sail-boat.

The remaining sailor saw the basket fall toward him and was alarmed, because it was heading right toward him. At the last second, the basket became hung up in the ruined rigging and didn't hit him.

"That really messes up the whole show," Karen Ann said.

"Captain, the chopper's calling us," Mr. Farber said.

"Very well. Bring us back into position. Mr. Farber, while I see how they want to perform this final rescue."

"Aye, aye."

She took the mic and said, "That was a close one, Captain."

"It sure was, but we still have one POB, and we had to dump the basket. We need to regroup and send in our swimmer for a water pickup using a harness, but our fuel is almost bingo."

"We'll be back in position as soon as we can, but we're so big, it takes time."

"Understood, Captain. Is it possible you can do the water pickup of our swimmer and the survivor if we have to return to base due to fuel?"

"I'd like to say yes, but I can't promise that."

Mr. Farber positioned the ship to give the helicopter the nec-essary lee almost as expertly as the captain. "We're coming up on the re-quired position, Captain, if you want to tell the helicopter to get ready."

"Very well, Mr. Farber, and well done."

"Thank you, Captain." He glanced at Hanratty and buffed his closed fist on his shirt.

Hanratty laughed softly.

"OK, Men," Karen Ann said, "we're back in business. Man your stations."

"Aye, aye, Captain," both men said.

The lee side lookout watched the rescue swimmer jump thirty feet from the chopper into the roiling water below. "Man, I wouldn't do that for any amount of money," he said.

The sailor on the *Natural High* was reluctant to get into the water, and the rescue swimmer swam toward the sailboat. The sailor tried to shout over the roar of the wind and the chopper, and he pointed at the water.

"What's he pointing at?" Karen Ann asked.

The lookout trained his binoculars on the spot. "Fins! Fins in the water behind the swimmer!"

Karen Ann couldn't believe it. The rescue attempt started out so well, then it devolved into a complete mess. What else could go wrong?

"Captain, they're dolphins," the lookout said. "One just cleared the water, and I saw its body."

"Very well. Has the survivor gotten into the water yet?"

"No, Ma'am. He must be really scared."

"He'd better build up some courage. That helicopter will be running on fumes to get home." She turned. "Mr. Hanratty, how are we with regards to dear old Peggy?"

"Skipper, the last report had it moving farther north. It looks like it'll now spare most of the Bahamas and Florida. The islands only received Category-Two winds, but it's coming right at us. She's plotted at ninety miles southeast of us, and her pressure is holding steady, but at least she stopped growing."

"Very well, Mr. Hanratty. Keep track of it and keep me up-to-date," she said tiredly.

"Captain, the guy on the sailboat finally got into the water, and the swimmer has him," Mr. Farber said. "They're moving away from the sailboat."

"Excellent. Now we can get this show on the road."

The rescue of the final sailor went smoothly after that. The rescue swimmer and the sailor were hoisted into the chopper without delay.

Karen Ann got on the radio to the helicopter again. *"Palm Princess* calling Coast Guard helicopter Two-Two-Whiskey-Bravo."

"Two-Two-Whiskey-bravo back," the pilot said.

"Great job, Captain. My compliments to you and your crew. Are your passengers OK?"

"Thank you, Captain. They're as good as can be expected. You guys were a real life-saver. I don't think we could've done this without your lee. Thanks again for the warning about that rogue wave.

"We still have a problem, though. We won't make landfall with the fuel we have left. I wasn't about to leave my swimmer behind. I'd like to take you up on that offer of a helio deck, if that's still good."

Karen Ann was momentarily speechless. Looking around, she saw shock on the faces of all the others on the bridge. "Of course, Captain. We need some time to get into position and get the crew to their stations. I'll get back to you when we're ready. What course and speed would you like from us?"

"I need you to get the wind broad on the port bow. I'll leave the speed up to you, but I need as little pitching as possible. Let me know when you're ready to receive us."

"Will do."

The watch wasn't ready to be relieved yet, which was good. That meant she'd have her most-experienced hands on the helipad to retrieve the helicopter. She had to make it happen. Otherwise, the helicopter would have to ditch in this weather and pray another Coast Guard helicopter would be able to find them.

She immediately began issuing orders for the proper personnel to go aft to the helicopter pad while getting the *Palm Princess* on the proper course and speed to reduce pitching to a minimum. Conditions had to be perfect before she'd be able to OK the helicopter's approach.

She was right to go over all possible scenarios with Chief Mate Carbini. *He and the rest of the deck gang will earn their money tonight,* she thought, giving him final instructions over the sound-pow-ered phone.

In the helio deck ready room, Carbini organized the crew and handed each one an assignment. Hanratty checked each crewman's safety harness and PFD to ensure he was ready to go on deck to help bring the helicopter aboard and secure it to the deck.

Once the crew was ready, Carbini called the bridge. "Captain, we're ready if you are."

"Very well, Jim. How does our motion on the deck look?"

"Captain, this guy better be pretty damn good. He'll need his best shot to put that thing down safely. We're rising and falling a good fifteen feet back here."

"OK, Jim. I'll give her some more speed to try to ease up on the pitching motion. Keep your fingers crossed that it works."

A minute later, Carbini said, "Captain, she's a little better now. We're oscillating only ten feet. That's as good as we're going to get."

"I'll let the chopper captain know the situation."

Lieutenant Commander Jacob "Jumbo" Garber of the U.S. Coast Guard was about to attempt the most-dangerous and challenging feat of his entire aviation career. The landing would take every ounce of talent he acquired during his seven-year military aviation career.

He set up a preliminary run at the tanker's helio deck to check the situation and make any final adjustments to his plan before he committed himself.

CHAPTER 13

At noon in Saudi Arabia, the Mullah just finished lunch and was ringing for his servants to bring his tea. Ali Mohammed Modula sat in his lavish estate in Mecca, watching CNN. They covered Hurricane Peggy almost as much as the Weather Channel in the U.S. did. He chose to live and operate out of Mecca, the holiest city in the Muslim world, because he believed he was the second coming of the Prophet Mohammad, and his followers were sure to protect Mecca if not himself.

He felt safe knowing it was almost impossible for the West to get a spy within the city limits, let alone place an assassin close to him. Hurricane Peggy, he believed, was sent by Allah to assist with the destruction of the Great Satan, the United States of America. Allah heard his pleas and would help him destroy America even faster than his plan would have. Ali Mohammed Modula, giddy with expectation, thinking it was like Hurricanes Camille and Andrew rolled into one. It would wreak terrible devastation on the East Coast.

He led the most-dangerous, most-secret terrorist organization in the world, so secret that not even the CIA knew about them until well after 9/11. "Allah Yad" translated loosely into "Hand of God," which was what the self-proclaimed Imam called his band of super hyped-up terrorists who had always been kept on a very short leash. So far, all he had done was train his men, and he paid all the other terrorists groups, like Al Qaeda, the Red Brigade, and Hamas, and more, to do his bidding against the Great Satan, which he hated with more passion than any man could invest in anything except his family and God.

He was ready to unleash his small but very-well-trained and financed band of destructive, nearly psychotic madmen. Some were already in place in the U.S., waiting for the order to attack their targets. In one fell swoop, Modula believed he could cripple the entire country and paralyze the rest of the world into full submission to his will.

Lieutenant Commander Garber received word from Captain Murphy that she was ready to accept his helicopter onboard her ship, which was as steady as she could make it. Jumbo looked left toward his copilot, Ensign Eugene "Jeep" Brighton and pressed the push-to-talk switch to the intercom channel.

"Gentlemen, this will be a first for us," he said. "I can say only two things for you to do—hold on, and if you know any prayers, start saying them. Here we go."

"If anyone can do this, Skipper," Ensign Brighton said, "you can. Let's go for a boat ride."

"Captain," Farber said, "the Chief Engineer's on the phone and wants to speak with you."

"Mr. Farber, I'm in the middle of air operations, and unless we're on fire or sinking, tell him I'll call back after we get that helicopter on the deck."

"I told him what you were doing, but he said he needed to speak with you ASAP." He handed her the receiver.

"This better be good, Chief," she said.

"Captain, I'm not sure what's going on up there, but down here, we have some serious problems starting to compound on us. You need to know what's going on. We have two bilge alarms from starboard number six wing double hull tank. The starboard shaft bearings are setting off high-temperature alarms. I'm requesting that you go to dead slow on the starboard engine, so I can get those temps down, Skipper."

"Chief, I'll slow down as soon as I can, but you need to do everything you can to keep that shaft turning until then. I've got a chopper trying to land right now."

The big sixteen-cylinder diesels produced two-thirds of their power output, and the strain on the three-foot-diameter shaft turning the twenty-eight-foot diameter propellers that kept coming half out of the water, spinning, and smacking back down as the *Palm Princess* rode the waves made the bearings do things they were never designed for.

The Chief Engineer could only hold on and pray the captain slowed down the engine in time to avoid the bearings seizing on the shaft and either breaking the shaft or destroying the reduction gears and main engine. He had the bilge pump lined up and online, trying to keep up with the water coming into the starboard number-six double-hull voids that were giving him alarms.

He had only one more trick left to try to avoid the starboard shaft from seizing and possible snapping in two. He turned to his third assistant. "Take two oilers to the starboard shaft alley where that over-heating bearing is and start spraying the bearing with a fire hose. Maybe that'll keep things under control until the captain can reduce the RPMs, and we can get those temperatures under control."

The Palm Petroleum Company hadn't taken the cheapest route when designing the ship, but neither had they gone the full monte. They decided to use a conventional twin-screw design, even though the new thought in ship design was to go with diesel-electric Azipods for a power and propulsion plant. With the conventional design, they had one large diesel engine connected to the propeller via a set of reduction gears/transmission, clutch, shaft, and bearings.

The *Palm Princess* had two of those sending her through the water, thanks to the U.S. Coast Guard pushing for the new requirements to have all ships over a certain gross tonnage be required to have twin-screw propulsion. Without that ruling, the ship would've come off the waves with the standard of one engine, one shaft, and one propeller, like most merchant ships of the past.

With a diesel-electric setup, they had several smaller diesels connected to generators that powered an electric motor connected to a shaft-and-nozzled-propeller combination outside the hull that could be rotated instead of using rudders like conventional ship power trains. That would have given the ship better handling and more fuel efficiency, but it was also more expensive to install and repair. It was the "pay me now or pay me later," syndrome that affected all accountants world-wide.

"Jumbo," the copilot said, "I'm following you on the con-trols."

The chopper inched its way down toward the helio deck on the tanker.

"Man, that thing's going wild down there," Jumbo muttered.

Jim Carbini stood at the forward end of the helio deck with a pair of landing paddles, trying desperately to keep them horizontal to give the pilot a reference to judge where the deck was at all times during his approach.

Jumbo was getting good at timing the deck's heaving and had already decided to nail the landing on the first attempt. He doubted he'd be able to try it twice. Sweat beading under his flying helmet ran down his face. He always said there wasn't anything he couldn't do with his bird, but he never dreamed he'd face such a situation—landing on the rolling, pitching helio deck of a floating bomb in the middle of a hurricane. Empty oil tankers with empty cargo holds carried nothing but explosive petroleum fumes.

The deck crew spread out around the edges of the helio deck and crouched down, waiting for the pilot to land, so they could rush out and secure the tie-down straps before the chopper slid off in the ship's motion.

Jumbo timed it perfectly. He crossed the threshold of the deck at six feet, just as the ship rose to meet him, and it was as if he landed the chopper on automatic. The second the wheels touched down, he shut down the throttle and collective, almost standing on the brake pedal to keep the helicopter from rolling off the deck.

Carbini and his men heard the engine noise drop and scurried out to secure the chopper. He was first to reach it and had the lead strap attached before any of the others even came close. After his strap was attached, he moved quickly to the others and helped the crew tighten them all down. After a final inspection to make sure the chopper wasn't going anywhere, he went to the starboard side and began helping the survivors from the sailboat and the helicopter crew.

He passed off each passenger to the next crewman in the daisy chain leading to the ready room. The last man out was Lieutenant Commander Garber. "Welcome aboard the MV *Palm Princess*, Commander. I'm the Chief Mate, Jim Carbini," he shouted into the fierce wind, as they shook hands.

They struggled to reach the ready room across the rolling, pitching helio deck.

"That's twice today you guys saved our butts," Jumbo said. "I'll owe this entire crew a steak dinner when we're back in port."

"You're on for that. I'll take mine medium rare with a baked sweet potato and a nice bottle of Chianti."

Once they reached the shelter of the ready room, they stripped out of their foul-weather gear and shook hands with the others.

"The captain would like to see you, Commander," Carbini said. "If you'll follow me, I'll take you to the bridge."

As he stepped out the door, he stopped and called back, "Hey, Boats! Call the bridge and let them know Helio Ops are secured for the day. We have steak dinners waiting for us when we get into port. I'm bringing our benefactor to the bridge to meet the captain."

"Aye, aye, Mr. Carbini," the Boatswain replied.

The others cheered. The crew began settling the newcomers in, taking them to the galley for hot coffee, chow, and a dry blanket.

Captain Murphy didn't have the luxury of celebrating the successful completion of the helicopter-rescue mission, because she had to assess the ship's condition based on what the Chief Engineer said.

"Dead slow on the starboard engine," Karen Ann ordered the Watch Office and rang up the engine room to talk to the Chief Engineer.

"Captain, I think I can keep up with the flooding in the wing tanks for now, as long as we don't open her up anymore and keeping the RPMs down to a minimum on the starboard shaft. We should make it to Norfolk for repairs."

"All right, Chief. Keep me up-to-date on any changes. I'll get us started toward port and will make arrangements for emergency hull inspection. Maybe I can have a spare bearing waiting for us. It'll be about twenty hours before we make port, as long as we stay away from this hurricane."

She turned to the Second Mate and hung up the phone. "Mr. Hanratty, please chart a course to Norfolk, Virginia, as soon as you can. Until we have a charted course, Mr. Farber, let's come to a course of 330 degrees. We need half ahead on the port and stay at dead slow on the starboard engine unless you hear we need something otherwise from the Chief. If you need me, I'll be in the chartroom."

"Aye, aye, Skipper," both mates replied.

CHAPTER 14

Lamar cruised around his neighborhood for twenty minutes without seeing any sign of the van with the New York tags Wendy saw across the street from the house. He began to feel safe and was ready to call her to tell her it was safe to return home when he realized it *wasn't* safe, even if the van wasn't anywhere to be found. He had to look for booby traps.

"What did she say about that guy?" he mused. "He was coming from behind the house."

He stomped down on the accelerator and headed toward home.

He slowed, as he approached the driveway, swiveling his head back and forth to look for anything out of the ordinary. He slowly got out of the black Navigator and walked toward the backyard. At first glance, all seemed normal, but he carefully examined everything to see if something was off about the yard or house.

The crawl space cover was ajar from its frame. He didn't want to get near it, but he had to look.

As he moved closer, his heart rate increased, and he began sweating on his forehead and palms. He felt clammy. Carefully inspecting the area around the opening for trip wires, he gently removed the lid and stepped into the recessed area to next remove the crawl-space screen.

He reached inside to turn on the light and look around, but he froze at the smell of gas. He realized he stood in a pool of natural gas accumulating inside the house. His finger was a fraction of an inch from the light switch, which would have provided the spark necessary to blow up the entire house. It was the attacker's way of killing him and his entire family and removing another loose end.

"Hi, Babe," Lamar said, parking the Navigator at the shopping center where he told Wendy to wait with the kids while he checked the house. "It was a good thing you saw that guy and got scared. When I checked the house, it looked like everything was fine. I didn't see any break-ins, but I caught a whiff of gas.

"I called the gas company, and they told me what to do and not do. I took Butch from the house. He's with me. Looks like we need to move out for a few days while they find the leak and fix it."

She began to protest, but he overrode her.

"I was thinking we should make a vacation out of it. School doesn't start for another week or so. You think your parents would be up for a visit from the kids and Butch for a few days? We could have a mini second honeymoon. We haven't been away without the kids since Sally was born."

Wendy's head spun. She didn't know what to make of the situation. Luckily for Lamar, she wasn't able to ask any questions, either.

Lamar was relieved. He had a chance to get Wendy and the kids out of harm's way and the people who wanted to kill them.

"But...," Wendy began.

"We don't need to go back to the house, even for a toothbrush. We'll buy whatever we need. You can buy some basics for us. I'll take the kids to the bank with me and get our passports from the safety-deposit box. I can have the plane ready to go by the time you meet me at the airport. We'll be in the air in five minutes.

"We'll make a short hop to Maryland to drop off the kids and Butch at your parents' place, then we can go wherever we want." He got the kids into the car, then waved Wendy toward the stores. "Don't buy too much. We don't know where we're going yet. You can call your folks and give them the plan. It'll be great, a surprise getaway."

He waved and drove off.

Agent Max Gordon pulled up at the Route 1 Super Wawa outside the Dover city limits, where the suspected disposable phone was sold. He would meet Detectives Sharper and Hobnobski to take possession of the video tape of the sale. Delaware law specifically stated that no one but a Delaware law-enforcement officer could be in possession of surveillance tapes.

Gordon didn't want to waste time squabbling with state authorities about how DHS trumped any such law and end up appearing in court to defend his case. He didn't want to involve anyone else, so he called the detectives to get the tape for him, and they'd view it together to identify the purchaser.

An unmarked dark-blue Ford Crown Victoria of the Delaware State Police pulled into the parking lot of the Super Wawa and parked beside the Ford Tempo Gordon checked out of the FBI motor pool and drove from DC that morning.

As the two detectives got out, Max, who leaned on the front fender of his Tempo, said, "Hi, Guys. It sure looks like I'm working for the wrong agency."

"Well, Hello to you, too, Agent Gordon," Hobnobski replied.

"I'm not in DC right now. How about we go with first names, Gavin. The fewer people who know the FBI is investigating anything around here, the better."

"That's fine with me, Max," Sharper said, getting out from the driver's side door. "Let's get the tape and get out of here. Maybe we can help you find your man while we get a bite to eat. I'm starving."

On the way inside the store, Max said, "I'd like to have the tapes from a week before the first call was placed on the phone in question." He gave them the information he had.

"Can I help you?" an elderly woman behind the counter asked.

"Sure can." Detective Sharper flashed his badge. "We need to see the manager."

She glanced at the badge and pointed nonchalantly toward a young man near the deli counter.

"Very good," Sharper said. "Thank you for your help...Ella." He read the name from her nametag.

The three law-enforcement officers walked toward the young man. Sharper spoke to him and asked if they could talk in his office.

The little room the manager called an office was very tight once all four were inside, and the door was closed. The young manager appeared nervous and concerned.

Sharper tried to ease the young man's nerves. "You've got a nice store here. I'm impressed someone as young as you is the manager. We need to see the security tapes for these dates." He gave the manager the time frame.

The manager calmed considerably at hearing that. "I'll get the tapes for you. They're in a storeroom."

He returned a few minutes later with seven tapes in a plastic Wawa shopping bag. Reaching into his desk, he took out a chain-of-custody form and filled in the number and date of each tape, then he asked Detective Sharper to cross-check the entries and sign for them.

"Detective, there's a time limit on how long you can keep them without a warrant," he added. "If you need one of them for evidence, you'll have to give me a warrant if you want to keep it longer than the time limit. That's the law, you know."

"We appreciate your clarifying that for us, Sir," Detective Sharper said with a hint of sarcasm.

The three lawmen left the store. Sharper told Ella they were thankful for her help. "Have a good day," he added with a wink and tip of his hat.

As the door closed, Warren looked at Max and Gavin with a sigh. "Well, that was a tough morning's work. I'm starving. Let's get lunch. I know a great little restaurant in downtown Dover."

They roared with laughter, and Max said, "Lead the way, Warren. Lunch is on me. You certainly worked hard this morning."

Gavin shook his head. "You see what I have to put up with every day, Max? It's all he thinks about. It's a wonder we get anything done. It doesn't matter where we're in the state, either. He always knows a good little restaurant within a fifteen-minute drive."

"Hey," Warren said. "I can't help it if I like to eat. I've been stationed at every barracks the State Police has in the great state of Delaware. A guy's got to eat, doesn't he?"

They shared another round of laughter.

Lamar fought to remain calm and concentrate on pre-flighting his trusty Piper Saratoga. He was being very conscientious and went over the checklist to make sure he didn't miss anything.

You have your wife and kids on this plane, he told himself. *Keep your head on straight. Fly the plane. Don't do their job for them.*

The door to the T-hangar opened, and Wendy walked toward the plane. "Hi, Honey," she said, seeming a bit more at ease.

Shopping always does that to her, he thought.

"I just got the kids some clothes and a toothbrush. My mom's ecstatic about having the kids to herself. They'll be spoiled rotten when we get them back."

"That's good. Grandmas need to do that once in a while. That's how they get back at you for what you did to them. I'm done with pre-flight. Let's stow what you brought and get in the air."

As the Saratoga taxied from the hangar toward the runway, Lamar pressed the remote-control button to close the hangar door and glanced back to make sure it was working. He hoped it wasn't the last time he saw that building.

A few minutes later, they were in the air.

Max put the last French fry into his mouth and said, "I guess that'll hold him, Gavin, at least until we get back to your office and re-view these tapes to see if we can name this guy."

Warren looked up from his plate. "I love you, too, Max." As he raised his middle finger.

CHAPTER 15

Larry turned off the TV, where he saw the latest update on Hurricane Peggy, and got ready to shower. He had to go to work, because it looked like New Jersey was spared the wrath of Peggy when the storm turned during the night. The latest predictions were for it to head northeast, farther out to sea.

The Bahamas also escaped most of Peggy's force. The hurricane was moving up the slot between Bermuda and America's East Coast. The only effect she would have on New Jersey was to make the surfers happy. The swells from Peggy were the biggest waves the New Jersey shore saw in many years.

He was stepping out of the shower when his cell phone beeped with a missed call. *Who'd be calling me at this hour of the morning?* he wondered.

When he checked caller ID, he said, "Well, Karen Ann, you must've made it through the hurricane OK. I doubt you'd be calling if you were still playing games with Peggy." He immediately called back.

Karen Ann just got into her bed in the day cabin behind the chartroom on the bridge deck when her cell phone rang. She almost let it go to voice mail, then forced herself to get up to answer, although she was dead tired. She hadn't slept in the last forty-eight hours.

"Captain Murphy," she said without checking caller ID.

"Well, aren't we formal?" Larry asked. "It's Larry, Karen Ann. You called. What's up?"

"Oh. Hi, Larry." She unconsciously reached up to fix her hair and primp a little. "I didn't know it was you. I thought it was the office calling."

"I guess you made it through the little blow OK."

"We're still on the fringes of it, but actually, I called to see about my next time in port and if we could get together sometime. I wanted to tell you I'll have a little port time in Norfolk, Virginia, starting the day after tomorrow."

"Whoa, there. What happened? I thought you were sailing to Venezuela."

"We had to make a little detour. We might've bent the boat a little, so we're going to Norfolk to visit the dry dock. I don't have time to go into all the details, but you're more than welcome to visit me while I'm in Norfolk if you can get away for a few days."

"I'm sorry, but I really have to get some sleep. I'll call you when I'm in Norfolk."

"I'll request some time off so I can meet you in Virginia."

After they said good-bye, she rolled over and felt her body shutting down in its need for sleep, although she had a tell-tale smile in quiet expectation of seeing the man who, she realized, still held a big part of her heart.

Larry hung up feeling there were plenty of unanswered questions and finished getting ready for work. He wouldn't have a very good day, because the bay was a churning mass of high waves in all directions. There wouldn't be a comfortable course across it all day.

He let his pup, Harry, out one more time to avoid finding a mess when he returned home from work. After bringing the pup back inside and giving him his usual treat with a pat on the head, Larry picked up his truck keys from the kitchen table, along with his coffee mug, and, shaking his head, went out for another day on the bay.

CHAPTER 16

Max was anxious to see the video tapes since he left the Wawa parking lot two-and-a-half hours earlier. He followed the two detectives from the Dover restaurant to their office in Wilmington. He had to wait while they set up the video equipment hopefully to locate the mystery person who bought the phone.

"Is there anything I can do to help you boys get set up?" he asked, hoping to speed up the process.

"No, no. You just sit back and prepare to enjoy the show." Warren knew they had at least 336 hours of boring customer footage to view. They weren't even sure they'd find anyone buying a phone, let along be able to ID him if they caught his face on tape. It would be a very long day.

"I'm just a little anxious, I guess," Max said.

"No pro-blame-o, Kemosabe." Warren used his finest broken Spanish/Apache accent. "That should do it. Who's got the popcorn?"

The three lawmen sat back in their chairs and began reviewing the tapes.

"You two be good for Grandma and Grandpa, you hear me," Wendy told Lamar, Jr. and Sally. "Mom, their bedtime is 1930 hours," she added to her mother.

Grandma began shooing Wendy and Lamar away. "Do you think I've forgotten how to take care of a couple young'uns? We'll be just fine. You two enjoy your little vacation. Kids, give your mommy and daddy a big kiss good-bye."

She patted her husband's arm. "Come on, Soldier. We have some bunk arranging to do."

The general looked at Wendy and Lamar, as he was dragged to the car. "Wendy, what did I teach you about following the orders of your commanding officer? Give me a kiss, my angel. I must go."

Wendy quickly kissed his cheek, then he did an about face and walked to the car almost in double-time.

Lamar looked at Wendy and chuckled. "I'll never get over how he is with your mom. I hope our love is that strong after so long being married."

Wendy looked up at him. "I believe it will be, as long as you remember who *your* commanding officer is."

"Why, yes, Ma'am. How could I ever forget?" He snapped to attention.

"Oh, knock it off. Let's figure out where we're going." She slapped his arm.

"Ouch!"

"All right. Let's go to the FBO and see where to go. We can get a flight plan submitted and be off before it's too late."

Max was just getting antsy in his chair when he saw a well-dressed Black man look up at the camera with a throw-away phone on the counter.

"Stop the tape!" He almost leaped from his chair. "I think we might have our man. There's something about him that doesn't look right. Look at how he's focused on the camera. I know it's him. Let's get the facial-recognition software running. I need to know who he is."

"Hold your water, Max," Warren said. "We'll need the techies up here to do that stuff. We'll call them." He turned to his partner. "You remember that guy who did that rape case a couple months ago? You think he might do us a favor?"

"Yeah. I've got his number on my cell phone."

"Good. Let's call him before our Fed has a heart attack."

The little Piper lifted off the runway, and Lamar glanced at his wife. "Honey, there isn't anything in the world I wouldn't do for you. Now we're off to San Juan, Puerto Rico, for a little R&R."

Wendy gave him her most-seductive look and reached into his crotch, gently grabbing his manhood. "That's right, Baby. You'll have to muster plenty of energy for the next few days."

Lamar was slightly shocked, but he was so engrossed with her actions that he didn't realize he over-rotated the plane until the stall warning chirped. He immediately lowered the nose and gently lifted her hand from his lap.

"Stop laughing," he said into his headset mic. "You could've killed us, and we aren't even out of Maryland yet."

She laughed almost too hard to listen, then she said, "OK, Top Gun." She reached over and patted his crotch again. "You calm yourself down and try not to put us into a spin. I'll leave you alone and read my book."

Howard, the DSP's computer whiz, downloaded the scanned picture into the facial-recognition software just as Max returned from a bathroom break.

"OK," Howard said. "If this guy has a DMV photo anywhere in the U.S., he's ours, but it might take awhile. We don't have the most-modern equipment here, you know."

"Yeah, yeah," Warren said. "All you have to do is look at our desks to see we're barely out of the typewriter stage ourselves. You do your magic, and we'll wait. What do you want on your pizza?"

The last slice of pizza was gone an hour earlier, and they were still waiting when the computer finally lit up with an alert like a slot machine hitting the jackpot.

For Max, it *was* a jackpot. He stared at the Delaware State Driver License of Lamar Weston and mumbled, "Gotcha. I've got you now."

Gavin nodded. "Do you want us to run him down and pay him a visit?"

"No, no. This is where we take the lead with Shock and Awe. It'll be a visit with about twenty SWAT guys storming in to get his attention. Of course, you'll be there. We don't want to get in trouble with some technicality and have the whole thing thrown out of court, if we get that far.

"I'm going back to Washington to set it up. I'll let you know when we're going in. I really appreciate all your help, Guys. I'll remember this. I'll see you later."

He walked out the door, pumping his fist in the air like a prize fighter who just scored a knockout.

CHAPTER 17

The ringing phone stirred Karen Ann out of a dream where she and Larry were just getting to the good stuff, and she didn't want to wake up. She forgot where she was for a moment and what was happening.

It took a second before she realized what was ringing, and she immediately regained her composure to reach for the phone on the bulkhead. "Captain, here."

"Captain, this is Hanratty. We're two hours out of Norfolk, and you left orders to ring you when we reached this position."

"Thank you, Pat. I'll be up in a couple minutes. Have you called the pilot tower to arrange for a pilot boarding upon arrival?"

"Yes, Ma'am. They're all set, and so is the yard. We really lucked out. The drydock was empty, and they had just enough time to get ready for us. We won't even have to wait before we go in.

"Also, Skipper, the office called and tried to make me wake you early, but I told them you'd call back when you were up. They didn't make much of a fuss, so it didn't sound like it was super important."

"Thank you, Pat. I'll be up in a flash. See if you can rustle up something for breakfast. I'm starving."

"You've got it, Skipper. See you soon."

She looked at her naked body in the mirror and cupped her still-firm, forty-plus-years-old 36C breasts and thought, *Not too bad, if I do say so myself. Let these babies out, and he won't be able to resist. Then nature can take its course.*

She shook her head. *OK. Enough of that. I have a busted ship to get into port.*

She uncupped her breasts with a soft caress that slid into a teasing nipple squeeze between her index fingers and thumbs, then she finished dressing with a big smile on her face, and thoughts of Larry lingering in her mind.

She just finished her last slice of toast and checking over Mr. Hanratty's preparations for entering port and putting in at the shipyard when Pat walked into the chartroom. "Is everything in order and to your liking?"

Karen Ann looked up from the table. "Pat, you do fantastic work. You've got everything in order. I couldn't have done better myself. Why haven't you gone for your Chief Mate's license? You'd make a good one."

"Skipper, if I did that, I'd have to sail for someone else. I don't want to do that at this stage of my career."

"You can stop shoveling manure. I don't have my boots on."

They shared a good laugh.

"Seriously, Pat. You'd make a good Chief Mate, and someday, a great captain. You should consider taking some classes and going after your license. The pay increase more than compensates for the cost of the courses."

"Thank you, Skipper. I'll look into it. In all honestly, though, I enjoy being your ship's navigator. I've never sailed for a better skipper, so it would be hard to move on from here." He smiled. "What I came in for was to let you know that the pilot boat is five miles away. We ought to be pretty close to the station by now."

They walked to the bridge and the serious business of coming into port.

Special Agent Max Gordon was just getting to his office after having to deal with the usual commuter-traffic snarls on the Beltway in

DC that usually left him in a nasty mood until his morning coffee break, but not that day.

He was heading to meet with a task force that would go to Delaware and apprehend Lamar Weston. He walked into his office and broke out the file he compiled on the man over the last few days.

It's not much, but my gut says he's the one I'm looking for, he thought. *You seem so squeaky clean, you* have *to be dirty.*

He went to the underground garage to meet the assault force he requested for the mission and go over the plan of attack. It was fairly simple, and the meeting ended quickly.

"Remember, everyone, and I mean *everyone.* We want this guy alive," he said. "He's our only link to the big picture."

The meeting broke up, and the team members went to their vehicles.

The beach in front of the luxury hotel was a wonderful refuge for Lamar for the past two days. He hadn't found the courage or the right words to let Wendy know what was going on. He had to find a way to apologize for endangering their lives.

He knew she would probably divorce him and request full custody of the kids without any visitation rights. His only hope was she wouldn't turn him in to the authorities, because he knew that would be a death sentence. He doubted he'd even get to a trial, let alone start serving life in prison, before the cartel had him killed.

He also knew that today had to be the day he confessed. They were scheduled to return home the following day and pick up the kids. Wendy needed time to figure out what she wanted to do after she knew the truth, and he needed to give her that time and space.

He promised himself he wouldn't break down and beg her to do anything except never doubt his love for her and the kids. He considered drinking some liquid courage early but decided against it. He needed his head clear.

When the beach waitress stopped by to ask if he wanted anything from the bar, Lamar said, "I'll just have bottled water."

"One bottled water for the gentleman," she said. "Will the lady join you soon? May I get her something?"

"I'm not sure when she'll come down. She was still asleep when I left the room. Just bottled water for now, thank you."

The deserted beach stretched far beyond the hotel grounds. When Wendy arrived, he suggested they go for a walk. She felt that was romantic, and she expected him to choose an isolated nook to make love, but he seemed oddly preoccupied, which saddened her.

She walked beside him, holding his hand, wishing he would take her up the beach and make passionate love to her like the previous night.

Finally, she couldn't take it any longer and dragged him up the beach to a little spot that indented into the shrubbery with the shade from an overhanging palm tree, where she flung herself down onto the sand and pulled him on top of her.

She looked into his eyes once he focused on her and said, "I want you right here and now. Whatever's distracting you can wait until we're done."

He complied with her wishes. Their lips met, and their hands explored each other's bodies as if they never touched each other before. Soon, their swimsuits were discarded, and their naked bodies enjoyed the pleasure only those truly in love could know.

She made him roll onto his back, so she could be in control. She rose up until they were almost disengaged, then she slowly slid down, knowing she had him in her power, and he was at the mercy of her whims. She could pull him out of whatever had him so preoccupied. Her eyes met his, and he stared at her, showing he was in his happy place.

"I love you so much, Wendy Lee Weston," he gasped.

They climaxed together and collapsed into a writhing mass of flesh, easing toward a slow finish to what was one of the most-extraordinary love-making sessions of their lives.

After they recovered their composure and dressed, they continued walking. About a mile farther down the beach, Lamar saw a large piece of driftwood above the high-tide line and pulled her toward it. She assumed he wanted an encore performance, which made her smile like a schoolgirl.

Once they reached the log, she saw the worried expression he wore since they arrived in Puerto Rico was back in his eyes.

"Wendy," he began, "I need to talk to you about something very serious. I can't put it off any longer. Please sit and listen without interrupting, and please, never doubt I love you and the kids."

"But.... What do you mean? Are you leaving us?"

"No, no. It's nothing like that. Now just stop. Don't try to figure anything out. I'll get to all of it. When I'm done, you can ask whatever you want, but you have to let me finish. I've been laboring over this, and I need to do this now. Honey, will you do that for me?"

She touched his cheek with a gentle hand. "Lamar, I'm your wife, for richer or poorer, in sickness and health, for the good times and the bad. You can tell me whatever you need to say. As long as you love the children and me, I'm on your side."

He prayed she would still mean those words after he finished confessing all the things he did that led to betraying his country and his family.

"OK, then. Growing up on the streets of West Philly when I was ten, I joined the Gangsta, a local gang. Either that, or Lester and I would be beat up every day when we went to school, so that's what I did. I had to keep it from my mom, because the one thing she preached to me when I was growing up was to stay away from gangs. I couldn't let her down when she worked so hard to keep a roof over our heads. I respected her and what she meant to me. She was my hero. She made Lester and me promise not to turn out like our daddy, a man who died in prison after getting arrested for a gang shooting over drugs...."

He talked for a long time, then he finished with, "So we did have a real gas leak, but it wasn't from natural causes. I'm so glad you saw that man coming out of the backyard. I knew I had to get you and the kids out of there before they came back to finish what they started.

"I'll figure out what to do once you tell me where we stand, or where I stand with you, in your life. Whatever your decision is, I will honor it to the extent I'm able."

"So that's it, every crime and treason I committed in the pursuit of money, power, and self-righteousness."

She hadn't moved during the long story, as if mesmerized by his tale. She was barely able to believe him. She stared in shock, and he stared back, waiting to see if she would turn him in or if she would rather kill him outright.

Her face filled with disbelief and confusion, but, to his amazement, he didn't see hate, which he expected. Wendy sat there, her mind reeling, trying to place what she learned into the perspective of what she always believed was their life together.

How could he do those things and claim he loves us and cherishes his family, when he almost got us killed, and we might still be killed when we go back? she wondered.

"I...I need some time to digest all of this, Lamar." Her voice was distracted and unusually calm, as she got up from the log she sat on for over two hours. "I need some time."

She turned toward the hotel and walked away.

He was so exhausted from the effort of telling his story, he couldn't respond. He knew he crushed her thoughts of her life with him they shared until that moment.

He sat on the log, tears streaming down his cheeks, watching her image grow smaller in the distance and wondering if he would ever be part of her life again.

Max checked his watch. It was nearing 11:00, and the mission wasn't going as planned. The stakeout agents spaced around the office building where Weston ran his consulting firm were beginning to chatter over the radio. No one had sighted him yet.

Max looked at Sharper and Hobnobski. "Looks like I brought us here on a wild-goose chase. It doesn't seem like our man will show up at work today."

He called the rest of the team over the radio. "Change in plan. I'll walk in as a would-be client and see if I can find out where Mr. Weston is."

Max strolled into the building and checked the directory board, thinking, *So this is how the other half lives.* He realized he was in the Weston Financial Building. He hadn't noticed the name when he walked through the front doors.

Weston Financial Services was on the fifth floor of the five-story building, one of the largest buildings in Milford.

"Does this guy own the entire town?" he muttered, walking to the elevator.

The square with the number five lit up a few moments later. As the elevator doors opened, Max found himself surrounded by gold and glass. The floor had a red-and-gold carpet, with the red portion leading to two frosted glass doors—the only way he could go.

How about that? This guy gives everyone the red-carpet treatment as soon as they leave the elevator.

Gold lettering on the doors showed the company name and a motto.

Weston Financial Services
We treat your finances as our own,
because, when you succeed, so do we.

Well. The file said he was good at what he does. Very impressive so far. Let's see where he is today.

Max reached for the door handle. As he opened the door, he heard Wagner's *The Ride of the Valkyries* and stopped to get his bearings.

This guy is something. He makes it seem like you're going into the ring as Rocky and Apollo better look out. I'd better look out. He gets people into the right frame of mind.

He stepped into a room with individual, classic, high-backed gentlemen's club seats for people to relax in and wait for their appointment. The waiting area wasn't large but still didn't seem cramped. A large but not overly big flat-screen TV filled one wall with the stock channel on. The volume was high enough to hear without being overbearing. On the opposite wall, a frosted glass door opened almost the moment he came in.

"Good morning, Sir," an attractive young woman said. "May I help you?"

He almost swallowed his tongue. She was stunning. He quickly regained his composure and used every ounce of his high-school acting ability. "I'd like to see Mr. Weston."

"I'm sorry, Sir, but he's not available today. He won't be in the office all day."

"I didn't know. I'm sorry. Could you tell me when he'll be back, so I can meet him?"

"I'm not sure, Sir. He's out of the country on a vacation with his family."

"Oh. He didn't mention that when we spoke the other day. I told him I'd stop by to see what he could do for me."

Hoping to be efficient, she said, "He left on an impromptu vacation when there was a natural gas leak at his home. I doubt he'll be gone very long. His children start school in a couple of days, right after the Labor Day weekend."

"Oh, that's right," Max said. "I almost forgot. I'll be back next week when he returns from.... Where did you say he went again?"

"I didn't say, Sir, and Mr. Weston doesn't let me divulge that kind of information."

"Oh. I didn't mean to seem nosy. I thought you mentioned something."

"That's quite all right, Sir. May I have your name and where you met with him, so I can let Mr. Westin know to expect you and to refresh his memory?"

Max felt tense. He didn't want to ruin his chances of meeting the guy. Then he remembered the file said Weston had a daughter taking swimming lessons."

"Sure," he said. "My name is Maxwell Houseman. We were gabbing while our kids took their swimming lessons about a month ago. I'm not sure he'll remember me. It's been awhile, and I rarely see him there."

He was surprised when she took out a notebook and wrote down what he said. "Thank you, Mr. Houseman. That's H-O-U-S-E-M-A-N, correct?" She didn't wait for an answer. "I'll be sure to let Mr. Westin know you were here and to expect your return. Here's one of his cards. You might want to call ahead and make sure he has time available when you want to stop back."

She showed him to the door.

"Thank you very much, Miss.... I'm sorry. I didn't get your name."

"It's not Miss. It's Ms. Jennings." She held the door open for him.

"Thank you again, Ms. Jennings." He walked through the door to the anteroom.

CHAPTER 18

Max returned to his office just in time to receive the information he requested after leaving Milford, Delaware, and his failed attempt to apprehend Lamar Westin. He spent five minutes with his nose buried in the material he was handed on the way into his office.

"I should've asked for this from the beginning," he said. "He has his own plane, and he filed a flight plan with the FAA that says he and one passenger flew from Miami to Puerto Rico on Tuesday. This is Thursday, so let's hope he flies home really soon. He'll have to file another flight plan to return to the States. I can have the FAA notify me when he does."

He lifted the telephone receiver, preparing for a new takedown.

Max didn't notice Tim Ferrow from the DEA, who was sitting in his office when he walked in. Tim held back his laughter as best he could.

Finally, Max looked up and saw Tim sitting in the corner, ready to bust out laughing, and almost jumped from his chair. "Jesus! What the hell are you doing here? Have you been here the entire time?"

Tim almost rolled out of his chair with laughter. He couldn't speak, so he nodded. When his laughter slowed down, he said, "Hi, Max. You were so engrossed with that file, I couldn't help letting you finish. I heard about your attempt to get that guy who might shed light on your case. I want to see if you were up for a quick, beer to console your ego."

Max finally joined in the laughter while flipping his middle finger at Tim. "I'll get really consoled if you're buying. Just let me set up getting notified by the FAA when Westin comes back. Now stop laughing so I can make some calls, then we can get out of here."

Tim finally calmed down, and Max set up his new plan.

"All right," Max said. "It's time for you to console me with beer. I hope you've got plenty of money in your wallet. I need lots of consoling. Let's get out of here."

The 1969 metallic-blue Chevy Corvette Twin Top 427 cubic-inch four-speed, which Larry had in convertible mode, pulled up in front of Karen Ann's condo complex by the waterfront portion of the town called Waterside. She told him she was staying there while her ship was being repaired.

He reached for his cell phone and called to say he arrived.

"Hello, Larry," she answered. "I'm still at the shipyard. I'll be here a bit longer. There's plenty of water to pump out. Do you want to come down here or wait for me there? I can't promise how long I'll be."

"I can come out there. I should be there in thirty minutes. Can you get me a pass at the gate?"

"You'll find one waiting for you. I took the liberty of setting it up already. Someone will be there to escort you to the graving dock. See you then."

He said good-bye, flipped the phone shut, and drove toward the shipyard. He was impressed with what Norfolk accomplished to the city's condition since the last time he was there to attend radar school in the early '80s. The place had come a long way. People seemed dedicated to keeping it a vibrant, living city. When he was a young man, the place was dying and on life support. The only people who went to Waterside were those who had to.

Over time, it became a destination for people to play, not just run from after work. He drove his 'vette toward Route 64, the road that led to almost everything around Norfolk.

The *Palm Princess* sat in drydock, dominating the surrounding buildings and other ships in for repair work or under construction. The only ship that could give the *Palm Princess* any competition was an aircraft carrier under construction and still far from completion.

The yard worker who drove Larry to the drydock pointed at the small figure standing halfway down the dock. "That's the ship's master down there," he said in a Southern drawl. "I can't take you down the dock, because vehicles aren't allowed. All the masters or ship reps get a golf cart while they're here, so they can get around the yard easier. Personal vehicles have been banned from the yard since 9/11."

"Thanks for the ride. I don't think a little walk will kill me. Have a good evening." He slid out of the car.

A moment later, he walked beside the largest manmade object that moved he ever saw. The ship was massive. It was astounding that the little galley girl who cried on his shoulder about having to go to college was the master of such a monster.

Karen Ann didn't notice Larry coming down the dock, because she was studying the hull, looking for the crack the rogue wave caused. From all indications, she and the Chief Engineer agreed it had to be on the side, not the bottom. She hadn't found it yet, but the water was still being pumped from the drydock. The ship had settled into its support blocks and was steady as a rock. Already, plenty of people were working on the big girl. Time was money in the oil business, and the faster the turnaround, the better it was for both parties.

The *Palm Princess* would return to her regular run and continue filling the coffers of Palm Petroleum, and the yard would be able to use the drydock for another customer to fill the shipyard's coffers. Getting them in and out as fast as they could was the motto of the shipyard workers.

As Larry walked toward the figure who'd been pointed out to him, he couldn't help checking her out. *Wow. She looks better than the last time I saw her, right before she went to SUNY Maritime, if that's possible.*

She'd been a fresh-faced, tight-bodied, stacked girl who could have gotten a date with any boy she wished. Much to the heartache of the boys in her class and the classes above and below hers, she didn't date much. Larry remembered how hard people worked just to get her to go to her senior prom.

The closer he came to her and the more her shape became clear , he started fervently hoping this meeting wasn't just two old friends out to share old memories.

"Hello, Captain Murphy." He came up behind her, as he spoke.

His words broke through the intense stare she directed at the hull. She turned and almost leaped into his arms, giving him a hug that made him realize he hadn't been hugged like that since he talked to her parents and convinced them to let her go to a maritime school, not a regular college.

When she released him, she said, "Let me look at you. I didn't think it was possible for a man to get any better looking than in his twenties, but you sure have."

"You haven't lost a step, either, Karen Ann. You're as gorgeous as ever."

"Larry, let me finish up here, and I'll take you out to dinner. You're hungry, right? Oh, you can drop that captain stuff. I owe this all to you. There's no way I can ever thank you for what you did for me."

"I'm famished. Getting a bite to eat works for me. Secondly, you don't have to thank me for anything. Seeing you in command of a ship like this," he waved his hand at the *Palm Princess,* "is thanks enough. You took yourself from a little girl flipping burgers on a ferry boat to being captain. I'm proud that I had a small part to play in your success. That's thanks enough."

He looked at the huge ship. "Is there anything I can help you with? You seemed pretty preoccupied when I came down the dock a moment ago."

"Oh, that's right. You don't know why I'm here, do you?"

"You said you bent the boat a little bit, but the answer is still no."

"I'm sorry, Larry. It's been pretty hectic the last couple days. I'll fill you in over dinner. To give the short answer, we have a small split on the starboard side, on number-six double-hull, wing tank, but I haven't found it yet. If you want, you can help me look for it. Then I can give the office a heads-up on what we find."

"Sounds like a plan. Let's get looking. I'm starving."

Lamar waited until Wendy was out of sight before thinking about walking toward the resort. He didn't want to go back to face her, but he had to know where he stood with her.

He gave her a long stretch of time, then he found the courage to begin walking back. his thoughts raced from one scenario to another, each worse than the one before.

Finally, he felt he needed to clear his head before facing Wendy. The only way he knew to do that was to be immersed in aviation. He needed to make his next flight plan, check the weather, set up for customs, and get the plane fueled for tomorrow's flight home.

It seemed like a good time to take care of all that. Maybe the work would help straighten out his head.

When he walked back to where they left their beach towels and other gear that morning, he picked all of it up and found a taxi in front of the resort. Climbing in, he looked at the cabbie and said, "The airport, please."

CHAPTER NINETEEN

"Karen Ann," Larry said, "I don't know where the crack is supposed to be, but I don't see anything. The whole hull is clear. You couldn't have hurt it that bad."

"I guess we won't find it now. Let's go to dinner and stop back here afterward, if you don't mind. By then, we should be able to get inside the drydock and get in close."

"Sounds like a plan to me."

They walked back to the dock, where she had a courtesy golf cart waiting.

The restaurant was busy, but they didn't have to wait too long. It was right after the early arrivals cleared out but before the late-night diners arrived. The evening was going pretty well for both of them. Catching up with small talk that flowed easily, and they seemed comfortable in each other's presence.

Larry ordered the waiter's recommended dish, the shrimp medley, which was very good. It brought back a memory of a past boss at the ferry, and he tried to give Karen Ann his best impersonation of him when he asked, "Ta...ta...ta....try some ah...ah sh...sh...shrimp?"

Her head came up, because she recognized the impersonation and laughed with him. They tried to quiet themselves, which brought on even more laughter.

Karen Ann's cell phone vibrated on the table. Her laughter subsided, because she doubted it brought good news. She grabbed her phone and walked toward the waiting area to avoid disturbing other patrons, hoping Larry understood. She didn't even pause to explain why she walked away.

"Captain Murphy," she said.

"OK. OK. What? Where? I'll be there in twenty minutes." She hung up and walked back to the table. "Larry, I'm sorry. I have to be at the shipyard as fast as possible. They found the crack, but they also found something I need to see."

She waved to the waiter and asked for the check and some takeout containers.

Larry, seeing her puzzled, worried expression, didn't press for information. She would share it when she was ready.

The ride back to the yard in the 'Vette with the top down and a warm summer breeze blowing didn't have any effect on Karen Ann. She knew Larry was driving as fast he could while staying close to the speed limit and within the traffic flow. Knowing a Corvette drew police attention anywhere it went, she didn't want him to get a speeding ticket for her.

The shipyard gate finally came into view, and Karen Ann was almost out of the car before he parked. He quickly raised the top and ran to catch up with her before she reached the gate.

They showed their ID to the guard, who allowed them into the shipyard, and Karen Ann immediately found a golf cart. A moment later, they drove down the streets of the shipyard toward the *Palm Princess*.

As they sped down Graving Dock Avenue, the huge tanker loomed in the distance, growing larger as they neared the drydock. When they arrived at the drydock, the scene was the opposite of what they left.

What had been a furious amount of activity to prep the ship for repair work and the ships on either side had become a ghost town. All work stopped.

Each department at the yard wore a different color hard hat to distinguish their workers, and each level of supervisor or management had a separate color, with the department color in a stripe down the middle of the hat. Only when someone reached the upper levels of shipyard management did the hat become all white with just the person's name and title on it.

Since anyone in the shipyard had to wear a hard hat when outside or even in certain buildings, Karen Ann was issued one with her golf cart. The color of the company representative's hat was international orange, which she also got for Larry. It wasn't quite a lie. He represented the Cape May Lewes Ferry, not Palm Petroleum. With an international orange hat on, he could get into the yard easily.

A small group stood at the head of the pier, with yard security vehicles flashing red and blue lights blocking the entrances to the piers on either side of the *Palm Princess.*

Karen Ann pulled up the golf cart to the group of men and got out, quickly followed by Larry. She approached the group, all of whom wore white hard hats, showing they were supervisors on an upper level of management.

The only nonwhite hat in the group was a powder-blue hat with red stripe down the middle, showing he was the foreman of the riggers assigned to work on the *Palm Princess* that night. Riggers did all the heavy lifting in the shipyard, and they also set the large blocks ships rested on when the water was pumped out of the drydock.

Karen Ann imagined many scenarios. "Was someone injured? I'm Captain Murphy."

The hard hats turned to stare at her. Word had already spread she was quite a "looker."

"Hi, Captain," one man said. "I'm Alfred Beamer, Vice President of Operations. I'm the one who asked you to be called to the shipyard. I'm sorry if we interrupted your evening." He glanced at Larry. "Please call me Al. I like to keep things as informal a possible."

She shook his hand. "That's fine, Al. I'm Karen Ann. This is Captain Lawrence Halsey."

Larry offered to shake Al's hand next. "Larry is just fine with me."

"Great." Al's expression turned serious. "We discovered an abnormality on your ship that we have no record of being installed when we launched her in February."

"What exactly do you mean, Al?" Karen Ann asked.

"It would be better to show you than explain. Come with me." He led them down the pier where the starboard-side gangway was located. "It's down there, under the gangway, almost right at the chine in the shadow. Can you see it?" He pointed at something that resembled a blister attached to the hull.

"What is it?" she asked. "It looks pretty small. Did it have anything to do with the crack in the hull? What's it doing on my ship?"

"We aren't sure what it is, but it's not as small as it seems. We can't take any chances, Karen Ann. The Virginia State Police bomb squad is on its way. All work within 1,000 feet of here has been stopped until the bomb squad arrives and lets us know what's going on."

He led the contingent of hard hatters back up the pier. Once they were back at the head of the pier, he looked at Karen Ann. "I'll try to answer your questions, but right now, we don't have anything definite."

"Fine. I understand. Tell me what you know and what your best guess might be."

"OK. Here's what we know. First, it's not part of your ship. Second, someone deliberately placed it there who didn't want you or your crew to find it. Third, it's very well made and engineered, because it stayed attached to your hull during the hurricane you went through.

"That's what we know for certain. As far as guessing what it is, it could be almost anything. That's why we called the bomb squad."

Al's cell phone rang. He answered quickly. "Beamer here. Great. Send them down." He hung up. "Good news. The bomb squad is here and should be on the scene in five minutes. By the way, Barney is the one who found the object when he was down in the dock checking the setup of the blocks." He pointed to the only nonwhite hard hat in the group beside her and Larry.

"Thank you, Barney," she said. "You've got good eyes. You could've walked right by that without seeing it."

"You're welcome, Captain. Just doing my job. By the way, Captain, they found a small split in starboard number-six double-hull tank. A weld seam split open about eighteen inches. It shouldn't be too bad to repair, just cut out the bad seam and weld in a patch."

"The shaft bearing might take awhile," Al added, "because we didn't get very far into the takedown to know what we'll need to repair it."

"That's a little bit of good news, anyway," she replied. "Now we have to wait for these guys." She nodded at the bomb squad van stopping nearby. "Let me know if I'll still have a ship when they're finished. Oh, and one more thing. Where is my crew? Have arrangements been made if we can't get back aboard tonight?"

Al checked his watch. "I believe they were transported to the front office. Your Chief Mate said he would contact you about any arrangements."

She pulled out her cell phone and realized she missed a call from Carbini before she answered Al's call. "In all the rush to get here, I forgot to turn up the ringer and missed his call. Thank you. Let me call him to make sure my crew is taken care of."

She walked a few steps away and called Jim.

The bomb squad supervisor walked over. "OK, Folks. We have no idea what we're dealing with here, so I need all unessential personnel cleared out. I'll start with a 1,000-foot perimeter, and we'll go from there. Right. I need someone to get us down there and advise us on what we're seeing. Who'll be the victim...er, the volunteer, who can help out?"

"That would be me," Barney said. "I'll get you and your men down there and advise you while we're working."

"I'd like to come along," Karen Ann said.

"Not this time, Little Lady," the bomb squad supervisor said.

Before she could reply, Al interjected, "Excuse me, Sir, with all due respect for your profession and authority, but you need to pay a little more respect. That thing you're going to look at is the lady's ship. She's the Master."

"I'm sorry, Ma'am. I mean, Captain. I didn't intend any disrespect, but I still want everyone back except for the gentleman who will get us down there and give us the basic info we need. Let's get you suited up in protective gear and get this show on the road."

He guided Barney to the bomb truck. His men set up their perimeter, shooing the people in white hats back.

"Sir," Barney asked the bomb squad supervisor, "do you want to take the fast way down or the slow way?"

"First, call me Bob." He shook Barney's hand.

"I guess if there's a possibility I might get blown up, I should at least know the name of the man standing beside me," Barney answered. "I'm Barney."

"Let me ask you a few things, and we'll go from there. Were any radios used within the vicinity of the object? If so, how close?"

"Sure they were. That's how we all communicate around here. I stood almost right under it when I called for someone to give me some advice about it. I didn't recognize it being part of her."

"OK, that's good. It wasn't set off by radio waves. My men will need to use your yard radios, because we know those are safe. Tell me what the fast way down is. Was it already used around this thing?"

"The fast way is to get a crane operator back here and use that basket to lower us into the dock," Barney said, pointing. "That's how I went down and up the first time. I was the first one down to check the stability of the blocks. It didn't send us all up in smoke, so it should be OK the second time."

"That sounds fine with me, Barney. Let's get down there and figure this thing out. Call your crane operator over for an elevator ride. I'd like several of your walkie-talkies to use, too."

Once all the white and orange hats were in the safe zone, Karen Ann thanked Al for taking care of her crew. "My Chief Mate will make arrangements for them at a hotel for tonight. One thing, though. What about transportation? Is there any way to get them all there together and bring them back in the morning?"

"Sure. We can handle that. I'll get the bus that took them to the office to take them to the hotel and bring them back in the morning. Let me make a call to set it up."

"Thank you."

The crane operator quickly lowered the basket beside the object. Bob and two of his men accompanied Barney down into the dry-dock, carrying all kinds of equipment Barney didn't recognize.

Jim, one of Bob's men, had a TV camera that transmitted its feed to the van, which had a TV and recording device to save the video for later diagnostics and dissection.

They stared around themselves as if they'd been dropped into an alien world. They wore Kevlar body armor and Kevlar helmets with thick, optically corrected Lexan face shields. Underneath they wore Nomex body suits for fire protection. They looked like a cross between a human tank and a fireman. It seemed a miracle they could move with all that gear.

Most of their equipment trailed long cables back to the van, where technicians watched the feeds to decipher what various instruments sensed or viewed. They could talk to Bob in the basket, giving him more than his own expertise to work with.

"Wilson, let's get the X-ray up and send the scan," Bob said. "I don't think it'll show much. This looks like a solid piece of gear."

"We might get something, Boss. It appears to be aluminum. Depending on thickness, this baby might see something." Wilson set to work.

Bob gave a continuous verbal description of the object to the technicians in the van, making sure it was part of the record to be analyzed later. "I have a silver oblong object that appears sealed against the hull. I'm not sure if it's a cover, a solid object, or something hollow."

"Bob, I'm ready for the radiation scan," Wilson said.

"What do you mean? You were supposed to have it on already. We aren't wearing any radiation-protective gear. Start it now. It stays running throughout the entire operation." Bob's voice was calm but firm.

Wilson realized he'd been sloppy at his job. "Yes, Sir. Starting the scan now. I don't see any readings that are off the charts, but it seems a bit higher than normal."

"Bob, this is Sam," a voice said. "I don't think it's solid. I got a picture from the X-ray, though it's not very good. I've gone over it a couple times already, and that's the best I can give you right now."

"Thanks, Sam. Gentlemen, what we have so far is one, light radiation, and two, we're probably dealing with an object that's either hidden under a covering or is hollow. Three, it's about six-feet long. At its widest, it's about one-and-a-half feet. It extends off the ship a foot.

"Four, it's metal. Best guess now is aluminum or an alloy. Five, it doesn't seem rigged with a vibration switch, nor does it seem to be radio sensitive. I'm going to touch it, Guys. Make sure the TV records this, Jim."

"On it, Boss."

CHAPTER 20

Lamar opened his eyes but didn't recognize where he was. Then it all flooded back, and he felt sick to his stomach again. He ran for the men's room and threw up. Afterward, he splashed water on his face in the sink and tried to clean up.

He glanced at his watch. *Oh, no. It's 0230. I've been here since six o'clock last night.*

He returned to the pilot lounge of the FBO, fixed base operator, and checked his work to see if he completed all the items he needed to log for his flight back to Florida and get checked in with U.S. Customs. Then they would go to Wendy's parents' house to collect the kids and get back into the air for the short hop home—he hoped.

He checked his cell phone but didn't see any messages or missed calls from Wendy. Which only started his stomach to churn again.

"I can't put it off any longer," he said. "I have to face her." He gathered his charts and gear to carry to his trusty Saratoga.

The airplane had always been his refuge and solace when he was bothered by a tough problem or just needed to get away for an hour or two. He often sat quietly on the tarmac outside the FBO.

As he focused on the plane, he ran his hand along the wing and down the fuselage toward the tail, thinking how whenever he had a bad day or something went wrong in life, he took his magic carpet up for a little trip. His mind always cleared the instant he sat behind the yoke. When he landed and shut her down, the answer to the problem that was bugging him would materialize in his mind. As his hand reached the tail of the plane, he shook his head in dejection. "My girl, we ran into a problem neither of us can fix with just a little air time."

He affectionately patted the fuselage and walked toward the plane's door. After he stowed everything and locked up his plane, he went to the front of the FBO to catch a cab back to the resort, and, he hoped, a life that might still include Wendy, his kids, and Butch, their cute little Sheltie.

"So far it's as smooth as a baby's bottom," Bob said over the communication line. "This is fine workmanship. I think it was hand-drawn the old-fashioned way with an anvil, hammer, a strong back, and an eye for detail. It's beautifully made so far.

"Let's move to the lower portion of this thing and see if there's any way to get inside. There's nothing on the top."

He gently touched every millimeter of the object. When he was at the middle at the lowest, widest point, his finger touched a small opening the size of his thumbnail no one had noticed before.

"Whoa. I think we have something. Jim, get a shot of my hand's location. If you can, drop down to see if you can get a picture of this for the van guys to analyze."

"Right, Boss. I see what looks like a machined opening that could house an attachment mechanism. I can't see what kind of mechanism it might be, but I see the opening."

Bob continued his physical exploration of the blister, as the crew had taken to calling it. "Sam, what time do you have up there?"

"I've got 0430 hours, Bob. Why? Got a hot date you want to make?"

"Nah. I'm just getting a little tired. That's all. I need to get out of this hole for a while, stretch my legs, get some coffee, and hit the latrine, if you must know.

"Gentlemen," Bob said, "I'll stop us right here. We'll take a break and get back at it. We've been at this all night. Let's get some breakfast and tackle trying to get into this little blister."

Barney coordinated with the crane operator to lift them from the drydock.

Max didn't sleep very well, so he got up early and went to the office. It was 0500 hours, and traffic was light, so he made it into the city early. He decided to stop for breakfast.

Five years before, when he first arrived in DC, he found a good breakfast and lunch joint, but, in the ensuing years, he was relegated to eating a power bar from a vending machine and dousing it down with a cup of coffee from the break room, because he never had enough time to enjoy a nice breakfast of eggs, bacon, and hash browns.

He decided to make the effort, thanks to the extra time from his insomnia. He pulled into his designated parking space in the FBI building's underground garage and took an elevator to the lobby. He could walk to the restaurant and make up for not taking the stairs, his normal routine and the only real exercise he got anymore. From there, he could walk onto the street and head toward the greasy spoon he liked.

He placed his order as soon as he was seated. Even the restaurant was a little slow that early in the day. It was a good time to go over some paperwork he'd been putting off since the case began to heat up. He reached into his briefcase for the latest edition of his WOOPSIE, *Weekly Overview Of Probable Security Interagency Events.* After the Department of Homeland Security was created, the agencies involved in making up the DHS were ordered to communicate with each other to rectify the lack of communication that allowed for situations such as 9/11, the bombing of several embassies, and the World Trade Center bombing in 1993.

The DHS created the WOOPSIE in an effort to keep everyone aware of possible breaches in security or events happening in the realm of each individual agency. The theory was, any little bit of information might link to something another agency was working on, and that bit could be the piece that broke the case wide open.

The WOOPSIE worked so well around the Beltway that it was expanded to include local law enforcement contributions. It was where Max found information about the death of Willie and Leroy with the bizarre twist of having their eyes glued open, which led him to his case. Since its inception, the value of the WOOPSIE proved itself many times. It was the brainchild of Director Tom Ridge, the DHS' first director, and it still took two months before it became reality. Trying to get the other agencies to agree to participate and appreciate in the new form of openness the White House demanded and wasn't going to back down from became a lesson in diplomacy that would soon be taught in political science classes in every college. All the agencies now loved getting their copy of the WOOPSIE, because all of them had stubborn cases that were eventually broken open by an innocuous piece of information from a different agency.

Max was a diehard supporter of the WOOPSIE. He often had information that didn't seem useful to anyone, but when he submitted it to the WOOPSIE, one piece was immediately picked up by the CIA, and they broke open an Al Qaeda sleeper cell that was very well hidden in Mexico, waiting to sneak across the border.

Most of the general public never heard about ninety percent of the fine work various organizations did to keep the nation safe from terrorists. The government would like nothing better than to pat itself on the back each time a plot to bring a terrorist into the country was defeated, but doing so would severely endanger the lives of many good informants and moles who were put in place with terrorist groups, not to mention revealing many of the country's operational tactics and tipping off terrorists about anti-terrorist agencies and their missions.

The liberal public kept saying not enough was being done. If something did go wrong, they immediately said the government was sleeping on the job or was too busy spying on its own citizens instead of protecting them. The men and women in the agencies had a thankless job, but they performed it despite the criticism, general dislike, and even hatred the public showed. It was similar to how the servicemen and women returning home from Viet Nam felt in the '60s and '70s.

The internal motto of the DHS was added to every memo and email sent internally:

The battles will be many, the war will be long, casualties we will have to endure, the enemy is hidden and well entrenched, the road must be followed to the end. Vigilance must not be forgotten, and victory will be ours.

Max couldn't believe how good his breakfast tasted. He savored every mouthful, as he perused the WOOPSIE. As he finished the last bit of egg yolk puddle on his plate, sopping it up with a piece of whole-wheat toast, he finished the back page of the WOOPSIE and slipped it back into his briefcase.

Nothing jumped out at him concerning his own case, but one article buried on page four caught his eye. It came from the NRC, Nuclear Regulatory Commission, stating there was a discrepancy in their end-of-month inventory. Five thousand pounds of radioactive waste turned up missing, its whereabouts unverified.

He decided to have another cup of coffee before heading to his office.

The atmosphere in the room was colder than a blizzard in Antarctica. Wendy refused to acknowledge his presence. Lamar finally broke the silence to tell her they needed to be in the air by ten o'clock if they wanted to clear customs and get to her parents' house to pick up the kids.

She didn't reply. He began packing the things he bought or brought with him into their carry-on luggage, leaving it open for her to add her own things.

By nine-thirty, she stood at the door, waiting for him to get the bag and call a cab to take them to the airport.

"Remember," the lineman told Lamar, as he removed the chocks and untied the Saratoga. "You need to call at least one hour before arrival in Miami, so customs will process you."

"Thanks." Lamar handed the man a twenty. "I've got it here on my flight plan on my kneeboard. I appreciate your taking care of my baby while we were here."

"No problem, Sir. Glad I could be of service to you and the beautiful lady." He waved good-bye and sprinted into the FBO.

Lamar closed the door and began preparations for takeoff and his flight into the infamous Bermuda Triangle. That didn't bother him as much as his own personal Bermuda Triangle with Wendy, the cartel and its backers, and the authorities back home who would be looking for him someday—or his dead body.

The cockpit retained its chill and silence long after the Puerto Rico Center handed Lamar off to Miami Center an hour earlier, and Lamar acknowledged the turnover. Not one syllable was spoken in the cockpit until he finally broke the silence.

"Miami Center, this is Saratoga November Oh-four-six-nine-Whiskey-Whiskey. We are one hour out and southeast of Miami. Request permission to enter the ADIS. Over."

"Roger, Sixty-nine-Whiskey-Whiskey. This is Miami. We have you scheduled for arrival into Miami International in one hour. Please squawk 1753 and ident when ready. How copy?"

"Miami, this is Sixty-nine-Whiskey-Whiskey. Copy. Squawk 1753 and ident." Dialing in the new squawk code, he pressed the Ident button on the Mode C transponder.

The transponder talked to the controller's radar, and his plane became a computer-generated radar blip on the screen. The controller was able to read his true course and speed, as well as his altitude alongside an individualized ID number.

Lamar pressed the Push-To-Talk (PTT) button on his yoke and said, "Miami, this is Sixty-nine-Whiskey-Whiskey. How read ident? Over."

"Just fine, Six-nine. Say intentions. Over."

"I have two POB (Persons on Board), and we are going to land in Miami to clear customs and refuel, then continue to our final destination in Delaware with a stop in Maryland. Over."

"Roger, Six-nine. I'll notify customs to expect your arrival. It looks like you'll have a trouble-free ride up the coast. The entire East Coast is CAVU (Clear Air Visibility Unlimited). Check in at thirty miles out for routing information."

"Roger, Miami. Thirty out, check in. If nothing further, Sixty-nine out."

"Miami out."

Bob gathered the team and reminded them of their duties and safety rules before they returned to work after their break. During their debriefing after they came out of the hole, the others realized they never turned on the Geiger counter. Bob, Jim, and Barney left Wilson in the van to assist Sam with the diagnostic.

The crane operator lowered them down to the blister.

"Jim, you have the Geiger counter on this time, don't you?" Bob asked.

"You only need to slap my hand once, Boss," Jim said.

"That's good. I don't think our friend Barney wants to become an X-ray negative."

Barney monitored the basket's position and did his best to ignore the consequences of any problem they might encounter with the blister.

"OK, Gentlemen," Bob said. "The inspection part of our night is over. Now we start to earn our paychecks."

He began experimenting with different tools to fit into the small opening they found and see if it opened the blister the easy way.

"Well, I'll be a monkey's uncle," Bob said. "That seems almost too easy. The second hex wrench I tried fits perfectly. I get worried when things seem too easy. Everyone, stay on your toes."

He turned the wrench.

As the elevator took him to his floor and the start of another Friday, Max savored the wonderful feeling of satisfaction from having a full belly, expecting his plan would come together, and the hope he would soon see the results of all his labors.

CHAPTER 21

Lamar finished signing off with Miami Center after reporting he was thirty miles out. He received clearance to proceed to his next fix when Wendy, without looking at him, spoke.

"I'll be staying with my Mom and Dad when we get to Maryland," she said. "I haven't told them why. You should be the one to explain why I can't take our children to their home. You can either be the man I thought I married, or you can be a coward and live forever on the run from everybody. You decide."

She returned to reading her book and didn't look up even when they landed and taxied into the holding area for international general aviation arrivals at Miami International. Lamar didn't speak, either, except when talking to the airport controllers.

The customs officer was very expedient with his inspection and clearing them into the U.S. He would have held them for some reason if the FBI expressed an interest in Mr. Westin, but the FAA never sent word to the customs department that the FBI wanted to question Mr. Westin. The inquiry was screwed up from the start. When Max contacted the FAA for help in tracking Lamar and notifying him when he had an active flight plan, that's exactly what he received.

Max contacted the DC office of the FAA, which was its political arm, not the division that dealt with the work of planes and controllers. His request was put into the system as a minor request without any real importance.

When the controller entered Lamar's flight plan into the computer to activate the plan, the computer spat out a request for notification that a flight plan was activated. There was no reason given, so he sent the notice to his section leader, who didn't know who to contact. He passed it up the chain of command, and it continued until it finally reached the office Max contacted for his initial request.

The whole process took a long time. The notice of an active flight plan began on Friday morning of Labor Day weekend. The office Max contacted had the weekend off.

Max finally received notice that Lamar Westin activated his flight plan for return to the U.S. on Tuesday of the following week at 11:30 AM. Max missed the perfect opportunity to question his primary suspect.

Karen Ann and Larry sat on a small couch in a little coffee-break room off one of the maintenance buildings a few blocks from the drydock that held the *Palm Princess*. She was still exhausted from her dealings with the hurricane and bringing her injured ship into port. The quiet atmosphere, being sequestered from all the action, was all her body needed to remind her of the need for sleep.

She rested her head back, thinking she could close her eyes and regroup, and quickly fell asleep. Larry looked through a magazine and didn't notice her drifting off until her head slid onto his shoulder. She readjusted and slid all the way into his lap. He stroked her long hair and let her stay there, because it felt right.

Lamar had many questions for Wendy, but he knew her answers would be based on his actions dealing with her parents. Since Wendy made her statement that she wouldn't go home with him, he tried to figure out what to do when he reached Maryland. Would he run, try to lie, or tell the truth and realize he lost everything that meant something to him.

Somewhere over Virginia, he made up his mind.

Bob turned the hex wrench in slow quarter turns, reporting to the van after each quarter was completed. Just as he finished a complete turn, he felt the screw suddenly lock in.

"All stop! I just felt the screw lock into place or something. I might have released the cover. Let's see what we can do with this."

The men in the basket felt their senses come alive, as they prepared to open the blister.

"Jim, let's try putty knives," Bob said. "See if we can pry this off. I think it's a lid of some kind, so who knows what's under it. We need to be very careful and deliberate with our movements. Since we don't know how heavy it is, be prepared for some weight in case we're wrong about the material or that it's hollow."

He glanced at the others. "Everyone ready?"

Barney and Jim, standing on either side of him, nodded, with putty knives in one hand while their free hands touched the bottom of the blister.

"OK. On my go," Bob said, "we each give our knife a push down to see if we can slip behind this thing. Ready...go."

All three putty knives slid under the covering about three-quarters of an inch until they struck something solid.

"All right. Hold that, and let's see what we've got."

A quick check indicated there was an equal space all around the object and the hull, about the thickness of their putty knives. Bob took out a flashlight and gently probed the crack with his knife.

"OK. Let's see if we can slide it off its base."

All three men set their putty knives into the gap and slowly applied outward pressure. After a few tense seconds, the blister's shell slid away from the base to reveal more of the interior. Once the cover was fully removed, they saw a large metal package strapped down inside.

The base consisted of a thick portion that supported the cover and where the lock attached. The bottom of the base, against the hull, was segmented into an open grid where individual strong magnets had been precision fitted to mate the base against the vessel. The bottom also showed hold-down attachment points where straps were attached to hold the cargo firmly against the base and keep it from moving or putting pressure on the cover. Each magnet had an individual handle and could be removed one at a time to make the whole thing easy to carry, though the process would be time-consuming.

After Bob gave the base and its contents a careful examination, he reported to the van team, "The blister is composed of a bottom laid in an open grid that looks like a cargo net. Each grid opening is three inches square, and the flat piece making up the edge of the square is a quarter-inch thick with a wall separating it from the next magnet. Around this grid is a half-inch-thick rim that sticks out about an inch from the ship. That's what the cover fit over and locked into place.

"There are locking pins on the bottom, top, and at each end. They are interlocking and operated by the hex screw located on the bottom of the cover. Each individual magnet is shaped to fit into its opening like a glove. The face of the magnet is three inches square, with an eighth-inch-thick lip extending all around the top edge to provide the support that holds the base onto the ship's hull.

"On the outer rim are strap hold-down bars molded into the rim. Straps attached to them hold whatever someone packs into the space between the cover and the top of the magnets, about nine inches in the center tapering down to an inch at the ends. The package inside the blister is metal, about two-feet-six-inches long by one-foot-eight-inches deep, with a hasp and lock."

They stared at the pieces of finely machined, carefully crafted artwork. It was ingeniously made, but Jim shook himself when the Geiger counter gave off an alarm.

"Boss, you need to look at this." He showed the meter to Bob.

"OK. Looks like something in the package is giving us the alarm," Bob said. "Let's put the lid back on this baby and get topside for better protection."

The men carefully slid the cover into place. Barney called the crane operator to bring them up from the drydock. Once they were moving upward, he looked at Bob and asked, "Why did that thing go off like that?"

"Don't fret about that little bit of exposure," Bob said. "You'd get more in a dental X-ray. We need to suit up and come back down to see what we're working with. Hopefully, we'll have this cleared up by this afternoon, and I can get these boys home."

"Exposure? To what? Radiation?"

The basket was setting down on the ground above when Bob replied, "Just a little, like I said. Don't pay it no mind. The Geiger counter was barely registering.

"I've got a question for you as a rigger. With that quick look we had, can you make a guess how much weight that thing could hold?"

"It was definitely made to transport something. A rough guesstimate, and do mean rough, would depend on the strength of those magnets. It could be anywhere between 500-1,500 pounds, depending on density."

"Wow. You could hide a lot of something that way."

They nodded at each other.

Karen Ann's head was in his lap. Her hot breath was directed at his loins, making him feel slightly excited. He felt his penis become engorged with the blood of passion. Just as he realized he would have to adjust her head and himself, he felt a hand massage him almost to the point of no return.

He looked down and saw her looking up at him with questioning eyes, seeking his approval. He smiled and stroked her cheek. "I'm not sure we should continue this right now. It's almost nine in the morning, and there should be someone coming along real soon to tell us what's going on with your ship."

Karen Ann sat up. "Oh, my gosh. I almost forgot where we are. I was having such a nice dream. You can guess what it was about."

"I don't know exactly, but I can make a good guess what I hope it was about."

They giggled, and she leaned over to kiss him, which sent his imagination into overdrive, thinking of what might come next.

Max felt pretty good that Friday morning, sitting at his desk with a belly full of good breakfast and knowing that his man was as good as caught. He still had a nagging thought about that blurb in the WOOPSIE about that missing radioactive waste that wouldn't go away, so he pulled the newsletter from his briefcase and reread it for the fourth time that morning.

He decided to call the agent mentioned in the article to get more background information to see if anything fell into place concerning his own case.

You never know, he thought, punching numbers into his phone.

CHAPTER 22

Barney, Bob, and Jim looked like they just returned from a trip to the moon, dressed in radiation suits and SCBAs, Self-Contained Breathing Apparatus. They were ready to investigate the object in the blister's cover that gave off those radiation readings.

Barney guided them into position by the blister to begin removing the cover a second time and see what was causing the Geiger counter to give such a reading.

Jim and Bob removed the cover and set it to one side. Bob examined the container attached to the inside of the blister and said, "This is definitely not a bomb. However, we do have a problem. This stuff is labeled as nuclear waste, and it's got an NRC tracking number. Sam, get the NRC on the landline. Wilson, prepare a containment vessel for the waste to control the radiation being emitted.

"We'll have the package up on the pier within ten minutes. The container in this thing actually has many small packages that have a total weight of about 1,200 pounds, including the container itself. I need the containment vessel right by our landing site so we can get it in there without traipsing all over and facing a bigger cleanup than what we've already got. OK, Wilson?"

Bob started work on removing the package without waiting for a reply.

Barney stood at the far side of the basket. He leaned away so far, the other two men worried he might try to climb out and ride the basket on the outside.

"Barney, you don't have to be afraid," Bob said. "As long as you've got that suit on and breathe self-contained air, you're good as gold."

"Just the same," Barney said, "I'll keep as far from that thing as possible."

"You realize we aren't done, right? We still need to pull off the base of the blister, then we need to decontaminate the area and the blister itself, although you don't have to help with that part. Just help us with decontaminating the ship and yourself."

"How'd I get wrapped up in this?" Barney asked.

Bob and Jim shrugged.

"Sam," Bob said, "tell the shipyard people and that cute lady captain that there was no bomb, but it'll be a little while before we can release the ship for unrestricted access.

"You might also tell them that the NRC people will come by to pick up some of their wayward waste. I'm sure they'll be interested to know it wound up on this ship."

The basket gently touched down beside the containment vessel that Wilson had waiting at ground level. Bob and Jim set the waste containers inside and sealed it shut.

"The vessel is sealed and ready for removal," Bob said to the van crew. "We'll need a decontamination unit set up to clean up any residual contamination."

Karen Ann and Larry were just readjusting their clothing when a shipyard worker came in.

"Captain Murphy, the situation at the drydock is almost wrapped up. They didn't find a bomb, but Mr. Beamer wants you to come to his office to discuss the situation. If you can join me, I'll drive you to his office."

"I have my golf cart outside," Karen Ann said. "I'll follow you to the office. Thank you."

All three left the building and got into their golf carts for the short drive to Beamer's office.

"Captain Murphy," Al Beamer said, as Karen Ann and Larry walked into the office, "I have some good news and some bad news. I'll give you the good news first. Here's what we know so far. There was no bomb on your vessel. The object you saw was, as far anyone can tell, a transporter. What it was designed to carry is anyone's guess, because it's been on there for a while. There was no marine growth under the base."

"You mean to tell me I've had that thing on my ship since we launched from here?"

"I can't say when it was attached, but we know it wasn't on your ship when we launched her, because we broke out the pictures from the launching ceremony, and we had several clear shots of the hull. It was clean at that time. Someone attached it soon after the launch is our best guess."

"That's the good news?"

"It's better than the rest of it. Your hull needs to be decontaminated before we can let your crew and our workers back onboard."

"What do you mean, decontaminated?"

"That thing had some radioactive waste inside, and it wasn't in its normal protective container, probably because it wouldn't fit inside the transporter in the container on your hull. Someone must have removed that and placed it in a small, more-regular metal container, then put it in there unprotected except for some metal foil wrapping which had NRC information printed on it.

"Whoever handled that stuff got a dose of radiation, but it depends on how long his exposure was. If he gets sick, the authorities might be able to track him down by searching the hospitals. For now, we need to decontaminate the area and all the equipment used to get it off the hull. The NRC is coming to collect the nuclear waste and check the area to make sure it's clean, but we don't have an ETA for their arrival yet."

"All right," Karen Ann replied. "I need to call the home office and tell them what we ran into. Then I'm going to our condo to get cleaned up, since we don't have a time frame for whatever comes next.

Could you call me as soon as you have any more information? I'll give you all my contact information."

"That'll be fine, Karen Ann. I'll make sure you're notified ASAP once we have something to tell you."

The Saratoga pulled up to the front of the FBO, and Lamar turned off the engine. It was a very quiet but stressful ride up the coast from Miami. The general opened the door leading to the tarmac, and Sally and Lamar, Jr. ran to the fence that separated the tarmac from the FBO building, followed closely by Wendy's mother.

Lamar looked at Wendy, as she got out of the plane. "Please let me talk to your father to explain some things."

She glanced at him, fighting back tears and doing her best to look impassive. "You can have all the time to do whatever you want." She went to hug her children.

After everyone exchanged hugs and welcomed them back, Lamar said, "General, may I have a moment of your time to explain some things?"

"Yes, you may. Wendy's mom and I wondered why she needs to stay with us, not that she and the kids aren't welcome, but she ought to be home, getting the grandchildren ready for the school year. Wendy, please take the children into the FBO, while Lamar, your mother, and I have a little talk."

Wendy nodded. "Come on, Kids."

They followed her inside.

Once they were out of earshot, Lamar said, "Mom, General, I can't begin to tell you how sorry and ashamed I am to have gotten my family into the dangerous situation we face right now."

Wendy's mother almost began hyperventilating, and the general did his best to help keep her under control. "Honey, why don't you just go inside and let the two of us get on with his story, so we can get it cleared up. Don't say anything in front of the children, all right?"

"Yes, I think that would be best, Horace. You men can figure this out." She turned toward the FBO.

The general regarded Lamar for a moment. "Just what kind of dangerous situation are we talking about?"

"General, the gas leak was real, but the part about the broken pipe fitting was a lie. We're targeted to be eliminated because of information I have. I need to get this information to the proper authorities as soon as I can take care of some unfinished business.

"Can you give me some time to get those items completed? I'd like your help in getting this information to the proper people. I really need your guidance on this."

"Lamar, I'm not happy to hear my daughter and my grand-children were almost killed because of someone you do business with over something you know or did or maybe didn't do. My daughter, however, loves you. She begged me to help you if you asked. That's what I'll do, but I'll tell you this, Son. Don't ever think about lying to me or anyone I introduce you to. Are we clear?"

"Yes, Sir. I hear you."

The general looked down the runway. "Then we can move forward from here. You let me know what I need to set up. We'll get it done. Now let's go say good-bye to your kids and wife. You do what-ever you need to do and get back to me. I expect to hear back from you soon, understand?"

"Thank you, General. You'll hear from me by the holiday."

They turned toward the FBO and their families.

"Hey, Karen Ann," Larry called from the guest bathroom, "do you have any shampoo? I must've forgotten to pack mine."

"I'm sure there's some manly shampoo in here somewhere. This is a company condo, and all the other captains use it when they're here on business. I'll look. You can use my girly shampoo if you're des-perate."

"I'm fine with whatever you have. I don't like using soap un-less that's all I've got. If you find it, just toss it in. I'll be in the shower."

Karen Ann found some manly shampoo in the vanity cabinet in the master bath and decided to deliver it personally. She slipped out of her uniform and gently opened the door to the guest bathroom.

"All I found was this bottle of hotel shampoo." She slid back the shower curtain and stepped into the shower.

Larry, pleasantly surprised, almost immediately showed his approval of her joining him.

"I thought we might conserve water by showering together," she said.

"That's a splendid idea. I didn't realize you were so...conservation minded."

Her hand found his penis. "I firmly believe in conservation. For instance, we should share the bed in the master bedroom, so we'll save on water needed to wash only one set of sheets, not two."

He wrapped his arms around her and brought his lips to hers in a passionate kiss that had their tongues exploring each other's mouths. Larry was all soaped up before she stepped into the shower, and both were quickly lathered. He guided the handheld shower head to rinse her and himself off, as she crouched down to slide his impressive rod into her mouth. She worked on him like he'd never been orally satisfied before.

The sound of water cascading down their bodies provided the music to accompany their erotic pleasure. Larry reached down and reluctantly brought her to her feet, then he turned her to face the shower head and guided himself into her pleasure cave from behind. Water beat against his chest, flowing down his front and Karen Ann's back. Each thrust and recoil added a refreshing, warm feeling to both of them.

"Larry," she moaned, "give me your all. Give it to me! I want it now. Make me cum, Larry Halsey. Make me cum!"

Unable to hold off any longer, he felt his own climax start just as she convulsed in her orgasm.

Later that afternoon, as they lay in bed with her head tucked on his shoulder, she looked into his eyes. "You don't know how long I waited for this to happen. I've wanted you ever since I was a teenager working at the snack bar on the ferry."

"You have no idea how hard you made it for all of the men back then. You were young and beautiful, and man, what a body! I must say, though, you've gotten even more beautiful since, and with an even better body."

"You sure know how to make a girl feel good...and I do mean good."

CHAPTER 23

Ali Mohammed Modula received the message that his foolproof plan experienced a hiccup, but he didn't expect anything more than a delay. He took the American sense of immunity and the resulting lack of security, even after 9/11, for granted. Still, the Americans were waking up and beginning to tighten their security while doing their best to retain the freedoms their forefathers fought and died to create.

One of the petroleum tankers missed its arrival date, which meant he might not have enough radioactive waste to make the dirty bombs dirty enough for a true catastrophe.

Well, Ali thought, *we'll just have to wait for the arrival of the last shipment and do the job right. I won't have anything except the biggest, deadliest, costliest attack on Satan.*

He wrote a reply to his field officer in Arabic, then he coded the message below the original. Giving it to a messenger, he said, "Get this to our agents," and dismissed him with a wave of his hand.

After the messenger left, though, Ali pounded his fist on the table, making a dish of fresh fruit bounce high enough to spill its contents. He screamed a curse at his enemy for failing to stay on time.

"How useless these Americans are!" he shouted. "I never should have let those drug pushers persuade me to use their stupid American smuggling stunt to carry out Allah's work. They'll get their reward as soon as that message reaches my trustworthy followers."

"Yo, Walter, we're getting some activity out of M12 again. It's going into the computer right now for decrypting. Maybe it'll spit out something useful this time," Roman said.

Walter and Roman, two NSA cryptologists, were trying to break a code of a suspected terrorist organization, the twelfth one identified that was located in the Middle East, was using to communicate with its field officers. They knew some of the code, and they were only able to read about every twentieth word, but they still needed their Rosetta Stone to enable them to understand fully the communiqués.

The two cryptologists had locked in on that group and labeled them as probable terrorists. Then they tracked them to definite locations, turning up the connection to the cartel, but that was all they had so far. They were stymied in making any further progress breaking the case or the code.

"Walter," Roman said a moment later. "You might want to come here and look at this. It might be trying to spit out something."

Walter rolled his chair to Roman's computer station to view what appeared on his screen. There on the screen was what they'd been looking for. The message had been sent half-coded and half in Arabic, a language in which both men were fluent.

"Jackpot," Walter said. "I can't believe they sent the first two lines in the clear. It appears they recopied it in code and sent that, too. What a break!"

"All right. Now let's get down to business and get these messages cleaned up and readable. We should be able to read ninety percent of this stuff now. This is the break we've been looking for."

"Let's see what we can come up with."

It was late afternoon, and Max was trying to fit the missing nuclear waste into his case. Every time he gave up in disgust and tried to move to another project, it came back at him like a boomerang. The idea refused to go away, so he finally decided to keep working on it.

"Sam, when you get some time," Bob said, "Log onto the NSDB (National Security Data Base) and get this information downloaded. Someone out there will want to know what we found."

The NSDB was the mother of the WOOPSIE. The DHS had every law-enforcement agency, as well as Interpol, providing them with information. Many local police departments put up interference when the idea first surfaced, but since then, many cases were solved when the database classified and digested the information. Suddenly, matches cropped up, and the system notified each department that more information was available about certain cases.

Sam dutifully typed in the information about the past night and day dealing with the false bomb scare caused by the blister, only to find they discovered the nuclear waste. The NRC was already on its way to retrieve the material.

Once Sam finished typing the information into the system, he secured his equipment in the bomb van for their return trip to home base, unaware of all the alerts he just triggered at several different agencies.

The first was the NRC, who added the info about the missing nuclear waste in the first place. They knew about the recovery and were on their way to take it back.

Another agency, however, that received notification of the blister and its contents was the FBI—specifically, Max Gorgon. The alert signal on his computer was programmed to sound like a submarine dive warning.

He was just about to shut down his computer and end his day when he heard, "Ah-oo-ga! Ah-oo-ga! Dive! Dive!"

He acknowledged the signal with a sigh. "It never fails. I can go all week without getting anything, then bam, Friday rolls around, and I'm ready to call it a week, and then...."

He swung his chair around to face his desk. "Let's see what the commotion is about." He clicked the icon.

Up popped a text box that read, *Your NSDB inquiry has been matched to a new posting by the Virginia State Police Bomb Squad, Yorktown Division. Click here.*

He dutifully clicked the next link and saw the homepage for the NSDB, where he could log in. He typed in his ID of *gordonm,* then he tabbed down to the password and typed *1flash#gordon.*

The computer dutifully took him to the Inquiry Hit Page.

He couldn't believe what he read. "Damn," he said repeatedly, as he looked at each piece of information.

Finally, he reached the end and hit the print icon to get a hardcopy of all the information he just received. As the printer hummed, he dialed the phone number for the Virginia State Police Bomb Squad, Yorktown Division's Officer in Charge.

"Bomb Squad, Captain Raburn," Bob said.

"This is Special Agent Maxwell Gordon of the FBI, DHS Division. I want to speak with you about the material you discovered on the side of that ship today, Captain."

"Wow. That's a quick pick up on that. How can I help you, Special Agent?"

"I need any details you may've left out or didn't elaborate on in the NSDB alert you filed."

"I don't think we left anything out, and there isn't much to elaborate on. Do you have anything specific in mind I might help you with?"

"Well, yeah, Captain, like what is radioactive waste doing attached to the side of a ship, and how did it get there?"

Bob shook his head as if to ask, *Where do they get these guys?* "Look, Agent Gordon, I can't give you anything about the why or how. I just defuse bombs for a living. Whoever put that stuff in there didn't leave a note addressed to anyone who might find it, if you know what I mean."

"All right. I guess I was carried away, Captain. I'm sorry. I know this fits into my case somehow, but I can't quite connect the dots."

"I'm sorry, too, Agent Gordon. I put everything I could into that alert. I can't speculate on the hows, whys, or who. I leave that for the investigators and shrinks. That's what they're paid for."

"I understand. I guess I'm just desperate and hoped you might be able to shed some light on my problem. Thank you for your time, Captain." He hung up

Bob flipped the cell phone shut and hung it on his belt, as he looked at Sam, who was driving the bomb-disposal van back to York-town. "I don't understand the Feds. They think you're a mind reader or something. Man, I just stop the bombs from going boom, if I can. Take me home, Sam."

Lamar landed the Saratoga and taxied to his hangar, where he pulled in after opening the door with the control in his cockpit. He shut down the electronics and the engine. After making sure the aircraft was secured, he went straight to his car, bypassing his usual routine of wiping down his baby and checking every last rivet and bolt before cleaning the interior.

He was a man on a mission. He drove to his office and took the private elevator up to his interior office. He had to find his CD of names, places, and facts for his nonexistent company that made him a very wealthy man, then he needed to make a few calls.

"Lic is back," he told the empty room, "and he's in charge."

He opened the secret door to his wall safe and used the combination based on Wendy's measurements—R 34, L 22, R 36. When he swung the handle over, he heard the reassuring slap of three bolts being pulled back into the door.

A yank easily opened the heavy door to reveal a large stack of cash and other documents, including some computer CDs. Taking out the money and setting it aside, he retrieved all the CDs and thumbed through them until he found the one he wanted and set it on the money on his solid oak, hand-carved desk.

He was so preoccupied, he didn't realize he was sweating until he leaned over to reach for the receiver and saw sweat drip onto his blotter.

Startled, he went to his private bathroom and dowsed his face with cold water, only to find himself shaking uncontrollably. When he reached for the towel hanging by the sink, he glimpsed himself in the mirror and was horrified to see a man he no longer recognized. His face looked sickly, and his bloodshot, puffy eyes were those of someone he didn't know.

That scared him more than the cartel or the Allah Yad terrorist group. Walking slowly to his desk, he sat down. "Get a hold of yourself, Man. Get a hold of yourself." He lowered his head into his hands.

When he looked up, an hour passed before he realized the situation alone would kill him. Everyone else would be denied their pound of flesh in retribution. He lifted the CD with all his illicit activities on its surface and inserted it into the computer. Taking a blank CD from a drawer, he put it into the CDR slot and made a copy with several keystrokes. That was the one he would give to the general.

Once it was finished, he took the CD from the slot and scooped up all the cash from the desk. Looking around, he realized it was probably the last time he would see his beloved office. His family would have to move to keep the kids from too much embarrassment and shame, because their father was a lowly drug pusher and now a traitor to his country.

"Lamar, you really made a mess of your life. You should've stayed a dumb punk like your old man and lived hard and died young before you screwed up too many other lives. No, you thought you could outsmart the entire world. I guess you found out different, didn't you?"

Shaking his head, he finished his preparations. An old briefcase in the coat closet was big enough for the money, which amounted to almost three million, as well as the original CD. He locked it shut and reached for the phone one last time to call his father-in-law.

"General? Lamar here. I will surrender myself to you when I arrive tonight. Just let me say good-bye to the kids and Wendy before you do whatever you have to do."

"I can do that for my grandchildren, Lamar, but I still don't know what this is all about or how to handle whatever mess you got yourself and your family into that they will have to go into hiding for the rest of their lives."

"I'll tell you the whole story when I arrive. This line might be bugged, so I can't say too much."

"That sounds like the smart thing to do. I'll see you tonight. Good-bye."

The line went dead.

Lamar hung up, grabbed his briefcase, and took the private elevator down to the garage, where the Navigator waited. He got behind the wheel to begin what would become the rest of his life.

"Roman, you have to see this," Walter said, walking to Roman's desk. "I can't believe we got this much from that little transmission they left in the open. We need to get this to the boys upstairs. This is red hot."

"Hold on, Walt. Let me see what's got your panties in a bunch." He took the folder from Walter's hand.

Roman got his name from his mother, who, as a little girl, had a crush on the quarterback of the LA Rams, Roman Gabriel, who was traded to the Philadelphia Eagles in the twilight of his career.

A quick scan of the folder showed that Walter was right. The information needed to reach the top as fast as possible.

"Shit, Walt. This isn't going to happen soon. It's happening right now! It's the holiday weekend, and that little idiot Pickle has the duty. He'll sit on this, because he's an idiot and a glory hound."

The two cryptologists sat down to devise a plan to circumvent their section boss and get the information into the right hands in time to stop the terrorist plot.

Max couldn't leave his office in light of the new development. He did what any good investigator did—he broke out everything he had on the case and spread it out on the floor.

After an hour of crawling around, rereading everything he had on the case, he said, "That's it. This has to be the key."

He reached for his cell phone, scrolled through his contacts list, and called Ferrow.

The phone rang twice, then a man's voice said, "Agent Ferrow."

"Tim, this is Max. You need to get over here and see this. I think I know how this all fits together."

"Max, I'm already on the Beltway headed for home. Is it so important that you want me to turn around and come back into the city?"

"Yeah. It's about the case we discussed a little while back. I need you to verify I'm seeing this the right way. If I am, we need to push this up the chain of command right now. This might be something that's happening right now."

"All right, but I'm ten minutes from home. I need to let my wife know that duty calls. She won't be happy about this. I'll stop home for a bite, pet the dog, slap my wife's ass, and head back into the city. See you in about two-and-a-half hours. That's the best I can do, OK?"

"Fine. I understand. You have to keep your home life happy. I'll be here when you get back. See you then."

He hung up and looked around at his office. "Now what? If Tim's going to have dinner, I might as well treat myself to some chow for a job well done."

He tiptoed past all the papers on the floor and locked the door behind him before heading toward the stairs. Maybe taking the stairs would burn some of his nervous energy.

CHAPTER 24

Lamar drove the Navigator from the garage onto the street. As he pulled away, a white cargo van left a side street parking space and followed. Too preoccupied with thoughts of his family, he didn't notice he was being followed. He was on his way home to retrieve a few things his mother-in-law asked him to get for the kids and Wendy.

The elevator doors opened, and Tim walked through the deserted office of cubicles to Max's office to knock on the door.

"Yo, Max. You in there?"

"Come in, Tim. You have to see this."

Tim opened the door and saw Max on his hands and knees in the midst of a paper mess. "I'm sorry, Old Buddy, but I'm not here to clean up your mess. What the hell are you doing?"

"Just shut up and come over here. Look at this and tell me I'm not crazy."

"I'll look, but I sure as hell won't tell you that. You look like a man who finally lost it big time." He dutifully weaved a path through the paper storm on the floor. "What's so damn important I had to come back into the city when I was already home?"

"I won't tell you what I think. I want you to look this stuff over and see if you come to the same conclusion I did."

"All right," Roman said. "You know what to do, right?"

"Just explain to me why I always have to be the one who plays the idiot."

"You're a better actor than I am. You know I'd just get mad and tell old Pickle how much of a complete incompetent smug asshole he is, then we'd both be fired for our conspiracy to leave him out of the loop and jump his precious chain of command."

"You're so full of shit, your eyes are brown. Let's get this moving."

Walter and Roman went to tell Pickle that Walter would send him a file he needed to read once it landed in his in box. What they would carefully not tell him was that when Walter sent the document, he would also CC it to Pickle's boss and DHS' Foreign Terrorist Division. Walter could conveniently forget to add Pickle's email address. Since they did that a few times before, Pickle would just assume they were being stupid nerds again.

The DHS Foreign Terrorist Division would alert the CIA's DHS detachment, as well as the DEA's DHS detachment, which would instantly alert all the agents assigned to the Middle East, including the newly assigned Agent Tim Ferrow.

"Max, are you sure all this is accurate?" Tim asked. "If it is, we've got a serious situation that's already in motion. There isn't much time to get assets into position to keep this from blowing up in our faces." He shook his head and continued.

"It looks to me that the drug connection is a delivery service for a sleeper cell that's already in place and has been activated with the robbery of the nuclear waste. Is that what you concluded?"

"Yes!" Max said, excited. "That's exactly the conclusion I came up with. Thanks, Tim. We need to get this to the DHS and get a coordinated response to this threat. Let's get this organized to present to the brass, so we don't look like a couple of idiots."

"Right you are, Max. I'm confident this is an active operation, and we need a most-rapid response with a counter-operation started ASAP."

Tim and Max's phones both gave loud triple beeps announcing an immediate threat alert message from DHS. All hands had to report to their sector chief immediately.

Lamar arrived at the entrance to his development. As he checked his rearview mirror, he noticed the same van that was behind him several stoplights earlier was still three cars back, with its turn signal on to follow him into the development.

Odd, he thought, continuing into the entrance. *If I want to stay alive, I'd better stop being distracted. I hope I can escape the firing squad my father-in-law would recommend and just sit in prison for a long time.*

He decided to put a few things to the test he saw on the spy movies he loved. He turned off onto the first street to avoid being caught in a dead end, with the emphasis on dead.

He kept one eye on the road. The development had plenty of little kids who darted into the streets at times. He kept another eye on the rearview mirror. He hoped he was just the victim of an overactive imagination.

Lamar was ready to relax when he saw the white van turn onto the same street. He forced himself not to panic and speed up. A street up ahead looped back onto the same road he was on. If the tail followed him, he'd have to find a way to shake him or get somewhere public and size up his options.

The van remained some distance behind, as Lamar reached the loop, and he turned and slowed to give the tail time to catch up. Just as he reached the corner to start the loop back to the first road, he saw the van turning onto the street.

Lamar continued driving, although he went slightly faster. *It seems I have a tail. Who is it, my cartel friends, their Arab friends, or the cops?*

He felt alongside his seat for his Tire Buddy bar that he kept handy in case he ever needed to protect his family from muggers or car jackers. The steel bar filled with lead and a grip wrapped with electrical tape would serve him well if necessary, giving the bar a little pat, *I might just need you today.*

He picked up a little more speed, watching for kids in the neighborhood, and went to his home.

The white van remained some distance behind. With luck, that would give him enough time to prepare for unwanted guests. If it turned out to be the authorities, he decided not to resist but go along peacefully and pay his debt to society.

Lamar turned onto his driveway and used the garage door opener to raise the door so he could drive right in and close the door behind him. He needed to buy time.

As the door closed, he jumped from the Navigator with the Tire Buddy in hand and ran toward the interior door. By the time he reached the living room window, he saw the van pass by the house and continue down the street, much to his amazement.

Am I being paranoid? he wondered.

Then he saw the van's brake lights come on. It parked alongside the street. He kept watching, but he didn't see any activity come from the van, so he felt he had time to gather a few things from the house.

Lamar made one more check out the window. The van was still there. He raised his binoculars and saw exhaust coming out the tailpipe. *Still running. They must be waiting for me to leave and are hoping I'll take them to Wendy and the kids. That'll never happen. I'll die before I lead you bastards to my family.*

He got what he needed, backed the Navigator down the driveway, and headed for the development's entrance at a normal speed, watching in the rearview mirror. The van began moving and did a K turn to follow him but still kept its distance. He hoped to lose them in rush-hour traffic without having to deal with violence, which he found distasteful. If it meant protecting his family, though, he wouldn't shy away from it.

Max and Tim exchanged worried expressions before answering their phones.

"This isn't good, Max," Tim said.

"Yeah. Are we behind on this, or is something else going on? Either way, it looks like a long night."

They answered their phones.

It was evening, and Lamar felt half-asleep. He was certain he lost his tail, so it would be safe to drive to his in-laws' home, but he needed a restroom. One was coming up in two more miles.

As he parked in the rest area, he felt drained by the long day and his emotions. Sitting there, he began crying, unable to believe what he did to his family and country.

He finally regained control of himself and went to the restroom to empty his bladder and throw cold water on his face.

As he came out, he saw a white van parked a ways down. *Could it be the same one?* he wondered. *Thank God I didn't go directly to the general's.*

He had to do something. He retrieved his Tire Buddy from the navigator and cupped it behind his arm, adding a dive knife and a tire valve stem removal tool into his coat pocket. He tried to act nonchalant, but his heart raced, and sweat beaded on his forehead.

He went to the restroom, shaking his head and patting his pockets, as if he left something, hoping the act would buy him a little time. As he neared the entrance, though, he slipped away and walked around the building toward a wooded area twenty feet away. He remained hidden in the woods, as he moved toward the van at the far end of the parking lot.

He hadn't planned exactly what to do or how he needed to approach the situation. He just hoped his memory of his Lic days wasn't too rusty, but he had a backup if he needed it. He was a 10th degree Black Belt in Kung Fu. Wendy pressed him to take the classes when he was in college, because she said his brain might not always be able to protect her and their future family.

She's always right, he thought.

He came to the end of the parking lot just beyond the van. It was almost pitch dark, because night had fallen, and the moon was still below the horizon. The nearest streetlight, ten parking places away, didn't shed any light on the passenger side of the vehicle.

Damn, he thought. *It's the same van. At least the conditions are perfect.*

Two figures sat in the front of the van, both staring at the restroom. There was no way to tell if anyone was in the back. He hoped it was like most cargo vans and didn't have any seats in the back.

When he reached the rear of the vehicle, his heart pounded so loudly, he wondered if they could hear it inside. They were playing music, though, something Middle Eastern, like belly dance music, and he heard the rumble of voices speaking Arabic or Farsi.

He eased down to the ground and inched along until he came to the rear tire on the passenger side. Slicing it would probably be too loud. It would be best if he could pull off the job without being discovered, so he reached for the valve stem remover and unscrewed the valve stem cap. He used the tool to loosen the valve stem enough to start a slow leak.

A hiss came from the stem. He slowly went to the other side, which involved a bigger risk, and did the same thing to the other rear tire, hoping nobody would pull into the rest area and hit him with their headlights.

When he finished, he backed away slowly and scurried into the woods. *Mission accomplished,* he thought. *I've still got the touch. I just might live long enough to face the general's firing squad.*

He pulled out of his parking spot and headed for the on ramp to take him back onto I-95 south. As he reached the start of the ramp, he saw the van leave its parking space behind him.

With a stomp on the gas pedal, he roared onto the highway, knowing the van would have to speed up to keep him in sight. The highway had heavy traffic even at night, and following someone in the dark was difficult, especially with only one chase car.

The van's driver saw Lamar's car race up the ramp and pressed his gas pedal to the floor, swerving to miss an elderly gentleman who stepped out from between two parked cars by the restroom.

The van felt different. He wasn't sure why, but there was no time to worry about it, because he had to keep that SUV in sight to finish what that stupid Colombian screwed up. At least the drug pusher wouldn't screw up anything ever again. He was on the bottom of the Hudson, swimming with all the fish.

In Arabic, he told his passenger to keep his eyes on the SUV. The man grunted.

Don't worry about me doing my job, the passenger thought. *You just keep from running over stupid Americans so I don't have to face the Mullah and say we failed. If I do, you won't be there. I won't be around much longer, either.*

Lamar slowed a little to let the van get onto the highway, then he sped up and slid into the left lane. The van quickly followed, although the driver kept what he thought was a safe distance behind to avoid being noticed.

Lamar began passing other cars, forcing the van to increase its speed. Soon, he was pushing eighty.

"Do you think he made us?" the passenger asked.

"No. He's just one of those rich, arrogant Americans who thinks he can buy his way out of anything. Just watch him and shut up!"

Lamar increased speed and cut all the way to the far-right lane. The van was coming alongside a tractor-trailer and had to speed up to get past it and find an opening to pull to the right. The tires were still losing air slowly, becoming increasingly unstable at the high speed.

The van driver spotted a good place, he hoped, to cut over in front of the truck and get to the far-right lane.

"I see him," the passenger said. "Right up there."

The driver turned his wheel sharply to the right. The combination of low air pressure, high speed, and a sharp turn made the van so top-heavy, it began to topple right in front of the truck.

"You God-forsaken bastard!" the passenger shouted. "You'll get us killed!"

The driver of the eighteen-wheeler never expected the van passing on his left to pull in front of him suddenly, let alone start to roll. He did his best to avoid an accident, but he had his foot on the accelerator, and there was no room to swerve. He was hemmed in by cars and trucks on both sides. His big Peterbilt was about to slam into the overturned van.

Lamar looked in his rearview mirror and felt a flush of satisfaction for a well-performed job. In the next instant, his heart went out to the innocent bystanders who would be caught in the accident.

He wasn't a church-going man, much less religious in any sense. He hadn't minded when Wendy had their kids baptized in the Lutheran faith and took them to church every Sunday, but that day, he prayed to some Supreme Being to protect the innocent ones who had become engulfed in his problems and to forgive him for what he'd done.

He eased his foot off the gas and slowed, as the scene unfolded behind him. The van rolled down the highway in front of the huge truck, leaving a trail of sparks behind. The tractor-trailer began to jackknife when the driver tried to avoid the van. A second later, they collided in a massive fireball.

Lamar slowly pulled away from the accident and drove into the night. Even if they had a second car following him, it would be stuck in a traffic jam that would take hours to clear up.

He set course for his in-laws' home and his day of judgment. Just to be safe, he planned to get off the highway one exit early and wind through town to check if anyone still followed him.

CHAPTER 25

When Lamar reached his in-laws' home, everyone was asleep except the general. He saw the Navigator's headlights flash through the living room windows and got up to meet Lamar at the door.

"Good evening, General. I'm sorry I'm late, but I was followed, and I had to get creative to get clear. To the best of my knowledge, no one knows I'm here. You and your family are safe for now. If I'd been thinking straight, I would've asked you to meet me somewhere else, but I think it's safe enough right now."

"It's too late for me to get anyone to help you with your problem, so why don't you come in and brief me on the details of your situation? Then I can sleep on it and figure out who are the right people to help you through this and protect my daughter and the children."

"Thank you, General. That's a start. I can't say how much I appreciate your help."

Lamar entered the house. The general closed the door behind him without another word and led him into the study before closing the door.

A large oak desk sat in the middle of the room, with a full-wall bookshelf from ceiling to floor filled with novels and technical manuals from the general's active duty days. In front of the desk sat two high-back plush chairs, canted at the corners to leave the center of the desk open. The setup looked ready for a soldier to walk in and report to the general, standing at attention in a very imposing situation for any low-ranking person.

The other walls were filled with the general's sword and flag, along with the awards he earned through his time of service. There was almost no space for another plaque. His life was displayed for all to admire.

Most men had a certain space on a wall, or, at the most, one entire wall, which the general often referred to as a "love-me" wall. The general had three, and Lamar knew those weren't all of his awards. They were his most-prized possessions. The man always intimidated him, but that night, he felt like a kid who ruined his parents' most-prized possession and had to account for it. The general had an imposing way about him. It wasn't a put-on or some chest-puffing on his part. It came to him naturally, and Lamar was in its full grasp, as he took one of the offered chairs in front of the desk.

"Sit, Lamar." The general patted a chair for his son-in-law, while he moved to the back of the desk and sat in his usual chair. "All right. You have my undivided attention. Let's hear what you've gotten yourself and your family into, so I can figure out how to protect them."

Lamar, swallowing hard, rubbed his face. He began relating his story, beginning with his early lawless days in Philadelphia. The concerned expression on the general's face grew deeper, as Lamar's life became more involved with increasingly dangerous characters, but he didn't interrupt except to ask for a clarification about a term, much to Lamar's gratification.

He absorbed everything Lamar said, not wanting to miss any detail. The young man who married his daughter was a loving, caring, brilliant, normal man who lived a secret underworld life of crime that would have intrigued him in another time and place. The current situation, however, wasn't fully Lamar's fault, and he was trying to do the right thing by turning himself in to the authorities.

Also, the general was impressed with Lamar's ability to stay so far under the government's radar that he almost forgot how dangerous the situation was for his daughter, grandchildren, and now his wife and himself.

Lamar finally finished his story. "General, you can see the mess I've gotten my family involved in, however unintentional it was. I hope you can provide me with some guidance about who do I see to stop this attack on our country and protect my family simultaneously."

"Lamar, I must first say how disappointed I am with your behavior and how you didn't see the danger you were exposing Wendy and the children to with those madmen from Colombia. Nothing is sacred to them if it gets in their way or can be used as leverage, let alone extremist Muslims.

"For being one of the most-brilliant men I know, you've been downright dumb and reckless with your family's welfare. I should have you arrested right now. You'd be on the first plane to Gitmo if I did.

"However, I like you, and my daughter happens to be very much in love with you. I won't have you arrested. However, I want you to know, and I've already told Wendy this. I'm not sure how much I can protect you. I'll do my best for you and your family, but I'm just a retired general.

"For Wendy's sake, I'll burn every bridge I ever made, but only if you give me and her your word you'll give up your life of crime and end your association with these criminals. You'll be completely frank with the authorities and give them one hundred percent of your cooperation. Do we have an agreement?"

"That's why I'm here, General. I plan to provide full disclosure and take whatever punishment is in store. I just don't want any harm to come to my family."

"That's what I wanted to hear. You need some rest. It'll be an early and long day tomorrow. Reveille is at 0600 hours. Lillian made you a bed in the family room." He stood and offered his hand.

Lamar stood as well and shook the general's hand. "Thank you, General. I won't let you, my country, or my family down ever again."

He found the bed his mother-in-law prepared. The moment his head hit the pillow, he looked up toward the ceiling and praised the people who loved him for not abandoning or turning their backs on him, vowing he'd never let them down.

He fell into an exhausted sleep, beginning his new, law-abiding life. Lic was dead.

The general replayed what Lamar told him and tried to create a plan, considering how he could help the young man and who he should call in the morning. He opened his computer and signed on to bring up his list of contacts. His days spent as a staff member of the Joint Chiefs of Staff were filled with making connections at the highest political offices and cabinet positions. Some of them would be valuable in protecting Lamar and also his country.

Once he created a list of calls to make, he closed the computer and went to bed, trying to slip in without waking Lillian, whom he considered his greatest asset. The smartest move he ever made was to marry her.

Word of the massive accident reached Washington early that night. Several of the agents who raced to their respective emergency recall meetings were caught in the traffic jam. They had no idea the accident was related to their recall, as they called in to report their dilemma and their late arrival.

It was early morning in Washington, DC, and Max was up all night conferring with other agents and sector chiefs about what he and Agent Ferrow were working on and how they felt certain items were connected. Tim did the same with his counterparts and sector chiefs.

The sector chiefs, in turn, conferred with each other and tried to create a plan to present to the Director of Homeland Security. There were differing opinions on the best way to proceed and which avenues were best to explore. They weren't able to agree on much so far, much less come up with a cohesive operational plan, because they couldn't agree on exactly what they were dealing with.

The only thing the FBI sector chief and his agents agreed on was they needed to interview the crew of the MV *Palm Princess*. Someone woke the CEO of Palm Petroleum at four in the morning to tell him he needed to bring his crew to DC ASAP.

Larry woke first at six o'clock, gazing at the golden hair splayed out on the pillow beside him. His mind raced. Was the previous evening a dream, or had he really been making love to that magnificent woman? Sliding out of bed, he went to the bathroom.

When he returned, he found Karen Ann awake, half-covered in bed, patting the empty spot beside her. "I hoped we could pick up where we left off."

He didn't need any more invitation than that. He got back into bed. "I hope you won't think me rude to have my breakfast first, but I'm famished." He disappeared under the covers.

Within seconds, Karen Ann was writhing and moaning with pleasure.

The cell phone on the nightstand vibrated. Larry raised his head and asked, "Do you want me to get that?"

She smiled and rolled off him from her reverse cowboy position and said, "No. You just save what you've got." She looked at his throbbing penis. "I won't be long, and I intend to finish what I started."

She picked up her cell. "Hello, this is Captain Murphy." She listened for a long time, then said, "Good-bye" and pressed the *End* button on her phone. Larry had been gently stroking his cock and rubbing her bare back to keep his attention from wandering.

His patience paid off. She replaced the phone on the nightstand and straddled his face before bending down to take his penis in her mouth. He turned his attention to her freshly shaven vagina that hovered over his face. He teased her vulva lips and clitoris, occasionally sliding his tongue inside her as far as he could.

He received an uncontrollable moan from Karen Ann and knew he was pleasuring her the way she wanted.

They made love for two more hours. Each time he approached climax, he gently moved her into another position and gave himself time to regroup before continuing.

By the time they finished, climaxing together in an uncontrollable frenzy of thrusting, pounding, and gasping for breath, they realized they had found the missing part of themselves and both were finally whole.

She led him to the shower, knowing the previous call would end their wonderful romantic interlude and praying it wouldn't mean the end of their romance and the love she found with him. Once in the shower, they soaped each other, which gave him an immediate erection, and she turned around and bent over, offering herself once more.

The alarm clock began its annoying sound. The general rolled over and slapped the *Off* button before it woke Lillian. As was his normal routine, he rolled back over and gently stroked her hair without waking her, whispering, "I love you, my darling."

He eased out of bed and visited the bathroom, his mind already running through what he needed to do to get his son-in-law through the situation as unscathed as possible.

He dressed in a suit and tie, making sure his lapel pin that distinguished him as a Retired Three-Star General was position just right. Walking into the kitchen, he prepared his morning coffee.

Once the coffee was ready, he took a bowl of fruit from the fridge for breakfast and sat at the table. After a second cup of coffee, he went to wake Lamar and found him snoring softly on the makeshift bed Lillian prepared.

The general cleared his throat, and Lamar came awake. "It's time to get to work. There's coffee in the kitchen."

The first call the general made was to an old friend he'd served with in the Army, who eventually became the Director of Homeland Security—retired General Edward B. "Yukon" Samson, who gained his nickname after his days as the Commander of the U.S. Army Northern Sector in Alaska.

Much to the general's surprise, Yukon's wife answered in a sleepy voice.

"Good morning, Audrey. This is Horace. I'm sorry if I woke you. I hoped to catch Yukon before his morning jog. Is he there? It's rather important."

"Hi, Horace. I needed to get up, anyway. I'm sorry to say that *Edward*," she added, because she hated nicknames and thought grown men shouldn't act like children, "isn't here. He was called in late last night and told me he probably wouldn't be home. It appears he was correct. You should be able to reach him on his cell. Do you still have the number?"

"Yes, I do, Audrey. Once again, I'm sorry for disturbing you. Thank you. Have a good morning. 'Bye." He purposely used Ed's nickname, because he knew she didn't like it, and he got a laugh out of making her cringe. He imagined her cringing right at that moment, mumbling about men and their childish ways.

He hung up with a chuckle and called Yukon's cell.

General Ed Samson, Director of Homeland Security, sat at his desk reviewing the information he received from various agencies concerning a new threat, when his private cell phone vibrated. He silently cursed. He didn't need an interruption and considered ignoring it. It was probably Audrey, and he didn't have the time to explain why he hadn't been home all night.

When he took out the phone, he saw Horace's caller ID and knew that if Horace was calling at 0630, it had to be important. He was willing to spare the time for one of his best friends, and he needed a distraction from the mess of an investigation he was reading. Maybe if he took a break, he could gain a fresh perspective.

"Good morning, Horace," Yukon said. "What has you up at such an ungodly hour, you old foot soldier?"

"Good morning to you, too. I should be asking you the same, except I just spoke with your dear wife, and she said you've been at it all night. I know it must be important to keep you in the office on a holiday weekend, but what I've got for you is pretty important, too."

"We do have an important situation here, but I need a break from it. What's stuck in your craw, Horace?"

"I need you to listen to my son-in-law, Lamar. He's involved in something that's urgent to national security, as well as his and my daughter's entire family."

"I'm really involved here, Horace. Maybe I can send over an agent to take a statement. I'll give it top priority once I get a handle on the current situation that's ready to explode in my face."

"Under normal circumstances, I wouldn't impose on you, Ed, but you really need to hear his story. This is happening right now, and there's no time to waste. I beg you to listen. You can be the judge of his story. If you say it can wait, it can. All we need is two hours of your time. I can bring him to your office in an hour."

"Fine, Horace. Get here as soon as you can. I'll inform security to have you and your son-in-law escorted to my office the moment you arrive. Give your name at the checkpoint."

"I can't ask for more, Yukon. I'll see you soon. Thank you."

As the call ended, Ed stared at his phone. "You jerk! Did you ask for Yukon when you called my house? I'll hear about this from Audrey when I get back. Now I'd better get back to this mess and see what I can make of all these bits of information."

Larry finished toweling off, and Karen Ann dressed in her uniform.

"Larry, that call was from my office," she said. "They ordered me to take my entire crew to DC, because the FBI wants to question us about that thing we found on the side of the *Princess*. I need to close the condo and collect the crew.

"I don't know how long this will take, so it looks like we'd both better get back to work. I'll call with any news. I'm sorry to cut short our time together like this, but I hope you understand."

He stopped drying himself and listened carefully, his expression concerned. "Honey, you be careful with those Feds. They can turn your words against you. If you even suspect they want to implicate you in something, you stop talking and ask for a good lawyer. I've had to deal with the Feds, and it's not pretty. I need to get home, anyway, so don't worry about me. I'll wait for your call."

She walked him to his Corvette to say good-bye. He held her and kissed her with more passion than she ever felt in her life.

As they slowly separated, she whispered, "I need you, Larry."

"I'm not going anywhere, Honey. All you have to do is call. I'll be there as soon as I can."

He got into his car, honked the horn, and blew her a kiss, as he began the long drive back to Cape May.

Karen Ann turned away with a tear in her eye. "I love you, Larry Halsey."

She took out her cell phone to start calling her crew and give them the news about their upcoming trip to DC.

CHAPTER 26

The general and Lamar got into Lamar's Navigator. Lamar didn't want to leave his vehicle at the house, in case the terrorists had the address of his in-laws and drove past just to check if he was there.

"Traffic shouldn't be too bad this morning, Lamar," the general said, "so let's take the major highways and make good time. General Samson's busy with something, and he's doing us a big favor by seeing us personally."

Lamar had already programmed the car's GPS, and it showed the route. "Is this what you mean?"

The general looked at the map. "Yeah, that look like it. Let's hit the road."

Max and his sector chief went around and around about Max's theory. The chief couldn't follow the logic Max and Tim used to formulate their theory of what was happening.

"Look, Peter, it's elementary," Max said. "Everything fits. The drug boys in Colombia jumped on a money-making scheme that Allah Yad offered, not knowing it would put them out of business. That's how this Lic character got involved. He was the importer and distributor for the drugs on the east coast. He used that thing found on that tanker to smuggle the drugs into the country, and that's how they got the nuclear waste out after it was stolen from the NRC. Don't you see it?"

Peter shook his head. The whole thing sounded too far-fetched. He couldn't imagine the Colombians and the Arabs in bed to-gether, and neither could any of the other agents involved. The other area of contention was how the stolen nuke waste would be used. There had to be a dirty bomb or bombs, but how would they be brought back into the country—by land, sea, or air?

What could they do to protect the country? Their response force was relatively small compared to the number of options the terror-ists had.

The emergency repair work on the MV *Palm Princess* was al-most done. The ship could be refloated within a day. Alfred Beamer, the yard's VP of Operations, was extremely pleased with his workers' output to handle the emergency repair.

Unfortunately, the situation would grind to a halt very soon and start costing the shipyard hundreds of thousands of dollars if the vessel couldn't be re-floated, because there wasn't a company represen-tative available to sign off on the repair work.

He was pretty upset about that and couldn't believe the entire crew was called to DC, leaving no one to sign the necessary work papers.

"Damn," he said. "This is turning into a nightmare. First, we get behind, because of that thing with the radioactive junk in it, then we have to deal with testing everyone for exposure, and now the Feds take the whole crew to Washington to play guessing games, as if they know anything. Now we have to wait for Palm Petroleum to send a new com-pany rep, who'll have to be shown around when Captain Murphy al-ready knows everything and could sign the paperwork that lets me have my drydock back.

"It's no wonder the government's broke and screwed up. What the hell do they think the crew can tell them about this?" He shook his head and returned to work, trying to find a way to avoid losing more money and time.

The security guard, with the general and Lamar, reached the top floor of the DHS building. As the elevator doors opened, the guard said, "Follow me, please."

He thought it odd that the director would receive guests. With everything going on, it seemed everyone in the building was getting crazy. It was just one more crazy thing in an already crazy day.

He knocked on the director's door.

"Enter," Ed said from inside, his Army days showing more and more under the day's increased stress.

The door opened. Before the guard could announce the visitors, Ed said, "Horace, you old coot, come in and tell me something good. I need to hear good news from an old friend." He dismissed the guard with his thanks. "That will be all."

The guard shook his head and closed the door behind the two men. "Fancy damn bigshots," he muttered, walking back downstairs to his regular duties.

"Ed," Horace began, "this is my son-in-law, Lamar." The two men shook hands.

Lamar was in shock, like a schoolboy hauled in front of the principal, not like the powerful man he usually was. When Ed heard Lamar's name, he immediately had a disturbing thought but dismissed it and gave his old friend the attention he deserved.

"He has vital information you need to hear firsthand," Horace added, "but I need your assurance there won't be charges brought against him. He's here of his own free will to provide information to you at considerable risk to his and his family's lives."

"I can give him as much protection as I'm able, Horace, but I'm not the Justice Department. They might have a different view of things. However, I can think of one way to protect him. How about I make him my informant? We'll sign all the necessary documents before he says a word. That way, the information will be classified. That's the best I can do.

"If that's satisfactory, I'll print the required paperwork, and we can get on with this."

Horace glanced at Lamar. "Is that satisfactory?"

Lamar nodded. It was a lot more than he hoped he would get. He expected already to be in handcuffs and halfway to Gitmo.

After they quickly went through the paperwork, Lamar began his story.

"I won't bore you with the very beginnings, Mr. Director," Lamar said, "so let's get to the meat of the situation I find myself, as well as my country, in."

"That's fine, Lamar. We have to work fast. I need to get back to another matter that's had me up all night."

"I've been the largest cocaine drug smuggler and distributor on the east coast for the last ten years."

Twenty minutes into his story, the director stopped him.

"I want to look at something," Ed said, quickly checking his notes and finding the two stories matched. "Oh, my God. I need to get some people up here. You're exactly what we've been here working all night trying to solve. Lamar, I need you to repeat what you just told me to these other gentlemen and ladies. To protect your identity as my informant, I'll set up a screen you can be behind with a voice modifier to hide your real voice. Once I get this set up, we'll continue. Is that all right? "

"Whatever my country needs, Director. I appreciate everything you and my father-in-law are doing for me. Thank you."

Lamar soon sat behind a screen with a light behind him to create a shadow. A microphone was in front of his mouth, ready to convert what he said into a random, distorted voice. The large office suddenly felt a lot more cramped. Twenty people crammed into the room, sitting on folding chairs brought up by maintenance workers.

These people included directors of the FBI, CIA, NSA, DEA, NCIS, USCG, CGCIS, NRC, and some of the assistant directors, too. Also in the room were Max Gordon, Tim Ferrow, Roman Naples, and

Walter Doring, the cryptologists. All had been very surprised to be summoned to the director's office after being unable to figure out a proper diagnosis of the problem, let alone create a plan to deal with it.

Lamar was given an alias of John Jones. The director told him what parts of his story to repeat and what to leave out, because not all was necessary for the business at hand.

The office was abuzz with chitchat. Once the director had everything in place for Lamar to relate his story, he called the room to attention.

"May I have your attention, please?" Ed asked.

The room fell silent. The people turned and straightened in their chairs to face General Ed Samson, standing in front of a screen.

"Gentlemen and Ladies, I believe what you will now see and hear will unlock what we've been trying to define all night and part of today. I present you my informant, John Jones. His story convinced me that we have a very, very serious threat on our hands and very little time to deal with it.

"Mr. Jones, may I call you John?"

"Yes, you may," Lamar replied, surprised at hearing his voice sound so foreign.

"I want you to relax and tell this group what you just told me, so we can devise a plan to thwart a terrorist attack on our nation." Facing the group, Ed added, "Please save your questions for the end of Mr. Jones' story. Mr. Jones, you have the floor."

He sat behind his desk, able to see Lamar and cue him if he needed any help.

"Good morning to all of you," Lamar said slowly. "What we're faced with is a drug-smuggling operation that has been taken over by terrorists who left a trail of dead bodies from here to Saudi Arabia. The drugs were smuggled in using magnetic containers attached to the bottoms of certain ships, very similar to the limpet mines of World War Two, making steady runs from the U.S. to Venezuela."

As he spoke, people took rapid notes. With each fact he added, someone raised his head in surprise as if thinking, *This is right on. I had this part of the information.* Then the person would return to taking rapid-fire notes.

Once Lamar concluded his account of the life he once lived, the room fell silent.

Director Samson stood from his chair. "OK. Those are the facts. We need to devise a plan to thwart this attack and put these terrorists out of business. Let's get cracking, Folks. First, are there any questions for Mr. Jones?"

The director of the DEA raised her hand. "Why would the Colombians jump into bed with the Arabs and destroy what has to be their most-successful drug-smuggling operation? That's the part I find hard to believe."

"The Colombians wanted to expand their operation to the Arab world," Lamar said. "The only way in was through the terrorists, who saw a chance to use the cartel to their own advantage. The cartel fell for it. Does that answer your question, Ma'am?"

"That's a probable explanation, but...."

"Madam Director," Ed said, "that's how it was done, but that's not why we're here. We need to focus on the threat and worry about peripheral events later."

Max raised his hand. "So, Director Samson, how can we figure out where and when the attacks will happen? We don't have the manpower to check every ship coming into harbor."

"That's our job, isn't it, Special Agent?"

"If the transmissions we've intercepted are accurate," Roman said, "then we have a little time, but I don't know how much. I don't know what caused the delay. If we knew the cause, we could plan for when it will be cleared up."

Max raised his hand. "I believe the delay was the ship that the Virginia State Police Bomb Squad found nuke waste attached to the hull. That'll definitely throw a wrench into their plans."

"If I may offer a suggestion," Lamar said, "I might be able to provide you with a way to stop everything from coming into the country." He looked at Ed.

Director Samson shrugged. "I don't know about anyone else, but I'm game to listen to just about anything if it'll get us going. Mr. Jones, you have the floor."

"The delay the gentleman mentioned has already been discovered by our people," Lamar said, "but it doesn't appear that the terrorists know that we know. I would reattach the limpet mine to the hull and give them some of the nuclear waste material to keep them from knowing about our discovery, then send the ship on its way.

"I'd have a team of Special Forces in place to shadow the ones who retrieve the material at the ship's final destination, then follow them to where they're making the dirty bombs to be attached to various ships. We can let them complete the bombs and reattach them to the ships. That should be safe. I doubt they'll arm the bombs until they reach port to avoid any trouble from an early detonation or a delay like the one the ship has already had.

"We let the ships sail for their U.S. ports of call and for the South-American cell to report back to their base that the bombs are underway. As soon as we get that message, we capture the South American cell.

"Once the ships are at sea, we stop them and remove the bombs. You can do whatever you like after that, maybe replace them with fakes and let the ships sail to their destinations, which we'll know about by then. We could have more Special Forces in place to monitor the cells that are waiting to activate the bombs and trail them to their safe houses.

"They will report the activation of the bombs, and once again, after we intercept the report, we can arrest those cells in succession.

"As for the leader of the terrorist organization, I think if we can get the cartel implanted into Saudi Arabia, they'll take care of him for us. They would obviously try to restart their drug operation, but it'll never be as successful as before, and they'll never be as powerful.

"Once they assassinate the leaders responsible for this, there will be a war of attrition. The Arabs will seek revenge, and the cartel will wind up at war with the terrorists. This is big enough it should spread throughout the world, which will keep their focus away from smuggling drugs and more on surviving. We could kill two birds with one stone."

Lamar, finally comfortable in his situation, felt the old feeling of power through intelligence. A new Lic was back and in charge, but this time, he was on the side of the good guys. That made him feel a lot better.

The room was silent after Lamar finished.

"I don't know about the rest of you," Ed said finally, "but that sounds like a plan to me. We'll need the cooperation of the Venezuelans and the Colombians, then we need to get the cartel to do our dirty work. I'm sure that can be arranged. This sounds like the best thing I've heard all day. What do the rest of you think?"

There was plenty of talk among the attendees, but no one had a better plan. Soon, the room cleared, and the others told Lamar how brave he was to risk his life for his country, as they filed out to work on their part of the new plan.

They needed to get the Department of State and the Department of Defense onboard with their plan. Calls were quickly made, and cooperation was assured. Most of the plan would be in place before the day ended.

Karen Ann and her crew waited in the FBI building for most of the day. When they first arrived, they were escorted to different rooms and were told it wouldn't pay for them to lie. Karen Ann was flabbergasted by the treatment she and her crew received. She demanded all interviews stop and asked for legal representation for herself and her crew.

She took Larry's advice about including a maritime lawyer as part of the legal team. Before she left Norfolk, she made a few calls and told some attorneys about her predicament. When she finally called them later in the day, the attorneys were already prepared and on their way to DC.

After the interviews were stopped by the request for legal representation, the crew members sat in their interrogation rooms, waiting.

Time passed slowly for all of them. Karen Ann was ready to scream at someone when the director of the FBI came into her room.

"I protest! I won't speak to anyone without a lawyer present!"

He raised his hand. "Captain, I'm not here to interrogate you but to ask a favor. You don't need to answer until your lawyers arrive in case you feel this is a trick."

She calmed down a little. "I'd like this conversation taped. Once it's over, I want to be in possession of the tape."

"That's fine." He left for a few minutes, then returned with a tape recorder and started it.

"You see, Captain Murphy," he said, hoping to calm her further, "we had a situation where we had to look at every lead to the fullest extent the law demands when our national security is in the process of being compromised."

"I understand the need for investigating every lead," she said, "but my crew and I are all loyal U.S. citizens who've been put through your background checks and fingerprinted every time we renew our documents and licenses. Right now, I don't know why my crew and I are here other than the fact that you people lost some nuclear waste and somehow, part of it was found attached to *my* ship.

"We were as surprised as the shipyard workers who found the damn thing attached to my ship's hull. All of us swore an oath of allegiance to defend the Constitution, and now we're summoned to the FBI building to be treated like terrorists, interrogated without proper legal representation? I will...."

"Captain Murphy, please. I can understand your frustration and feelings of mistreatment from my agents, but please believe me they were acting only for the good the country. We were desperate for leads on this case. I apologize to you, and I'll apologize personally to each of your crew before you leave the building today.

"However, your country needs you and your crew to do it a favor. Can we depend on you, Captain?"

CHAPTER 27

The director's office of Homeland Security was quiet after the others left. The only people still in the room were the two generals, Ed Samson and Horace Washington, and Lamar. All the chairs, the screen, the microphone, and the voice-altering equipment were still in place.

Horace and Lamar sat in the two chairs closest to the director's desk. Samson relaxed on one corner of the desk, telling a story about the time he and Horace were fresh-faced, newly minted railroad-track captains in the Army, in Saigon on three-day passes after a hard month in the jungle hunting Viet Cong.

"We were in a bar knocking back a few cold ones, talking about how we'd run the war if we were in charge and sounding like bigshots, when this guy dressed in civvies sitting in a mixed group of Americans and Vietnamese at two tables pushed together suddenly came over to sit with us," Ed said. "He says, 'So you guys think you know how to run this war better?' Horace says, 'You're damn right, Buddy.'

"Neither of us looked at the guy, Lamar, and we had no idea who we were talking to. Horace elaborated on how this or that could have been done better or how to make the South Vietnamese take more responsibility for their war. He went on for half an hour.

"The guy bought us another round of beer. When Horace finally got off his soapbox and looked at the guy, the next thing I knew was his beer flew off the bar, and he jumped right off his bar stool.

"I thought we were in a bar brawl for sure, Lamar. I turned to get a good look at the guy and almost choked on my beer. Horace stood at attention in front of General William C. Westmoreland, wearing four stars! We'd been telling him how to run the war!

"We were two scared ground-pounders, both of us as erect as flagpoles. We didn't even breathe. Old Westmoreland looked at us and said, 'As you were, Gentlemen.' He told the bartender to set us up for another round, then he told us, 'Thanks for being so frank. You have some good ideas there. I want you to give your names and unit numbers to my assistant. I think I want both of you on my staff.'

"A week later, we were pulled from our unit and bam! We started working for General Westmoreland."

Lamar looked up at him. "The general really told General Westmoreland how to run the war?"

"No, Lamar. *Captain* Washington told a four-star general how to run the war," Ed replied. "I didn't tell you that story to make you feel impressed about your father-in-law. I wanted you to know the moral of the story. Sometimes, there are better ways to do things, and those answers can come from the people closest to the problem, but they have to be heard by someone who can actually change the game. Those few must be willing to listen to the ones working for them. That's the moral of the story."

Lamar, silent for a moment, thought that over. "So the moral is, the higher you get in an organization, the farther you are from the action. You need to listen more to the ones who are in the action, correct, Director?"

"Absolutely. I wanted you to know that story before I asked you a question."

"OK."

"I like how you formulated that plan to thwart the terrorist threat. I had the top minds in the country, with access to all sorts of materials and facts, but they were groping in the dark until you gave us that plan. I love that kind of straight thinking and quick assessment of a situation. I want you playing for the good guys, not the other team."

"General, I meant what I said about being finished with illegal activities. You said yourself this isn't over, and I could still be prosecuted. I'm not sure how to answer you."

Horace sat there, dumbfounded, guessing where the conversation was going.

"Lamar, to be truthful, I can make all the drug stuff go away and get you through a security check. You could have an office in this building where we can have regular meetings and discussions about the way we do business. I know this is a lot to digest, so I don't expect an answer right now. Go home and sleep on it. Discuss it with Horace and that beautiful wife of yours."

He turned to Horace. "How long has it been since I last saw her? She was going off to college, right?"

"That sounds about right, Yukon."

"Does that sound all right to you, Lamar?"

"Of course, Mr. Director. I'd be honored to deliberate on this offer. May I get back to you after Labor Day, when the kids are back in school?" Lamar felt shell-shocked, unable to believe he was going home instead of jail or being shipped off to Cuba, let alone that he'd been offered a job.

"That's fine. Take your time and do what's right for you. All right, Gentlemen, I need to get home before I'm in divorce court, thanks to you, Horace."

Horace looked up at Ed. "I don't know what you're talking about, Yukon."

As all three men stood, the director said, "Lamar, you let Horace know your answer. He can let me know, then we can arrange a meeting."

They shook hands, and Ed escorted his friend and hopefully newest employee to the elevator. All three rode down. The director used his key to go directly to the garage and avoid letting anyone see him with Lamar and blow his anonymity.

Lamar still couldn't believe he was going home to his family. The director promised him security for him and his family while they were in the DC area. If Lamar wanted to go home before the holiday, he should contact the DHS office and give his informant name to tell them where he was going, so security arrangements could be adjusted.

Karen Ann, taken aback by what the FBI director asked her to do, forced herself to remain focused on his words. He spoke about how it would be for the good of the country, and how she and her crew would be in no danger from the nuclear waste, even after it was made into a bomb, because the bomb wouldn't be armed until they returned to U.S. waters.

By that time, the Navy would send someone to remove the bomb from her ship and replace it with a dummy that the terrorists would try to arm when they were back in the States.

She didn't know what to say. The only thing she finally said was that if the company agreed to risk the ship and its crew, she was willing to command the ship, but she refused to speak for her crew. The director would have to make his pitch to each crewman. There were married men with children involved, who needed to make their own decisions.

With all the agencies involved and being brought into the operation, the activity level was on overdrive. Many people worked to organize their part of the plan. Max was back at the FBI building to help set up the takedown. Federal law dictated that the CIA and the Army and Navy Special Forces weren't allowed to operate on U.S. soil, although the underwater surveillance of the terrorist activation of the dummy bombs would be conducted by Navy SEALs, then communicated to the FBI, who conducted the land surveillance and landside takedown portion of the operation.

Over at NSA, Roman and Walter set up their surveillance equipment to monitor transmissions from the terrorists, including any cell phone communication channels coming into or out of Saudi Arabia from South America and the U.S.

The operation was coming together more smoothly than anyone hoped. The Navy put their SEAL teams on alert. One was already en route to Venezuela, with others being deployed to ports Lamar told Director Samson where the ships would arrive. Since all the ships belonged to Palm Petroleum, the director spoke with the CEO of the company and received the company's full cooperation for access to the ships.

So far, no ships were in port. All were either still loading cargo in Venezuela or were at sea, heading toward the U.S. According to the latest intercepted messages, all material except that from the *Palm Princess*, which carried the majority, had not been received, though the South American cell was preparing as many units as possible with what they had.

The story on the news, TV, and in the newspaper didn't mention the *Palm Princess* being in drydock after its heroic rescue mission during Hurricane Peggy. It was mentioned the ship needed some repair work due to the storm before it could resume its voyage to Venezuela.

The media, hungry to interview the female captain, were told she was busy preparing her ship. One news company even sent its traffic helicopter over the shipyards, hoping to see the *Palm Princess*, but the moment they landed, FBI Special Agents greeted them and escorted them to the local office, confiscating all their cameras and erasing any video of the ship in drydock by invoking the Patriot Act.

The news story provided the Mullah with an update of when the final, crowning shipment would sail for the day of reckoning, when he would finally destroy the Great Satan, making him the most-powerful leader in the world. All nations would be cowed before him, and he would rule the world.

Mohammed would reward him with eternal life, and Allah would grace him with riches unknown to any man in history. He called in his servant and handed him a coded message to be sent to all his men, telling them to be patient, that their time was near. They must remain vigilant.

He knew of the accident where two of his army gave their lives for the cause, but not even that deterred him from feeling good about how the overall mission was going. Those two men were probably receiving their just reward in heaven, enjoying their seventy-two virgins.

Mr. Pickle was in the cryptologist's lab ever since Roman and Walter returned from the meeting with the DHS. He wasn't very happy about Walter forgetting to add his email address when he sent off the coded messages that had everyone in an uproar. Walter tried to explain how in the excitement over the discovery and breakthrough, he made a mistake in the rush to send it out to everyone.

Pickle camped out with the two to keep from being forgotten again. He didn't want to look like a fool to his superiors any more than he already did. He had no idea what the two men were doing, so he sat there. Anytime it looked like they were doing something important, he demanded full disclosure.

Just as Walter and Roman were finishing up for the day, their sector alert rang to tell them their site was active. Pickle almost fell off his chair trying to get up, and the two cryptologists almost died holding back their laughter.

"Roman, let's see what old Allah Yad has for us now," Walter said, pulling out the translated copy. "Look at this. He's buying everything old CNN is giving him."

"Well...." Roman began.

"I need to provide the brass with my new discovery of the terrorists buying into the plan," Pickle said quickly. "I'll take that."

He grabbed the paper from Walter's hand.

"Ouch!" Walter said. "Watch it. You almost gave me a paper cut. It wouldn't look good on your record if you make me go out on an OJI would it, Mr. Pickle?"

"I'm so sorry, Walter," Pickle replied sarcastically, almost running for the door in an attempt to regain some of the glory Roman and Walter stole from him.

The FBI director gathered the entire crew into a conference room to make a personal apology to all of them for the behavior of the special agents, then he tried to explain what they hoped to accomplish with their actions. He went over the plan to thwart the terrorists and the fact that Palm Petroleum was backing the plan with all the ships and crews, who agreed to stay working on their ships.

"Your country needs you to carry out this plan, so we can avert an attack of the greatest magnitude from our enemy. I and your company will understand if you have any reservations regarding your involvement with the plan. You won't be looked down upon in any way if you choose not to take part.

"We need your answer quickly, though. It can be a simple yes or no as you walk past me. The ones who say no will be kept in a safe house until the mission is over. That's strictly for security reasons and your safety. Innocent people have already died in this operation, and we don't want any more if we can help it.

"Please file past and give me your answer. Those who say yes remain in the room. Anyone who says no can leave. The agents outside will assist you to a safe house. I want you to know your country appreciates what you do every day, and we hold you in the highest regard.

"Let's begin."

The men stood and filed by, each giving the director his reply.

CHAPTER 28

Despite feeling wronged by the way the FBI treated them, the entire crew agreed to the mission. All were members of the U.S. Merchant Marine, a very loyal and historically valiant and brave, though unarmed, civilian branch of the military. The U.S. Merchant Marine served honorably in every major conflict that involved the U.S., from the American Revolution through the two World Wars and on to Granada, Panama, the Gulf War, and the Afghan and Iraq wars.

The crew was rushed back to Norfolk, Virginia, as fast as the FBI could make arrangements. Once back on the ship, they prepared to refloat their battle-tested, battle-hardened supership. Each crew member knew the mission was important to the country, making it doubly important to all of them as patriotic Americans. They didn't want terrorists to use their profession to bring harm to their country, and they were willing to fight back any way they could.

Before they began to refloat the *Palm Princess,* Captain Murphy called them to the mess deck for a meeting.

"First, I want to tell you all how proud I am to be your captain. Second, all we have to do is our jobs like we'd normally be doing. That's our mission. We're just another big, fat tanker going to Venezuela for a big ol' drink of crude oil that we can take back to the States. Third, when we reach Venezuela, I want everyone to do your normal jobs. Don't spend any time looking over the side to find bubbles or anything else. Play it cool.

"We'll get in and get back out. Then we meet the Navy and let them do the bait and switch with the package we'll be carrying. Let's get going, and have a good voyage. By the way, there are no hurricanes forecast for this trip."

She received a rousing round of applause, then Hanratty called for three rounds of, "Hip, hip, hooray for the best captain!"

She gave him a dirty look, although she was just joking, to let him know he managed to embarrass her. *You'll pay for this,* she mouthed.

He smiled. "I know, Captain. I'll put myself on report and make sure it's in triplicate."

The crew laughed before filing out of the mess deck to their duties.

Larry slept soundly in his bed in Cape May, dreaming about a deserted beach with Karen Ann naked on a beach towel, when someone woke him by pounding on his door. Harry barked loudly, as Larry reached for his watch on the nightstand and saw it was 0625 in the morning.

The house better be on fire, or whoever this is will be sorry he's pounding on my door, he thought, pulling on his pants, hopping on one leg toward the front door, as he pulled on the other.

"I'm coming!" he shouted. "Stop pounding, will you?"

He reached the door and desperately tried to zip his pants shut over his erection and control Harry simultaneously. Finally, he opened the door. Seeing two men in dark suits told him the news wasn't good.

"Can I help you?"

They both flipped open their wallets to reveal badges. The man on the right spoke first.

"We're sorry to wake you, Captain Halsey. I'm Special Agent Kent, and this is Special Agent Clark. May we come in?"

He blearily stared at the badges, wondering why two FBI agents were on his doorstep at 0630 in the morning. *Why did someone assign these two to work together with names like Clark and Kent?* he wondered.

Shaking his head to banish the last cobwebs of sleep, he said, "Let me put the dog in the backyard, then I'll invite you in."

Once he put Harry outside, he turned on his Mr. Coffee machine, which he prepped the previous night, and let the two agents in through the front door. "Have a seat in the living room."

"Captain," Special Agent Kent said, "we're sorry to be visiting you so early in the morning, but it's a matter of national security. You know Captain Karen Ann Murphy?" He didn't wait for an answer. "Were you with her during this past week?"

"Yeah, I know her," he replied in confusion. "Yes, I was in Norfolk with her. What's this about? Is she in some sort of trouble?"

"No, she isn't," Special Agent Clark said. "If you were there, then did you see the object on her ship?"

"Yeah. What was that thing, anyway?" He scratched his head under his unruly hair.

"We're not at liberty to divulge that information. Just the fact that it was there is considered confidential. We're requesting you to keep it secret.

"We have a confidentiality document for you to sign. It says you won't divulge anything you saw in Norfolk this past week. You haven't spoken to anyone about it yet, have you, Captain?"

Larry wasn't even thinking about the blister on the hull of Karen Ann's ship. His mind went straight to thoughts of being in bed with her. "Ah, yeah. I mean, no, I haven't said anything to anyone. I don't see any problem with signing a confidentiality document. What's so special about all this?"

"It's an ongoing operation that needs to be kept quiet," Kent replied. "As you can tell from the news reports we've allowed, nothing has been mentioned about the ship being in drydock, either. That's all part of the confidentiality document."

"Let me find my glasses. I'd like to read it before I sign."

He read it over, signed, and handed it back.

"Thank you for your cooperation," Kent said. "Have a good morning."

He opened the door for them and said, "It *was* a good morning until you two came in to play Superman. Really? Clark Kent knocked on my door?"

The two agents chuckled and left. Larry, still wearing only his pants, stood in the doorway with the aroma of freshly brewed coffee drawing him toward the kitchen.

The counteroperation was named Murphy's Heroes. All aspects came together nicely as far as Director Samson could tell from the reports he received. He watched the heroic ship and crew leave Chesapeake Bay on TV. The news reports still discussed the dramatic rescue of the Coast Guard helicopter and the crew of the sailboat from Hurricane Peggy. With the departure of the ship, Allah Yad would know its shipment of nuclear waste was on its way to Venezuela.

The Mullah watched the news carefully, especially when the broadcasters were so excited about a female captain who saved a helicopter from having to ditch in the sea with her expert ship-handling skills and the courageous and skillful Coast Guard flight crew.

As he watched the ship sailing south from Chesapeake Bay, he said, as a servant poured tea for him, "Finally, my plan to destroy America, the Great Satan, will be completed. I, your Mullah, will forever be remembered as the righteous one who took down America when no one else could.

"That fool of a female captain cost me, but Allah looked out for us. He wants our plan to succeed."

He suddenly realized that the servant wasn't the same one who usually brought his tea. "Where is my regular servant?"

"He's sick, Master. He didn't wish you to catch whatever he has. I'm Ahmed, his cousin, and I told him I would gladly serve you in his absence until he can return to his duties."

"Fine. Tell your cousin I will pray for his well-being and speedy recovery."

"If there's nothing further, Master, I'll see about your dinner." Ahmed bowed and backed from the room.

The Mullah sipped his tea amid smug feelings of impending victory. He felt invincible, although he was suddenly tired and decided to take a nap. He lay down in his California king-sized bed with satin sheets and goose-down pillows to rest. As he fell asleep, he smiled.

The following morning, a servant found the Mullah in the same position and was saddened by the man's passing, although he was relieved that he could live his life as he saw fit from then on. He swore not to become another man's servant ever again, especially someone so arrogant, thankless, and self-righteous.

Ahmed resumed his life as a street drug pusher in Riyadh. His powerful overseas connections ensured him the finest quality drugs to sell to his customers and earned him a fat bank account. The body of Sahib, the servant he replaced in order to get close to the Mullah, would never be found in the vast sands of Saudi Arabia.

CNN covered the Mullah's passing, noting he was a powerful, wealthy man in the Arab world. Speculation about his death was rampant, as was concern over who might succeed him to lead his followers.

Ari Bohanni sent a new message to all agents in the field.

The Allah Yad did not die with Ali Mohammed Modula. We must continue with our plan.
Ari Bohanni

The message was received by all of the Allah Yad cells along with the NSA.

Director Samson saw the CNN broadcast about the Mullah's death and learned how he'd been schooled in the U.S. from childhood, attending Harvard University, then MIT, for his Master's Degree in Engineering. He was interested in the story because of the part of the world the man came from. Also, the Mullah was on a watch list because of his radical views, and his recent anti-American preaching gained him many followers.

One down, and God only knows how many more to go, Samson thought. *At least we can chalk him off the list.*

Ignoring the rest of the story, he returned to Operation Murphy's Heroes.

Director Samson wasn't the only one watching the CNN coverage of the Mullah's death. Marco Raimondo, the latest leader of the Colombian cartel, had recently seized the reins through a coup and gave swift cartel justice for the ineptness of the previous leadership. He'd been waiting for a report from Saudi Arabia to verify the message he received from Ahmed that his mission was completed. Ever since he disposed of the fool who allowed the Mullah access to the inner circle of the cartel and create the huge problem that held the cartel captive to the Mullah's wishes, he planned to remove their most-dangerous enemy.

With a smile, Marco turned off his TV and returned to his most-pressing problem—how to rebuild their successful smuggling network and resume the flow of drugs to America. He also had to consolidate several factions of the cartel that broke off after his coup.

He had unfinished business in Saudi Arabia, but he would return to that later. Ahmed was allowed to think he was safe and rich—for now.

The MV *Palm Princess* ran at her full speed of twenty-five knots, trying to make up a small part of the delay caused by her unexpected need for drydock. She cruised through the warm Caribbean waters, and Captain Murphy felt mixed emotions, as she sat at her desk in her stateroom.

She missed Larry very much. She relived their time together in her daydreams as well as her dreams at night. She was also glad to be back at sea, feeling the gentle rise and fall of the swell. It always gave her comfort and a feeling of reassurance, as it meant her ship was alive and well.

There was also the mission she and her crew were tasked with completing, and the fear of the unknown that lay ahead. She was ready to make her rounds and check the bridge watch to see if all was going as smoothly as it seemed.

It's a beautiful day, she thought. *It feels good to be back at sea.*

Before she left her stateroom, she tucked the picture she'd been holding and unconsciously rubbing with her thumb back into her desk blotter. With a satisfied smile, she left to make her rounds.

CHAPTER 29

"Tim," Max said into the phone, "I know Director Samson told us to drop whatever we had and concentrate on the new operation, but I can't stop thinking about what we had and who the informant was who suddenly came out of the woodwork. Can you?"

"Yeah," Tim replied. "That's been bugging me, too. I didn't want to say anything, but we had the whole thing nailed, and then everything went crazy. I guess we should drop it for now and concentrate on the operation."

"Maybe you're right. Let's have coffee once this is over. I'll call, all right?"

"That sounds like a winner, Max. Take care." Tim hung up.

Max tried to return to work, but he couldn't get the oddity out of his head. Somehow, that guy named Lamar Weston, or Lic, was involved in the situation up to his eyeballs.

Later that afternoon, Max had a revelation while sitting at his desk, reviewing the data that had been flowing into his office ever since Operation Murphy's Heroes began.

"That's it!" he muttered. "That son of a bitch is the informant! It's the only possible explanation. How else could that informant know so much about the entire operation? It's like he was inside the organization.

"Then how did the director get him to rat out his buddies? Hmmm. That can wait. Now that I finally cleared that up, maybe I can get some work done. I'll check the finer points of all this after we kick Allah Yad's ass back to the sands of Saudi Arabia and out of the western hemisphere."

He began checking and double-checking his assignments to make sure everything he was responsible for was swiftly completed.

The MV *Palm Princess* lay at anchor in the harbor of Puerto Cabello, Venezuela, waiting for her assigned berth to become available. A special guest aboard wasn't mentioned on any roster or crew list, although he rated a small note in the captain's log.

The guest had been in the radio room since the ship entered port, watching a TV monitor that was specially installed, connected to tiny minicams attached to the hull to watch the limpet mine.

Petty Officer 2nd Class Joseph "Sledge Hammer" McCahan was assigned to monitor the limpet and alert the other members of his SEAL team whenever there was activity. He would dispatch the divers to follow the men taking the nuclear waste and transporting it to their exit point from the water. From there, the surveillance duties would pass to the rest of their team, who would follow the material to the terrorist's safe house where the bombs were being manufactured.

Captain Murphy opened the door to the radio room and asked, "Any activity yet?"

"Well, Captain," McCahan replied, "we've got only ten feet of visibility down there. I won't see much until they're right on top of that mine. Aside from a couple fish swimming by, there's not much happening."

"I wish they'd hurry it up. I want to finish this and get out of here, so I can get that thing off my ship."

"Understood, Captain."

"Sorry if I'm getting fidgety, Petty Officer. I just want this over and done." She turned to leave, then asked, "Do you want anything brought up to you?"

He lifted his empty cup. "A cup of coffee would be wonderful, Captain, if it's not too much of a problem."

"No problem whatsoever. I'll let the steward know to bring you a cup. I believe you like it black, right?"

"Yes, Ma'am. That's how I like my coffee. Thank you very much."

Karen Ann left the radio room and returned to her stateroom the long way, via the galley, to tell the steward their passenger needed a cup of java.

Two men studied the harbor from a secluded area far from the hustle and bustle of the docks and ship traffic. Half a mile out in the harbor, directly in front of them, lay the biggest ship either had ever seen, the MV *Palm Princess.*

They wore lightweight wetsuits. With a look and a nod at each other, they unloaded the necessary tools for their job from the van. The van held two powerful underwater scooters, the rest of their dive gear, and several heavy-duty burlap sacks, as well as a special Allen wrench.

Once they were geared up and lifted their scooters into the water, they donned fins and slipped silently under the surface to begin their run to the *Palm Princess.* They weren't stupid and knew prolonged exposure to nuclear waste would eventually make them very sick, then they would die a painful death. If they allowed themselves to get that far, which they didn't plan to, they would use any extra explosives and radioactive waste left over from making the bombs to kill themselves. They would die knowing they helped destroy America's infrastructure, and, ultimately, America itself, striking a blow for the Great Jihad and their late, great leader.

Near where the two men slipped into the water, two other men in wetsuits waited, part of SEAL Team 2 based out of Little Creek, Virginia. They were brought to Venezuela via submarine, along with their SDV MK VIII, their SEAL Delivery Vehicle, Mark 8. The SDV was mounted on the outside of the sub's hull for the trip down from

Norfolk, Virginia, and the two SEALs used the sub's emergency escape trunk to exit the sub while still underwater a few miles from shore.

They entered the escape trunk and secured the hatch below them. The sub was only under 100 feet of water, which wouldn't give them too much discomfort. Chief Petty Officer Lucas "Pooky" Ryan flooded the escape trunk with water. Air pressure and the water level in the trunk rose to equalize with the pressure of the water on the outside of the sub.

Once the air pressure equalized, and both men donned all their gear, Petty Officer Second Class Daniel "Bam-Bam" Freeman opened the outside hatch, letting in a rush of water to replace the remaining air in the trunk. He slipped quietly into the dark, crystal-clear water of the Caribbean followed by Chief Petty Officer Ryan. They slowly swam past the sail of the submarine to their chariot, as the men of the SDV Squadron affectionately called their craft. The name came from the British frogmen of World War Two, who attempted to use similar craft, called X-Craft, nicknamed Chariots, to sink the German battleship *Tirpitz* in a Norway fjord.

The two men methodically prepared their craft for launching. Chief Ryan made sure all was in order and asked PO Freeman over the intercom if he was ready for release.

"Let's go take out some bad guys, Chief," Freeman replied.

Ryan pulled the release handle, and the SDV lifted away from the submarine's hull. Ryan used his guidance system to navigate them into the harbor and find their lay station in secrecy. The sub would rendezvous with them once they received a radio message saying the bomb had been placed into the limpet mine.

Chief Ryan had the name *Turtle* painted on his SDV out of respect for the first submarine ever used in battle. In 1775, in Connecticut, Patriot David Bushnell invented the submarine *Turtle* to be used against British warships. He planned to use a screw drill to bore a hole in the ship's hull and attach a keg of 130 pounds of gunpowder to be detonated by a time-delay fuse.

On the night of September 7, 1776, Sergeant Ezra Lee attacked the HMS *Eagle* in New York Harbor but had difficulty controlling the sub against the tidal currents.

Sergeant Lee was discovered and chased by men in rowboats. He had to abandon his attack and jettison the keg of gunpowder. The first and only attack by a submarine on an enemy warship during the war failed, stifling submarine development until the Confederated States Submarine *H. L. Hunley* was used in the Civil War. Although that had even more disastrous results, it began a long history of American submersibles that led to American subs being the most-feared and deadliest ships in the world.

The SEALS didn't use traditional scuba gear like sport divers. They wore the latest technology in underwater stealth, the Lambertsen's Amphibious Respiratory Unit, LARU. That type of breathing gear allowed them to proceed undetected from the surface, because there was no trail of bubbles to give away their position. It was almost silent, and the SDV was supersilent, too, meaning the SEALs could stay out of visual range while tracking their subject using the SDV's own passive sonar.

They had been waiting for word from their teammate, PO McCahan, of any activity around their target so they could begin tracking the terrorists since before the *Palm Princess* arrived and anchored to await her turn at the pier.

The SDV, a complicated machine, required a three-month school in Coronado, California, to train a SEAL to pilot it. It required constant practice to remain efficient, which meant SEALs who volunteered for training on the craft usually remained with the squadron and were attached to whichever SEAL team had a mission requiring the use of an SDV for insertion or surveillance. That was how Chief Ryan found himself on his assignment with SEAL Team 2. He deployed with that team once before to perform an insertion and extraction into another harbor in a different part of the world, so he knew the men and their capabilities. He was comfortable with his teammates' ability to accomplish their task and keep their comrades alive to fight another day.

The two frogmen did very little talking while waiting for word to move into position and begin their surveillance of the terrorists. They silently watched their area, using hand signals for communication. PO Freeman raised two fingers toward his eyes and pointed up the coast, indicating Chief Ryan should look.

Chief Ryan turned and spotted the disturbance in the water near the shoreline, then he whispered, "Looks like it'll be showtime real soon, Bam-Bam."

Freeman nodded. They saw the two terrorists use their sea scooters in the shallow water where they couldn't remain below the surface, and they created a visible wake that few would have noticed, although a SEAL's trained eye would spot it half a mile away.

Suddenly, the radio crackled in Chief Ryan's earbud. "Pooky, we have shoppers entering the mall."

Ryan gave a thumbs-up to Freeman, who reached forward and tapped his right shoulder twice to signal he was ready. Ryan gently sent the *Turtle* toward the *Palm Princess* and the start of their mission.

McCahan stared intently at the TV monitor, watching the two terrorists work diligently to remove all the nuclear waste and deposit it into burlap sacks. He worried Pooky and Bam-Bam might miss the show, because the divers worked quickly and would be finished shortly.

He finally heard a double-tap from Pooky in his headphones.

Man, that's cutting it close, Guys, Sledge Hammer thought.

He watched the divers work as if they were picking up abalone from the ocean floor on the Pacific Coast on a Sunday afternoon like he did before he enlisted in the Navy with his diving buddies. It wasn't abalone, though. It was very radioactive, unprotected nuclear waste that would kill the two men eventually, but they didn't seem in the least concerned. Either they were stupid or didn't care they would die a slow, horrible, painful death.

The men finished unpacking the limpet and began reinstalling the cover when one suddenly spun around as if he heard or saw something. Sledge Hammer quickly checked his other screens, but Pooky and Bam-Bam weren't visible.

If I can't see them, they can't, either, Sledge Hammer thought.

A six-foot bull shark filled one of the camera screens, making him jerk back in his chair a little. *That must've been what made the diver jump.*

He's not afraid of unshielded nuclear waste, but a little shark nosing around spooked him. He chuckled.

T-1 and T-2 finished removing the cargo from the limpet mine and began their return run to their van, and, in their eyes, Allah's waiting arms.

Pooky and Bam-Bam heard the sea scooters start up and fade away, as the targets moved toward shore. Chief Ryan waited until the sound was gone before tailing the men. As he moved away from the ship, he called Sledge Hammer.

"They're heading in the general direction of the spot where we reported the water disturbance earlier. The shore detail should move into surveillance range based on this information."

"Acknowledged, Chief." Sledge Hammer relayed the information to the rest of SEAL Team 2. "Rendezvous and prepare to execute Operation Spanish Moss."

The team would shadow the van to the terrorist bomb factory and observe the operation while planning to close it down for good once they received authorization.

While the landside SEALs prepared, Chief Ryan gave a running narrative to Sledge Hammer on the position of the two targets and their direction of movement. Sledge Hammer relayed the information to the SEALs waiting ashore, helping them stay in the proper position to observe the targets leaving the water and loading their van without giving themselves away.

Lieutenant Marcus "Spunk" Gateman used all the information to deploy his men perfectly to cover all angles for observing the operation from the moment the targets left the water to begin their journey back to the safe house to construct their bombs. He had two mobile units ready to begin the tail, based on what he learned from the tracks the van left on the dirt road leading to the secluded spot the terrorists chose to park and retrieve the goods.

The two Arabs slipped silently from the water with their packages and placed them in the van. They loaded their scooters and scuba gear, then dressed. One looked at his watch and pointed at the time to his companion.

They went to the front of the van to retrieve something. Spunk watched through his binoculars and thought, *It must be time for prayers.*

Soon, both men unrolled prayer rugs and faced east toward Mecca, where they knelt to offer their afternoon prayers to Allah. They prayed with vigor, both knowing they would soon join Allah face-to-face.

As soon as they finished their prayers, they stowed their rugs and finished loading the van before driving off.

"It's showtime," Spunk told his men via their radios. "Get ready to tail the suspects. They're on the move."

He packed his gear and gathered his men who would accompany him in the trail car, then he drove toward the highway.

The first trail car picked up the van, as it left the dirt road and moved toward the mountains, away from the city. The four-car team planned to leapfrog each other to maintain surveillance without letting the terrorists know they were being followed.

It proved easier than when Spunk drew up the plan and reviewed it with his squad. The terrorists had become complacent. They had no reason to worry. The cartel was under their control, and the cartel controlled the police.

Amro, the van driver, looked at his partner, As'ad. "I'm glad the Mullah chose you to be with me on this mission of Allah's."

"Why is that?"

"I studied ancient Arabic when I was younger. Your name means Lucky. What would be more appropriate for a mission like this? I feel invincible with you at my side."

As'ad asked, "What does Amro stand for? Should I be the one worrying about the mission?"

Amro turned off the main highway from the city and headed toward the safe house. A car hung back behind him far enough that he couldn't see through its windshield. That was very strange. In Venezuela, all drivers were impatient and crowded the car ahead of them. That infuriated him, so he had reservations about a polite driver behind him.

As he turned, he kept watching the corner to see if the car followed him onto the road.

"So what does Amro mean?" As'ad asked again.

Amro saw the car drive past the turn-off and keep going, which relieved him. He thanked Allah silently before saying, "Amro doesn't mean anything. It's just an old Arabic name from when we were nomads living in tents and going from one watering hole to another. My friend, I am nothing but tradition. You're the Luck of Allah, praise Allah."

Another car turned onto the side road, but Amro didn't see it, nor did he think of looking in the mirror again until they arrived at the safe house.

It was twilight when they reached a very remote house and outbuilding. Only one light was on in the main house. The sun was down, and darkness covered the foothills. Ghazi stood guard and welcomed Amro and As'ad with the traditional words, *"Assalamo Alaikum."*

To which Amro and As'ad replied in kind.

"What does Ghazi's name mean?" As'ad asked.

Amro thought for a moment. "Conqueror. I think the Mullah had a plan. He put the Conqueror, Luck, and Tradition together on this project to ensure success. Allah be good to the Mullah, for he is wise and good."

The other two agreed with him and began unloading their precious material so they could work through the night. They would take the finished bomb back to the harbor in the morning and plant it on the ship. They couldn't let the ship set sail without their package. That would be disastrous to the plan.

Lieutenant Gateman slowed his convoy of vehicles to a crawl, so he could deploy his experimental miniature surveillance UAV (Unmanned Aerial Vehicle). The tiny radio-controlled helicopter was the size of a large grapefruit and equipped with a miniature FLIR (Forward-Looking Inferred Radar) camera, and it was so silent that at 200 feet in the air, people on the ground would mistake it for nighttime jungle noise.

He planned to send the UAV up ahead to monitor what was taking place and remain far enough back to maintain the stealth their mission required. He didn't want to send his men too close and let them be discovered, compromising the mission.

Spunk watched the tiny 5x4-inch monitor showing what was in front, above, and below the little helicopter. He had a heads-up display showing attitude, altitude, and speed overlaid on the screen while he used a small joystick to control the UAV.

He watched the terrorists' van stop at a cleared compound that held two buildings. An unsuspecting terrorist leaving the van was greeted by another figure that showed as a white heat signature carrying what appeared to be an AK-47.

"Must be the guard," he whispered to his fellow SEAL, Petty Officer 2nd Class John "Blockhead" Oatman, who drove the lead vehicle in the small convoy.

The rest of the squad heard the words via the squad's comm net.

"I'm not getting any other heat signatures from the area, so it appears this is a very small cell consisting of only three targets, Block-head."

Spunk heard no reply, which was correct. Their orders were that no one spoke unless directly spoken to or had a situation the others needed to know about.

Spunk made sure the little helicopter stayed above the 200-foot limit to avoid giving it away. The three men unloaded the van and carried the material into the smaller of the two buildings.

"Dismount," Spunk told the men. "Drivers, position your ve-hicles back in the clearing we saw on the way in to the safe house."

He positioned his men to scout access routes to the safe house for the capture sequence of their mission.

"Warning, booby-traps," he added.

The men spread out and circled the compound to find and disarm any booby-traps left in the area and to establish the most-advan-tageous route to capture the compound. They also looked for any out-posts or escape routes the terrorists might have set up that were out of range of the tiny helicopter.

One-by-one, the men gave the signal they were in position. No one found any booby-traps, and they settled in to watch the com-pound.

Inside the assembly building, the three men listened to tradi-tional Arab music. Spunk couldn't make out the words, but the instru-ment that came through clearly was an *aoud*, a predecessor to the lute. Since most Arabic music was about love songs, he assumed the three men were pining for the seventy-two virgins Allah promised them when they died.

He and his men settled in for a long night. He kept in touch with the men occasionally to make sure they were safe. Much to his re-lief, it was a very boring evening, but in their line of work, boring was a good thing.

Around midnight, the three Arabs finished making their bomb and walked to the house to rest before morning and the last step of their mission. Amro and As'ad needed it. Even with the sea scooters, the dive would be difficult and dangerous. They needed their wits sharp to deliver the package and reinstall the limpet mine correctly to keep the package safe during its return voyage.

As the three men exited the small building, a flurry of reports came to Spunk from the men around the clearing.

"Easy, Boys," he said softly. "Maintain your positions. Let's see what they're up to. They're probably getting ready to bed down for the night. Wait it out."

He sent the UAV back up for a bird's-eye view of what happened inside the house and to make sure his men weren't about to be ambushed. Since the little screen was bright, it needed to be covered, as the UAV flew. Blockhead held a lightweight tarp designed for covert operations.

Whenever Spunk had a night operation, he remembered his boyhood days of perusing his father's collection of girly magazines under a blanket with a flashlight to avoid drawing attention to his room if a light shone under the door.

His parents never caught him, and he prayed his record remained that clean. He was alone, dependent on one man to protect him while he performed his duties.

The little UAV flew well. Spunk saw the three targets going about their nightly routines before settling down in bed. Once assured all was quiet and the targets were secure for the evening, Spunk brought the UAV back to check the men's security. No one else was about in the night, and he felt they were secure enough for the moment, so he brought the little copter back.

It was still dark when one of the outposts alerted Spunk he saw movement in the house. It looked like showtime.

Spunk prepared his helicopter for another flight to get a better idea what was happening inside the house. It hovered over the building, transmitting an image to his screen.

It seemed like the normal routine of a household getting up and preparing for the day. The three men used the bathroom, dressed, and made coffee and breakfast. Finally, they left the house for the out-building.

They were loading the bomb into the van when Spunk told his men, "Return to your vehicles. Prepare to follow the bomb and get the waterside part of this operation underway. Blockhead and I will stay here to monitor anyone who's left behind and possibly check out the compound."

Amro and As'ad drove the van down the main road and didn't even glance into the small clearing as they passed. It wouldn't have mattered. The SEALs hid the vehicles back far enough to be out of sight and added camouflage. No one from a passing vehicle would ever notice them.

The men quickly uncovered their vehicles and followed the two Arabs as before.

Spunk and Blockhead moved closer to the compound to get a better feel for the land. He carried several listening devices he wanted to plant, but it wasn't imperative to the operation, because the signals from the cell phone were constantly monitored. He didn't like depending on spooks to let him know what was going on, so he hoped to plant his own devices while Blockhead kept watch and covered him.

Ghazi helped his companions load the bomb in the van. As soon as they left, he decided to take a nap and went into the house to find his bed. He loved the life of ease he blundered into when the Mullah selected him for the mission. He was one of the Mullah's prize pupils, a radical's radical, with devout reverence for his religion and leader, although he saw that the life and the people in the west weren't as bad as Mullah said.

With Ghazi in bed and asleep, Spunk slipped into the compound and placed three listening devices where they should provide the greatest coverage and keep him informed of any activity in the camp.

After planting the last device, he regressed from the compound to rejoin Blockhead for their long wait for the return of Amro and As'ad.

On the highway, the team caught up with the van and its package. Soon, they neared the area where the terrorists would covertly enter the water.

Chief Petty Officer Ralph "Wallstreet" Landon picked up his mike and said, "Sledge Hammer, this is Wallstreet. Package is headed for K-Mart's return counter."

Sledge Hammer almost jumped when he heard someone speaking. It was the first sound he heard over the radio since Lieutenant Gateman reported they had visual on the target.

"Roger, Wallstreet." He changed frequencies and spoke to the waterside element. "Pooky, the shoppers are returning the merchandise."

"Roger, Sledge Hammer. Will insure package is returned and restocked. Out."

Chief Ryan reached over to shake Bam-Bam awake. "It's time to make sure everything is tucked away for a sea voyage."

He woke to the first touch from Pooky and nodded, then helped the chief prepare the *Turtle* for its mission.

Just as they entered the water and dived to retrieve the *Turtle*, from the bottom where it lay hidden, the van pulled in to the same spot it parked before.

As'ad and Amro donned their wetsuits and prepped their scooters for the half-mile swim to the tanker.

Pooky had the *Turtle* prepped in a short time. He and Bam-Bam were waiting when they heard the two terrorists enter the water and swim toward the *Palm Princess.*

Pooky had the *Turtle* underway the moment he heard the scooters race toward the tanker. "The show is starting," he told Sledge Hammer. "You've got a front-row seat. We'll be in the balcony."

He heard two clicks of the mic as Sledge Hammer's reply.

Petty Officer McCahan sat at his video terminal, waiting for the action to begin. It was a peaceful view, like peering into a large aquarium. Small tropical fish swam by, when suddenly, they raced out of view, as something approached them.

The two terrorists came into view.

"That wasn't very nice of them," he commented, keying his mike. "Pooky, we have shoppers returning their gifts." He settled in to watch.

He heard a double click in return from Chief Ryan to verify he received the message.

The two men used a special Allen wrench to unlock and pry off the limpet mine's cover, letting it hang by its connecting wire. They gathered their bomb carefully. Using the hooks inside the mine base, they bungie corded the bomb into position.

Their next move came as a surprise. Sledge Hammer watched as they appeared to pray over the bomb, then they removed their mouthpieces and leaned in to kiss it.

After finishing their strange ritual, they reattached the cover and locked it down, pushing on it to make sure it was secure.

"Shoppers have completed their exchange," Sledge Hammer said over the mike, hearing two clicks in reply.

As the two divers scooted away, Sledge Hammer stared at the limpet mine, knowing what it held was very deadly, indeed.

Many thoughts ran through his mind about what he saw. He felt all terrorists should be strung up by their thumbs, while the families of their victims should be allowed to walk by, each allowed one slice of a knife. That would ensure the terrorists died slow, painful deaths.

Then he realized they were so dedicated and committed to their cause, they would sacrifice themselves by working with radioactive gear without any protection, knowing their lives would end in a very painful way. They did such things freely and with vigor. He couldn't believe it. People were willing to work with radioactive material and possibly blow themselves up in the process, then kiss it when it was sent on its way.

"The vultures are getting back to dry their feet," Pooky said in his ear.

He double-clicked in reply then radioed Spanish Moss that they had returning shoppers.

Pooky waited for the two men to leave the water before turning and heading back out to sea. He called Sledge Hammer and requested he notify the sub to return to the rendezvous for pickup.

Sledge Hammer passed on the message, then passed confirmation back to Pooky and wished him a safe trip.

I just hope the rest of this operation goes as well as this part, he thought.

Finally, he called the bridge. "Captain, the terrorists have completed their delivery. They re-secured the limpet mine."

"Thank you, Petty Officer."

A minute later, the captain spoke on the PA system. "Set the anchor detail and man maneuvering stations. We are cleared to approach the wharf for our cargo."

That was good timing, Sledge Hammer thought.

Max was in his office almost all night, coordinating the U.S. landside portion of the operation. He finally had all the players in place, from Houston, Texas, to Delaware Bay.

Maybe I can finally go home and sleep, he thought, standing from his desk.

His FBI agents were using the same frequencies as the SEAL teams who would take care of the bomb removals and coordinate when and where the terrorists left the water, so the FBI teams could track them to their safe houses and make their takedowns.

There was just one more thing to do. He had to tell the incident commander at the Department of Homeland Security office that all his teams were in place and ready for when the first of the ships that couldn't be intercepted while out to sea to have their bombs removed and fake ones set in their places finally entered port.

As he walked down the stairwell to the parking garage, he made the call.

General Samson at DHS headquarters had everyone working on overdrive. People went over every detail of Operation Murphy's Heroes. The news from Max that the FBI and SEAL teams were in place was welcomed. That reassured the entire operation leadership. At least there wouldn't be any bombs going off even if the terrorists lost their FBI tails. He was pleased that the operation was going smoothly, but he was still very worried that he covered all the bases.

He needed another set of eyes on the operation, so he reached for his phone and punched in the number of an old friend.

CHAPTER 30

Retired General Horace Washington reached for the vibrating cell phone in his pocket. It was early, and he set the phone to vibrate to avoid waking his wife, a light sleeper. As he retrieved it from his pocket to see who it was at such an early hour, he frowned.

It's Ed Samson. Well, considering what's going on, I don't think this will be good news.

He walked toward the bedroom door and went into the living room to answer the call.

"Morning, Ed," Horace said. "What has you calling at such an early hour?"

"Horace, I hope I didn't disturb the family, but I need Mr. Jones here to give me new eyes on the situation. I want his perspective to make sure we've covered all the bases. Can you get him down here pronto?"

"I'm sure he'll do whatever is necessary to assist you. Let me wake him. We'll be there as soon as we can."

"Fine, Horace. I look forward to seeing you. I'll tell the guard to expect both of you and escort you to my office."

Horace ended the call and went to where Lamar slept, tapping his shoulder to awaken him, saying, "We need to get down to DHS right away. General Samson needs you."

Lamar stared back groggily. He'd been dreaming about making love to Wendy on the beach on their recent vacation. That was the last time she spoke to him lovingly. He had trouble focusing on Horace.

"What's going on, General?"

"We need to go downtown right now. You have to get dressed, so we can get on the road." Horace left the room to get ready.

Lamar lay in bed for a second, trying to recall his dream. When he felt an erection starting, he dragged himself to the bathroom and started to prepare for the day.

Spunk told his men to don their NBC (Nuclear, Biological, and Chemical) gear. "The entire property is contaminated, as are the terrorists. I don't want it getting to any of you."

He waited at his radio all night to receive confirmation from the NSA that the signal from the hidden terrorist center had been sent and received by someone in Saudi Arabia. Then he could close down his portion of the operation.

Though the signal still hadn't come through, he and his men dressed in their gear. They felt hotter as the day progressed to mid-morning. They knew how important their mission was, and they suffered their discomfort in silence. The jungle around them was active and noisy, as if the inhabitants knew something would happen soon.

Roman and Walter were on duty since the beginning of the operation. Standing eight-hour watches, they tried to sleep in the break room, a small anteroom with a couple of cots for such situations. It even had a small shower, so they could freshen up.

It was Roman's watch. Nothing was happening, and he was bored. He could do only so many crosswords puzzles and reread the newspaper so many times before it palled.

Suddenly, his detection gear beeped. He almost jumped from his chair to grab the readout. There was an incoming signal from the South American portion of the terrorist operation.

All units are now in place for the anniversary feast to the take-down of Satan. Awaiting further orders.

That's better than expected, Roman thought. *Now we've got a date. At least, I think we do. It has to be 9/11. That's when they'll set their plan in motion.*

He immediately called Pickle to advise him of the new information. He knew the man would become excited at the news.

It'll probably give him a hard-on, but at least I know the intel will be passed up the chain pronto.

Ari Bohanni accepted the printout of the coded message from the South American cell and smiled. "This is good." He dismissed his servant with a wave of one hand.

The new Mullah felt very grand with his newfound power. He couldn't believe his luck when he heard of Ali Mohammed Modula's passing and didn't give the idea of foul play a second thought. He didn't care.

He planned to formulate a response to his agents, but he needed to check with the other cells in America and make sure he understood all the finer points of the operation. The Mullah had been very close-mouthed about the details, even with his second in command. Ari wanted to give his people the impression they were in good hands, building their confidence that he was an even-better leader than Modula.

The three terrorists in Venezuela waited for confirmation that their message had been received. Their conversation turned to concern about their new leadership.

Spunk listened to them talk and soon learned they had a plan to use some of the leftover explosives and radioactive waste. They intended to board three airplanes flying to America, filled with American tourists and businessmen, hoping to repeat the events of Pan Am Flight 103 from Lockerbie, Scotland, except they would do it over downtown Miami when the plane was on its final landing approach.

They assumed the second flight would be diverted to Orlando, and they hoped to use that one to take out Disney World, which was filled with tourist infidels. They would claim responsibility for the attacks by sending a letter to the *Washington Post* before they boarded the plane.

They looked forward to their reward of seventy-two virgins and a guarantee into heaven.

"Walter? Walter!" Roman shook his friend to take over the next shift. "Come on, Man, wake up. I need to get back to the crypto room. We've got some activity about to happen, and I don't want to miss anything. Let's go. Get up!"

He left the bunk room, as Walter slowly woke up. When he realized what Roman just said about activity, he sprang up from his cot and almost fell into the tiny shower to brush his teeth and pee. He would forego his usual morning routine and simply dress before swinging by the cafeteria for a cup of coffee and a bear claw before heading to the crypto room.

Wendy, getting up later than usual, wandered into the bathroom, which she was still not sharing with her husband, to splash water on her face and brush her teeth before checking on the kids and her mother to see if anyone else was up yet and wanted breakfast. She had to get the kids back home. School started on Tuesday, and she didn't want them to miss the first day.

Thank God Labor Day was late this year, she thought.

She was still very conflicted about Lamar and his self-induced troubles that affected her entire family. As she walked to the kitchen for a cup of coffee, she saw a folded piece of paper on the dining room table and read it.

"Good morning, Wendy," Lillian, her mother, said cheerfully. "What's that, a note from the boys?"

"Good morning, Mom. It appears they needed to go to town to meet with Uncle Ed at DHS headquarters. Do you want a cup of coffee?"

"Sure, Honey. Have you decided what you're going to do?"

Wendy poured her mother a cup and fixed it the way she liked, then made a cup for herself before sitting at the breakfast bar.

"The only thing I know for sure is that I need to get the kids back in time for school. I'm still pretty messed up about that business Lamar is, or was, involved with. I don't know which way to turn."

"That's all right, Honey. You don't have to rush into anything. Just figure it out for yourself. I'd like to tell you something your father said. Lamar's attempting to do the right thing now, and that's why Horace is supporting and helping him.

"Don't let your father influence your decision, though. That has to be yours. Let's drink our coffee on the patio on this beautiful morning."

The two women carried the cups of coffee through the French doors and onto the patio to embrace a beautiful, sunny morning.

Ari Bohanni drew up a message and sent it to all the operating cells in America to learn their status in the execution of the plan. As he waited for their response, he recalled how he always had an eerie feeling about the plan from the start, although he praised it like all the others, because the Mullah was a vengeful man. Anyone who didn't follow him enthusiastically usually ended up missing one morning.

The Mullah once said, "You can be placed on a forever vacation if you don't have the fortitude to be part of Allah Yad."

Slowly, he read over the incoming replies. Everything was on schedule. The first ship would enter port in less than two days. The divers would set the timer for the appropriate date and time.

Like clockwork, the other ships would arrive in their own ports within hours of the first. Finally, the *Palm Princess* would arrive, and the plan would be set in motion. It would begin thirty hours after the first ship reached port.

The anniversary of the great attack will be honored by an even-greater one with longer-lasting, more-devastating results. We will cripple and eventually destroy the Great Satan. The Mullah did well to set it up this way. He chose the right warriors to handle the job. Even with his passing, the plan moves ahead smoothly.

The new Mullah was firmly seated in his chair of power. All the messages he received ended with the words, *We will not fail our new and trusted leader. Long live the Great Mullah!*

He decided to bring home his trusted bombers, because their mission was completed. He quickly wrote out his message.

You have done Allah's will. Report back to your home as soon as possible. Allah be with you. You will live as heroes for all your days.

Ari Bohanni,
Your grateful Mullah

Those last words would entrench him in their hearts even more. He didn't know the raw conditions under which the men worked, nor that they were dead men walking. The other teams could be saved, because their exposure to the radiation was minimal, and the most harm any of them might receive would be mild sickness from their short exposure while underwater, which helped provide a little more protection.

The *Palm Princess* sat at dockside. The cargo hoses were connected for ten hours, and they had over half the load aboard. The ship was performing as expected, and Captain Murphy felt everything was all right, as she made her rounds to keep tabs on her crew and ship.

She walked toward her stateroom when she decided to have a cup of coffee, so she went into the officer's mess. While she poured a cup, Petty Officer McCahan came in, looking for his morning coffee. He'd been sleeping since his part in the mission ended.

"Morning, Captain," Sledge Hammer said.

"Good morning yourself, Petty Officer, but it's only 2200 hours. I take it you're just getting up from some well-deserved rest?"

"Yes, Ma'am. I haven't been to the radio room to check in. I thought I'd get some coffee first."

"That's fine. Could I trouble you for an update once you're up to speed, and we're underway? I'm curious how things are progressing. I'd like to give the crew an update, too, if that's possible."

"I don't see why not, Ma'am. I haven't been told to keep you out of the loop, and you're the captain. Your wish is my command."

"Very good, Petty Officer. Thank you."

They finished preparing their coffee and went their separate ways.

Roman told Walter what took place while he slept and added what they were waiting for, then went to get some sleep. His turn back in the box would come again all too soon.

He wished Walter a pleasant, successful watch before leaving the room and heading to the break room to grab dinner and dive into his rack for some well-deserved rest.

Walter sat down to start a crossword puzzle when the computers suddenly beeped. He almost fell over backward trying to get his feet off the desk and see what gifts he might have received.

As he read the message from Saudi Arabia, he was shocked. The guy was dumb enough to use his own name! That meant they could target him or neutralize him and his organization.

This is what we've been looking for. He called Pickle, who had gone home, to advise him that he had new intel and was going to pass it along himself, because Pickle didn't have a secure line, but he had one more thing to do. He quickly encoded a message and sent it into cyber space. It bounced off a satellite and returned to earth in a spot in the South-American jungle.

Spunk's leg vibrated. When he took out the phone and saw the text, he said, "Well, it's about time. We've been sitting in this sweltering jungle long enough."

With confirmation that the terrorists had been told to pack up and go home, all he had to wait for was the execute signal from command.

"Shouldn't be long now, Boys," Spunk whispered in his mic. "They've been given the go ahead to break camp. Stay ready to go at a moment's notice. Out."

He knew from the conversation he'd been hearing inside the house that they had a plan of their own in the works. There was way too much activity for them to just be packing to go home. He notified command of his suspicions to see if they wanted to revise his orders, but there was no reply. That meant his original orders stood unless he heard differently, although he still had the American option of using his own initiative.

Lamar and Horace were at DHS headquarters all day, going over various aspects of the operation at General Samson's request.

"General," Lamar said, "you've got a lot going on here. It seems to cover almost everything."

Whenever Ed received an update about the operation, he passed it along to Horace and Lamar for review. He looked up at Lamar's words. "I smell a but in here, Mr. Jones. Spit it out. That's why I called you two in. I want this done right the first time. We can't afford any fuck-ups. What are you thinking?"

"General, there are a couple items I would consider revising if I were running this. The first is, I'd let the SEALs in South America get more intel on their suspicions about the terrorists going rogue. It sounds like there could be something else happening down there."

"I've been mulling that over myself. You indicated there was more, so go ahead."

He gave a few more details about various parts of the operation, but he didn't have a lot to recommend.

"One thing," he said finally. "The State Department and the Department of Justice want to act on bringing down the new Mullah through diplomatic channels. We could get more mileage out of this organization if we leave him in place and monitor his people. We broke the code. If we go in there and bust up the organization, all that effort is for naught.

"You know as well as I do that when you bust a drug pusher on a street corner, two more pop up on corners two blocks away, and you start all over. It seems like a lot of wasted effort if we bust them now instead of using what we have to break up more cells.

"Who knows how many cells are in the country connected to this guy? Once we stop them this time, they'll just try again. Someone new will take over and start a new organization. We can be on top of this one the whole time. We just have to keep them guessing as to how we get our information. See what I mean, General?"

Samson rubbed his chin thoughtfully. "That has a lot of merit, Lamar. I'll see if I can get the DOJ and State to back off and let us see if we can beat them to the punch. It sounds like a winner, but we've still got the mission at hand. This is good. Anything else for me?"

"I can't come up with anything more with the present data, but if more comes in, which I assume will start happening at a rapid pace, I'll be glad to give you as much help as I can. I can't believe I helped get this country into such a mess. I'm truly sorry, General."

"Nonsense. You were just a useful tool to these bastards. I'm just glad you came forward when you did, considering what you risked sacrificing. I appreciate any further help if you want to stay. You're more than welcome."

"I just need to call Wendy and let her know I won't be back to help pack up the kids and get them home for school. Speaking of their going home, is there any way you can arrange protection for my family, at least until I get home, if she still wants me?"

"Lamar, your family has had twenty-four-hour protection ever since you left this building the first time. That will continue until I tell them to stop. They'll be fine, so don't worry."

"Thank you, General. I didn't know." He reached for his cell phone to call Wendy, hoping she'd answer when his caller ID showed up. If not, her father would have to give her the news, and he would have to hope for the best.

So far, the situation was better than he imagined. He just prayed his home life would be the same.

Ed Samson, mulling over Lamar's ideas, decided to run with a few of them. He would let the men on the ground in South America decide what was best concerning the capture of the terrorists and dealing with their plans. He called the Department of Defense and informed them to let the in-place commander make the call in the field when it came to dealing with the terrorists.

Spunk felt itchy waiting for the call from command to tell him what to do. He occupied himself as best he could drafting a new plan based on the information at hand. He was ready to follow whatever command decided.

Finally, his encrypted SAT phone beeped, and he read the message. "Damn," he muttered. "They've got some people up there with some brains."

He quickly redeployed his men for the revised mission plan. Instead of taking the terrorists at the house and then having to smuggle them out of the country, which was always risky, they would follow them to the airport and see which flights they booked and let them get aboard. Photos of the men would be sent to command to use in apprehending the terrorists in Miami, but first, their luggage would be intercepted by two of his own men.

They were of Latino descent who spoke fluent Spanish. They would have fake *Policia* IDs and would be appropriately dressed. The luggage and bombs would be taken to a safe area to be disarmed, then they'd be taken to the U.S. for proper disposal and to be used as evidence in the tribunals.

Once the terrorists were onboard the planes and in the air, the airline would be informed they had fugitives onboard, and the planes would be boarded upon arrival in Miami. As long as the luggage was intercepted, the plan was sound.

Spunk's men were well trained and very good at their jobs. He had no doubt they could do it. He sent the two ahead to make preparations. Most of the remainder would follow the bombs, and two would stay back to set up the area for decontamination with a team standing by offshore aboard the aircraft carrier USS *Ronald Reagan CVN-76*, waiting for the signal to come ashore and sanitize the area. The U.S. didn't want any member of the Venezuelan government to know that the SEALs, the terrorists, any U.S. nuclear waste, or U.S. explosives were on their soil. President Hugo Chavez wasn't very friendly with the U.S. and would love a chance to create an international incident over such an invasion of his country's privacy.

Amro, As'ad, and Ghazi were quiet since receiving the signal to break camp and return to Saudi Arabia. Their minds turned inward, and they dealt with their own thoughts and demons that began to haunt them about the families they were leaving behind and would never see again until they reached heaven.

Each man begged Allah for forgiveness for the sorrow they were about to bestow on their loved ones, but they moved ahead with the mission, preparing bombs and installing burner phones to be used as detonators. The bombs were vacuum-sealed in heavy-gauge polyurethane bags to hide the scent of the explosive materials inside, mixed with some of the leftover radioactive waste to create an even-bigger catastrophe.

The plastic explosive was shaped into a piece of modern art with various metal pieces added to camouflage the detonators during X-ray analysis.

Their plan, although simple, was brilliant. When the planes were on arrival and just over their respective cities, each man would call the burner phone's number. Then all three of them would be on their way to heaven and their reward for being good Muslims and martyrs of the Great Holy War against the Great Satan.

They were almost finished, but it was late, so they decided to forego leaving until morning. That meant their flights would be landing around noon American time, which would produce a higher number of casualties and worse effects on anyone who witnessed the event.

Oh, great, Spunk thought, as Amro told his comrades they would leave in the morning. *Another night out in the jungle. We can put the time to good use and touch up the plan to make sure all bases are covered.*

He gathered his men to talk over the details and make any necessary revisions, then he sent his two fake *policia* the information about the delayed departure.

"Hi, Wendy," Lamar said. "The director asked me to stay here until the mission is complete, so I won't be able to help you get the kids ready to go home. Will you be OK by yourself?"

"The kids and I will do just fine. Thank you for the note this morning. Mom will help get things ready. You have our car, though. Will Dad bring it home and take his own car back, so I can get on the road as fast as possible?"

"He's on the way now. There's one thing I want you to know. You and the kids have a security detail assigned to you for the duration of this operation. Please don't worry. General Samson sent a team to search our house and make sure it's safe. You and the kids will be protected. Just go about your regular day, and the agents will take care of security.

"Wendy, I love you and the kids. I'm truly sorry for all of this."

"Tell Uncle Ed thank you for me. I know you love us, but we need to get through this first, then we'll discuss the future. Lamar, thank you. I'll see you when you're done. Good-bye."

Lamar hung up and stared at his phone with conflicting feelings. *She answered the phone, so that's a good sign. She was amicable, too. Still, it could go either way. Her tone wasn't hateful, but she wasn't raised to be hateful. She didn't say she loved me back, which is a bad sign. I don't have any more information than I did before.*

Karen Ann looked up from her desk when she heard someone knock on the stateroom door. "Come."

206 - RICHARD MCCANN

The door opened, and Petty Officer McCahan entered her stateroom and stood at attention. "Reporting as requested, Captain, with an update of the operation."

"At ease, Petty Officer. Come in and be seated, pleased."

"Thank you, Ma'am." He sat down and thought how hot she must've been in her younger days. She was still pretty hot for a woman her age, and she didn't bother doing anything to emphasize her looks, but she was still beautiful.

He took the chair she indicated beside her desk. "Captain, it appears things are coming together, but there have been some revisions to the original plan, although it's mostly about other areas of the operation. Some of these terrorists might be going rogue, but...."

Her attention was squarely focused on the man.

"...as far as I can tell, our plan remains the same. We will meet with the sub at the agreed-upon location, swap the real bomb for the fake, and leave. Other than that, it seems to be going well, Ma'am."

"I thank you, Petty Officer. The crew will be glad to know things are going smoothly for now. We'll get underway shortly."

She stood and shook his hand, then opened the door to let him out of the compartment.

"Thank you, Captain." Sledge Hammer left with thoughts of her lingering in his mind, as he walked toward the radio room.

Max worked all day and into the night when the new order arrived on his desk from DHS to revise the details of Operation Spanish Moss. His people in Miami needed to be mobilized to round up some inbound terrorists for the suspected bombing of the planes they would arrive on.

Won't that be a hoot, he thought. *They'll get all giddy and think they're going off to their reward, then nothing happens.*

"I'd sure like to see their faces when they press the switch, and nothing goes boom. Then they land, and bam! My guys slap cuffs on them, as they exit the cabin."

Max called Miami and set up airport coverage, telling his people they would receive the accompanying photos and details about the flight and the manifests as soon as he had them.

Great, he thought, hanging up. *I'll be here all night waiting by the computer, and I thought I might actually get to go home and sleep in my own bed at least once this weekend. Oh, well. That's the life of a special agent. We get months of regular, boring stuff, then it's a ninety-six-hour marathon of craziness.*

CHAPTER 31

The sound-powered phone gave its annoying ring, waking Karen Ann from her needed rest and bringing her back to reality. "Captain," she said, pressing the button on the side of the handset.

"It's Hanratty, Captain. You left orders to wake you when we're fifty miles from the rendezvous point."

"Very well, Pat. I'll be there in a couple minutes. Please ring Petty Officer McCahan and tell him our position, so he can man his equipment. Soon we'll be done with this part of the operation. I'll be glad to get back to the hum-drum routine of transporting crude oil and dealing with Mother Nature."

"Yes, Ma'am. I understand that sentiment one hundred and ten percent. See you when you get here, Captain."

Hanratty hung up, then he called Petty Officer McCahan's stateroom.

"This will be a first for me, Rene," he told the helmsman on watch with him.

"Me, too, Mr. Hanratty.

"I'd better ring the chief engineer to tell him we'll need the engines on standby for maneuvering." Pat liked to verbalize his tasks to double-check himself. It was a running joke among the crew, and Rene gave a very soft laugh that wasn't loud enough to be heard by Mr. Hanratty.

"Captain on the bridge," Hanratty said a moment later, when Karen Ann appeared.

"Good morning, Pat," she said. "Good morning, Rene."

"Morning, Captain," they replied in unison.

"Skipper," Hanratty said, "we're forty miles from our rendezvous, but I already gave the chief notice that we'll need the engines shortly and to prep for maneuvering."

"Very good, Pat. Do we have anything on the long-distance radar yet?"

"Not yet, Skipper. They don't give much of a radar signature when they're on the surface. If my Navy time serves me well, I don't suspect they'll come up until the very last minute. Those sub boys don't like being on the surface if they can help it."

"Fine, Mr. Hanratty. I'll check with our guest and see if he's heard anything more from his command."

Rene loved being at the wheel when the captain came into the wheelhouse, then left before his relief arrived. He loved watching her walk out the aft bridge door. He was definitely an ass man, and she had an ass worth watching.

The intercom speaker in the control room came alive, "Con, Sonar. We have target number twenty-five heading 005º true, speed twenty-six KTS, range is 30,000 yards. I'm not completely sure, but I believe that's the tanker *Palm Princess*. Those civilians are on schedule and in the right part of the ocean."

The OOD, Officer of the Deck, picked up his mic. "Con, roger Sonar. Let me know when you have confirmed the target's signature as the MV *Palm Princess*." He hung the mike back on its hook.

"Diving Officer, make your depth 300 feet."

"Roger. Making depth 300 feet, aye." The diving officer was the COB, Chief of the Boat, the most-senior chief petty officer assigned to the sub.

He gave the planesmen orders to raise the submarine to the depth of 300 feet.

"Messenger of the Watch, please advise the captain and our guests that sonar has a target they believe to be the *Palm Princess* at 30,000 yards."

"Aye, aye," the young seaman said, walking aft to the captain's stateroom to deliver the message from the OOD.

Captain Blainey was a graduate of Notre Dame University and the NROTC (Naval Reserve Officer Training Corps) Unit, which was how he could afford his tuition, because he didn't come from a wealthy family and hadn't been recruited for sports, even though he starred in sports in high school. He was a walk-on for the football team. In his senior year, he led them to the BCS National title game but was injured in the second quarter when there was a breakdown of protection, and a free linebacker sacked him, dislocating his throwing shoulder and ruining a possible professional football career.

Blainey saw his beloved team defeated from his hospital bed, along with his potential NFL career. He decided to continue with the Navy, because he enjoyed the experience and the lifestyle. He chose submarines when given the chance, and he never regretted his decision.

At six-feet-four-inches tall, he barely made the height limit, and he maintained his physique from his sports days. The crew was glad to have him as their captain. He was raised to be fair and just, and they knew where they stood with him at all times. He gave one hundred percent at everything he did. Being the captain of one of the U.S. Navy's finest submarines was another example of how he led his life. His men would follow him anywhere he took the boat. They had faith he would always bring them home.

When the messenger knocked on the captain's door, he heard stirring inside, then a voice said, "Enter."

He opened the door and found the captain lying on his bunk. He gave the OOD's message and asked if there would be a reply.

"I'll be there momentarily, so no," Captain Blainey said.

The messenger went to the torpedo room to tell the SEALs it was almost showtime. It seemed they were always cleaning, inspecting, and reassembling their equipment. No matter when he passed them on his rounds, they were always doing something.

The SEALs didn't show any emotion at the news that their target was close, and they would soon be diving under one of the largest ships ever built to work on a dirty nuke device. The only thing in their favor was, it was daylight, and they were in the Caribbean, with crystal-clear water, so visibility was good.

The messenger saw the SEALs laughing and kidding, never showing any concern. They could have been going to the movies instead of getting ready to work on a live dirty nuke. If he were part of the Team, he would've been terrified.

After he gave the message to Lieutenant Penfold, he saw the man raise his index finger to head height and twirl it from his wrist about four times, like telling someone to start a car engine.

The men immediately stirred from their preoccupation with cleaning their weapons and started prepping for the mission. The messenger, shaking his head, returned to the control room.

The Miami FBI office buzzed with activity after receiving Max's mobilization notice. Special agents were recalled from home, and the Operations Command Center was activated. The Miami Bureau section chief was alerted and was on his way back to the office to run the operation himself.

Many ongoing operations from the Miami FBI section were suspended until the section chief arrived and assessed the new alert received from Lead Special Agent, DHS, FBI Section, Max Gordon. When anything came in from DHS, it was SOP (Standard Operating Procedure) to supersede routine ongoing investigations until the section chief ascertained the full impact and manpower necessary to accomplish the DHS mission.

All was proceeding smoothly. The duty agent sent an alert received message back to Max, so he could notify his superior that Miami had been activated for its role in the operation.

Max's computer gave a soft *ding* when the incoming email from Miami arrived, and a text balloon popped up that read, *You've got mail.*

He was in the office, reviewing the information he and Tim gathered on Lamar Weston, when the alert went off. Max spun around and headed for his desk.

Spunk spent the night catnapping, checking his troops, and making sure the targets were still in place. Dawn came slowly to the jungle, bringing overcast skies with the threat of rain.

Great, Spunk thought. *Just what we need, stuck out here waiting for these yo-yos to get moving, so we can pass them off to the Feds in Miami. We've been sweltering here for two days and nights, and now it's gonna rain. We haven't even fired a shot. At least they should be ready to go to the airport soon...I hope.*

One of his mini-microphones registered activity in the house.

"Look alive, Boys," Spunk whispered into his com mic to make sure all the men were alerted.

Spunk listened to the three men say good-bye to each other. Once they reached the airport, they would split up and take different airlines, all scheduled to depart within minutes of each other for Miami.

Four of Spunk's men were already positioned at the airport as tourists to shadow Amro, As'ad, and Ghazi, as they booked flights and report which airline and flight number they were taking. Spunk would pass that info along to headquarters, so the takedown could be accomplished as smoothly as possible. He sent the other squad members back to the last vehicle to be ready to tail the trio to the airport and give his men inside the signal their charges were arriving.

Everything was coming along fine, which made Spunk feel a bit nervous.

As'ad was the first to exit the house and toss his gear into the back of the van. He called for his comrades to hurry, so they could be on their way.

Ghazi and Amro came out together and loaded their bags into the van. The trio exchanged final hugs before getting in.

Once the van engine started and moved away, Spunk took his remaining gear and sprinted back to his men, taking a predetermined route out of sight of the road.

Jake looked over at Juan and asked, "The old man still has it, doesn't he? Look at him go."

Juan gave a thumbs-up. "Yeah. He can still match any of us step for step, man."

Spunk arrived just before the van passed the tiny clearing where the car was camouflaged. He waited until the van passed him before getting in. It would take the van time to reach the main road. There was little chance of losing their target.

Juan started the engine and eased out of the hiding spot to tail the van.

"Don't get too close," Spunk said. "We don't want to blow the tail."

Juan didn't need the reminder. He was fully trained in tailing another car, but Spunk couldn't help himself. He reached for his SAT phone and sent a quick encrypted message to the USS *Ronald Reagan* that contained his previous coordinates and the word *Vacated*.

The length of time the message took to leave his phone was less than a millisecond. It would never be traced, nor would it show up on any surveillance equipment. That would set in motion the next mission, where a cleanup crew would arrive soon to scour the area for any evidence and to decontaminate the location until no one would be able to tell what happened there.

"Captain," Hanratty said, "five miles to the rendezvous point. Permission to reduce speed to avoid overshooting our arrival point?"

"Granted. You may maneuver at will to put us into position, Mr. Hanratty."

"Aye, aye, Skipper." He rang the engine room for half ahead on both engines. The big ship lost some of its vibration, as it slowed from full speed to fifteen knots.

"Conn, Sonar. Target number twenty-five just reduced turns and is now doing fifteen knots."

"Sonar, Conn. Aye, aye," the OOD replied. "Diving officer, ease us up to periscope depth. Messenger of the Watch, let the captain know we're coming to periscope depth due to the slowing of the *Palm Princess* at 10,000 yards."

"Aye, aye," the messenger of the watch said, walking aft toward the captain's cabin.

Soon, he rapped on the captain's door to deliver the OOD's message.

The captain suddenly walked down the passageway and asked, "You looking for me, Dorning?"

"Yes, Sir, Skipper. The OOD wanted you to know we're coming to periscope depth due to target number twenty-five slowing to fifteen knots at 10,000 yards."

"Very well. I'm on my way there now. Thank you, Dorning."

Dorning stepped against the bulkhead to let the captain pass, then he followed him to the control room.

"Well, Ron," the captain said when he entered the room, "is she in sight yet, and are our guests ready for swim call?"

"Good day, Captain," the OOD said. "She's just coming over the horizon now. I received word from Lieutenant Penfold that he's all ready and standing by."

"Very well. We'll surface 200 yards to her starboard when she has slowed to four knots. Carry on. You still have the Conn, Mr. Smetana."

"Aye, aye, Captain. Surface when the *Palm Princess* is at four knots at 200 yards to her starboard. Mr. Smetana has the conn."

"Mr. Smetana has the conn, aye," the diving officer repeated.

The *Palm Princess* slowed her engines to all stop, letting her drift at five knots half a mile from the rendezvous coordinates. Hanratty did an excellent job bringing the ship to a specific point in the open ocean right on time.

An even-finer bit of coordination was happening right beside the huge ship without anyone knowing except those who stood in the control room of the USS *Philadelphia SSN 690.* She was a Los Angeles class fast attack sub. At the time she was commissioned on June 25, 1977, she was the stealthiest submarine in the world. Nothing could compare with her.

Lieutenant JG (Junior Grade) Ron Smetana brought the sub to within 200 yards of the huge ship and matched her speed exactly. Blainey was proud of him. Ron came aboard the *Philadelphia* as a fresh ensign from submarine school, and it was his first sea duty. He qualified on subs and earned his gold dolphins in record time. A determined student, he queried the captain every chance he had about ship handling and navigation, which pleased Blainey immensely.

Watching his protégé work, Captain Blainey was very satisfied.

Amro, As'ad, and Ghazi pulled into the airport's long-term parking lot, which seemed appropriate, because they were taking a one-way trip to heaven soon.

Spunk sent a text to his men in the airport to alert them the targets were coming out of the long-term parking garage, and they could pick up their tails from there. While in the car, Spunk changed into civilian clothes and used wet wipes to get rid of the jungle smell he acquired after three days in the bush. He would tail the targets to the terminal to ensure all were picked up by his men.

Juan dropped him off near the parking garage entrance. He followed the van up three levels without being seen, as they looked for a parking place. The trio wasn't looking for a tail, but Spunk didn't know that, and he refused to take any chances.

Ghazi was the first one out of the van. Amro followed him to the rear, so they could unload their bags and begin their journey to heaven. As'ad met them. Each man grabbed his bag. Closing the door and locking the van, they walked toward the terminal in silence.

Spunk wondered how three obviously intelligent young men could do what they did and were seemingly about to do without care for their welfare, then decide to finish their lives in what they believed would be a blaze of glory. They planned to blow up themselves and close to a thousand travelers when they were on final approach to their destinations.

There was no longer any cover for him, so he was out in the open. He watched his targets call for an elevator.

Now what? he wondered. *Should I keep following, or....*

The elevator door opened, and, as they turned to press the button to take them to the terminal, As'ad stuck out his hand to keep the door from closing. Much to Spunk's surprise, he waved him into the car with them.

He couldn't turn back, although he wasn't carrying a bag like he was flying somewhere. His mind reeled for a second, then he waved and began trotting toward them.

Upon entering the elevator, he said, *"Gracias,"* and stepped to one corner, hoping to be unobtrusive.

He kept wondering what drove men like these to do what they did or were about to do, yet they were willing to hold the elevator for a stranger who'd been too far away to reach it in time.

The elevator stopped and dinged. The doors opened, and Spunk saw his own three men waiting outside. They glanced at him in confusion.

He quickly held the door for the three Arabs to get out. Each replied with *"gracias"* and what appeared to be a genuine smile. Spunk left the elevator and walked off in the opposite direction of the men picking up their tails. All three wondered how their boss ended up on the same elevator with the terrorists.

"Surface, surface, surface!" the 1MC blared throughout the boat.

The diving officer gave orders to the planesmen, and the *Philadelphia* broke the surface beside the *Palm Princess.*

"Captain," Hanratty said, surprised, "we have a visitor right off the starboard side, and they're *really* close aboard."

"I would have to agree with you, Mr. Hanratty. Those Navy boys really like to show off. I guess they're ready for us, so you'd better get us stopped. Be careful, Pat. Neither I nor the company would like to buy a submarine today."

Figures appeared in the sub's sail cockpit, then the deck hatch popped open, and men filed up onto the deck.

"That's quite a welcoming party for us," Karen Ann observed.

"Yes, Ma'am," Hanratty and Rene replied.

Karen Ann watched, as a seaman pointed a device at the *Palm Princess'* bridge and began blinking a light at her. "Oh, my God. They're giving me Morse code? I haven't done Morse code in years!

"Mr. Hanratty, how's your Morse code? Please get me the ship's handheld blinking light."

"I think it's back in the chartroom, Skipper. I doubt my blinking light is any better than yours, but if you want me to try, I will."

"No. Just get me the blinking light, and I'll give it a go." Then she had an inspiration. "Rene, use the ship's PA system to pipe Petty Officer McCahan to the bridge on the double."

Rene reached for the mic. "Aye, aye, Skipper. Brilliant idea, if I do say so myself, Ma'am." He spoke into the mic. "Petty Officer Mc-Cahan to the bridge on the double."

Karen Ann studied the incoming signal. "I'm getting some letters, but it's too fast for me."

Thirty seconds later, PO McCahan came to the bridge, followed by Pat from the chartroom with the handheld signal lamp.

"Finally," Karen Ann said. "Can you read what they're saying, Petty Officer?"

"Sure thing, Captain. I used the outside ladders to get here and was reading it on the run. I got most of it, which is just a repetition of *Stop, please.*"

"Tell them we're trying, but a ship this size takes awhile to stop. They're pretty close, and I don't want to shear toward them. Thank you, Petty Officer. You're a godsend."

"On it, Ma'am." He took the blinking light and began flashing their reply.

"Skipper," Hanratty said, "we are DIW (Dead in the Water). I just rang up All Stop, and the engine room answered with All Stop."

Karen Ann, who stood 110 feet away on the bridge wing, said, "Thank you, Mr. Hanratty. Petty Officer, please tell them we are DIW and engines are stopped."

He was well into the message before she finished saying the words, almost as if he were taking dictation. "All sent, Ma'am. They're putting the Zodiac in the water now. It shouldn't be too long."

Forty-five minutes after the Zodiac was launched from the *Philadelphia,* the mission was completed. All the SEALs were back aboard the sub, and the dirty bomb had been neutralized, removed, shielded, and replaced with a fake bomb. The *Palm Princess* could continue on her assignment.

Captain Blainey turned to his quartermaster. "Send the following message. 'WMD safe. You may proceed. We will escort you as far as Norfolk, Virginia. Nice doing business with you.'"

On the bridge of the *Palm Princess,* McCahan read the message as it was signaled. "Any reply, Captain?"

She thought for a moment. "Please send the following. 'We have to stop meeting like this. I owe you and the boys a beer on me the next time I'm in Norfolk. Thank you for your assistance. Godspeed."

Blainey read the message as fast as the quartermaster did and began chuckling. "Send this reply. 'Sounds good to me, but I'm a bourbon guy. Don't know about the SEALs, but I'm sure they're a thirsty bunch. See you in Norfolk.'"

Sledgehammer laughed, as he read the sub's reply. "Captain, you'd better bring your checkbook. I've had drinks with those guys, and they can really put it away."

"Thank you. It's worth every penny to know I won't be blown up just for doing my job. Mr. Hanratty, set course for the Delaware Bay entrance buoy and make best speed."

When she looked back where the sub was, it had already moved well away from her ship, and jets of air came from her vents, as she submerged.

"That's something you don't see every day. At least, I haven't seen it. Watching a submarine go under is something."

All she could see was the sail of the sub and the top of its rudder, which vanished quickly, leaving just a swirl of water on the surface. She was back in her realm, where she was master of the deep, second to none.

"Mr. Smetana," Captain Blainey said, "please bring us around into a shadowing position of the *Palm Princess* and take us down to 400 feet. We've had way too much sunshine today."

"Aye, aye, Skipper. Helm, twenty degrees right rudder. Diving officer, make your depth 400 feet. One degree down bubble, and ring up half ahead," the OOD ordered.

"Aye, aye. My rudder's right twenty, Sir," the helmsman said.

"Making depth to 400 feet," the diving officer said. "One degree down bubble and half ahead, aye." He gave his planesmen their orders to bring the boat to 400 feet and had the helmsman dial in half-ahead on the EOT, Engine Order Telegraph. The USS *Philadelphia* began her shadow escort of the *Palm Princess* for the trip back to her home port of Norfolk, Virginia.

In Miami FBI Headquarters, the activity slowed from the original DHS alert when another round of message arrived from Washington with photos of the three terrorists, their flight information, and confirmation that all three suitcase dirty bombs were accounted for, neutralized, and in U.S. custody.

Spunk and his squad of SEALs did their job, and it was up to Miami FBI agents to apprehend the three terrorists when they arrived in Miami. Three agents were quickly assigned to each suspect to ensure apprehension would go as intended. They studied the picture and description of the terrorist's clothing and went over the flight number and arrival gate and time.

Max received updates of the Miami operation as well as making arrangements for transportation to Guantanamo, Cuba, for interrogation and internment, but first, the terrorists would be taken to Los Alamos, New Mexico, for decontamination and to receive as much modern medical attention to save their lives as the U.S. would do for one of its own. Doctors and equipment were already flying toward the base to prepare for the arrival. It was the American way. America always tried to give as much medical attention to its enemy's wounded combatants as it did for its own.

General Samson had only one- or two-hour catnaps since the operation began. He hadn't been able to go home to see his wife, but she understood his dedication to his country. Ed was accustomed to long hours and stressful situations from his Army days. This situation was no different, except he wasn't on the front lines where he wanted to be, leading his men and women.

He received constant updates as fast as they arrived, then he forwarded them to Lamar, who had only slightly more sleep than the general. Lamar, too, felt the drive and rush he used to feel with his unlawful pursuits, and those fueled his determination to make sure the terrorists failed.

The latest update reached the director's desk. He looked it over and jotted down a few notes when he got up from his desk and walked to the door to the private anteroom where Lamar lived since his father-in-law brought him there the second time at Ed's request.

He walked in and saw Lamar curled up asleep on the sofa with the latest reports laid out on the floor so he could study them.

You've been wasting your talents, Son, the general thought. He reached down and gently shook Lamar' shoulder.

"Mr. Jones, it's that time again. We have new reports to go over."

Lamar stirred, but the long hours of sleeplessness, and the weight of what he might have done to his country and family, had worn him down.

Ed shook his shoulder a second time. "Rise and shine, Soldier," he said more loudly. "Drop your cock and grab your socks. We have work to do."

Lamar sat upright. "I'm up, General," he said groggily, as he rubbed his eyes. "What's up with the operation now, Sir?"

"Get some coffee and drain your dragon, Son, then we'll go over the new reports."

As the general left the room, Lamar slowly gathered his energy to drag himself from the couch and walk to the small restroom.

CHAPTER 32

Wendy Weston and her children arrived at their Delaware home safely. The FBI sent an advance team to sweep the house and stake out the neighborhood. All was quiet and peaceful for a few days. The kids returned to school, and, as far as the FBI could tell, there were no threats in the area, but they would stay on the job while the mission was in play.

Wendy, still confused about her feelings toward Lamar, had been living on autopilot while getting the kids off to school each day. She kept to herself since her return, and her concerned friends began talking among themselves. Others expressed jealous envy. All wanted to know what was going on. Wendy was usually very outgoing and open about her life. Word began to spread that Wendy kicked Lamar out, and a divorce was in progress.

While in the supermarket one day, Wendy learned what some of the rumors were. She didn't care what was said about her, but she desperately didn't want her children to hear such things.

Once she was back home and put away the groceries, she decided it was time to stop waffling about Lamar. She still loved him, didn't she? She didn't understand all the reasons for his actions, but if her country could forgive him and even embrace him for his courage in turning himself in to the authorities no matter what, she could, too, couldn't she?

That and many other questions raced in her mind until she began to feel a headache. Ultimately, she had to choose. As she lay on the couch, she fell asleep, but her mind kept working.

Suddenly, she woke up and sat bolt upright. There was only one thing she could do. She needed to talk to her mom and discuss the situation. After that, she would tell her mother what she decided. She also realized she needed to know if her parents had heard anything from Lamar and whether he was still OK.

Amro, As'ad, and Ghazi had uneventful flights so far. Ghazi chatted with his seatmate about America and how he went to MIT for his bachelor's degree in engineering.

It was almost time to sacrifice himself for the Great Jihad, and his thoughts turned inward, as he became silent. He wouldn't be able to say good-bye to his mother or baby sister.

As'ad and Amro amused themselves on their individual flights with games on their phones, so no would notice when they called their respective bombs.

Amro had an hour left, while As'ad had thirty minutes.

Ghazi was also careful to use his phone between conversations, giving him the necessary cover for the call that would take him to heaven.

As the flight attendants prepared for landing, Ghazi raised his phone and pressed 1 on speed dial. He saw the icon that showed the phone was trying to connect, but nothing happened.

What's wrong? he wondered, hanging up and trying again.

He was still redialing the number when he heard the plane's tires squeal as they touched down on the runway. He felt like a failure. A tear slid from his eye to roll down his cheek.

"Well, I'll be," said the man beside him. "You didn't seem afraid to fly, but those look like tears of joy for landing. Son, you can relax. It was another uneventful flight. We're here safe and sound." He slapped Ghazi's knee.

He turned to look at the man. "Yes, another uneventful flight. Nothing to worry about at all."

As'ad waited for the sound of the engines spooling up to show they were aborting their landing after Ghazi's bomb went off, but nothing happened.

"Flight attendants," the captain said over the intercom, "please make final preparations for landing."

Something must've gone wrong with Ghazi's bomb, As'ad thought. *Did it fail to go off, or did he lose courage to make the call. I certainly won't lose courage.*

He turned on his phone and pressed 1 on his speed dial.

A second later, he said, "This cannot be." He watched the phone try to make the connection but fail repeatedly.

The chirp of the tires meeting the runway brought his attention to the present. He realized he must've spoken louder than intended, because the woman sitting beside him was desperately pushing the call button for a flight attendant with a desperate look on her face.

As the plane slowed, the flight attendant came over. "What's the problem, Ma'am?"

"He was trying to make a call, Miss, while we were still in the air. You're not supposed to do that."

"All right, Ma'am. Excuse me, Sir, but you know cell phones aren't supposed to be used in the air, and not even on the ground until the captain says it's OK."

As'ad felt relief flood through him. He looked up and quickly apologized. "I was in a rush to tell my mother I was landing and would be ready to be picked up soon." He leaned toward the woman beside him. "I hope I didn't frighten you. I haven't seen my mother in years. I guess I was too excited. I'm sorry, Ma'am."

She gave a forced smile. "Next time, just wait for us to land, then call her. Five minutes won't matter one way or the other, Sir."

He smiled, turned away, and thought, *Five minutes matters more than you think, Bitch!*

The Miami FBI team was in position and waiting for the three terrorists to exit their planes. Two agents dressed as tourists joined the flow of people disembarking from the flights and ended up on either side of Ghazi and As'ad.

Once the cluster of people thinned out, the agents flashed their badges and told their captives to follow them to security. They ducked through a side door, unnoticed by all the passing travelers.

As'ad thought it was his attempted phone call and tried to explain it was just a misunderstanding. Ghazi knew instantly they were discovered, and all their work was for naught. They failed, and they would die a coward's death.

When Amro realized his flight wasn't being rerouted, he jumped to his feet with his cell phone in hand and shouted, "I'm hijacking this plane! I have a bomb onboard. We're going to Cuba, or I will destroy this plane!"

Many heroes are born in a crisis. A man sitting two rows ahead of Amro slowly released his seatbelt. With the agility of a cat, he leaped up and tackled Amro. His first action was to punch a crushing blow to Amro's shoulder, making him scream in pain and drop the cell phone. It slid under the seat of a woman who lost control of her bladder at the thought that the phone itself was a bomb, and her life was over.

The second blow was a kidney strike delivered with such force Amro was lifted off his feet to land three rows back. He was still semicoherent enough to reach for his phone, which brought down the wrath of the woman with wet panties to lift her four-inch stiletto heel and come down on his hand hard enough to go right through. The other passengers cheered.

"Now land this plane," the lady said, "so I can get this dog shit off my shoe!"

The other passengers roared with laughter and cheered.

The first man leaped on Amro and pinned him down just as the aircraft's wheels touched down, bringing another round of cheers and applause from the passengers and flight crew.

The FBI team assigned to Amro was stunned when TSA agents stormed the boarding tunnel just as the plane arrived. The lead agent grabbed one of the TSA men and flashed his badge.

"What's going on?" he demanded.

"We've had an attempted hijacking. The passengers subdued the perpetrator." He ran down the tunnel, leaving behind the FBI agent with his mouth open, shaking his head.

He hurried back to his team and explained, "There's been a situation on the plane. Keep your eyes peeled."

The lead agent called his boss, who by then had Ghazi in cuffs sitting with As'ad in a security room. When he heard from Team 3, he gathered his men and explained, then he went to the terminal where Team 3 waited for the situation to quiet down before apprehending their man.

Special Agent Benjamin Mathis was right behind the Rescue squad that ran down the tunnel to the plane. He met with Team 3's leader, Special Agent Alan Wilson.

"What's up, Al? Why are they here?" He pointed at the TSA men.

"I don't know, Ben, but nobody's come off the plane yet. I was hoping you'd know something."

"All right. Let me get on the horn with headquarters and see if they know anything about this. Everything seemed to be going like clockwork."

"Captain, this is Petty Office McCahan. We've received a message from the *Philadelphia.*"

"Go ahead, Petty Officer,"

"Captain, they say they loved our meeting but must take their leave now. They'll be thirsty when they see you in Norfolk. Any reply, Captain?"

"Please send the following: 'Godspeed, thanks, and I guess I'll remortgage my house.' That will be all, Petty Officer."

She hung up the officer's mess sound-powered phone and shook her head. "I just might have to, Mr. Hanratty."

"Skipper, it's not like the old days. My money says you can hold your own with those sub boys in any drinking contests."

"Thanks for the vote of confidence...I think." She returned to her breakfast.

Hanratty did the same but ate faster, because he had to relieve the watch soon.

Once she was alone in the officer's mess, she thought of Larry, realizing they would arrive first at the sea-lightering area, then move on to the Delaware Bay pilot boarding area in sixteen hours.

She checked her cell phone to see if it was getting a signal. *Good. I have some reception. One bar is better than nothing.* She typed a short text with the details of their impending arrival and possible meeting.

She hit *Send* and hoped he got it and was still interested in an old sea dog.

General Samson just finished lunch when a messenger knocked on his door.

"General, it appears we have a situation in progress in Miami."

"I knew this was going too smoothly. What is it, Miss?"

She passed him a piece of paper.

He read it and said angrily, "Airport TSA? We kept them in the dark on purpose, and now they're in the middle of this operation. Do we know who the hijacker is yet? From first reports, it seems the passengers wouldn't stand for any of this guy's bullshit.

"Get Mr. Jones. I want him to review this with me, so we can figure something out and continue the operation."

She walked across the room to the general's anteroom and knocked. "Mr. Jones? The general wishes to speak with you."

No one answered. Lamar still wasn't accustomed to being called Jones.

"Mr. Jones?"

"Yes! I'll be right out."

The messenger returned to the general. "Is there anything else you need?"

"No, thank you."

The messenger left just as Lamar opened the door.

"Yes, General? What's up?"

"We have a situation growing in Miami. There was an attempted hijacking on one of the flights that held one of the bomb makers. The passengers subdued the man, but we're blind on the ground. I can't get too involved, because that would raise red flags with TSA in Miami. How can we resolve this without tipping our hand?"

Lamar, sitting in a chair in front of the general's desk, read the note the general handed him. "It does seem to be a problem, General. If we go in with just the FBI agents who are there, we can say it was a routine operation. Correct me if I'm wrong, but isn't a hijacking under the FBI's purview, anyway?

"We can figure out if our man was involved. If not, we take him into custody as a witness. That would get us off the hook with the TSA, and the local boys won't be any the wiser. What do you think, Sir?"

The general mulled the idea over. "I believe you're right about it being the jurisdiction of the FBI, but I need to check with them to make sure. If that's the case, you've got a solid plan. Thank you, Lamar. God, it's been a long week so far."

"Yes, it has been, General."

Max received the same news as the general and was trying to reach his boss and ask him to get General Samson's permission to let the FBI take over in Miami. Unfortunately, the preliminary information was very sketchy, so his boss was reluctant to give the go-ahead to contact the general.

Ten minutes after Max's request was denied, they received word from General Samson to begin taking over in Miami. They would sort out the details concerning jurisdiction later.

Max immediately called Special Agent Mathis. "Ben, this is Max. We need to take over down there. Find the guy in charge and let him know, in no uncertain terms, that it's our case. They need to back off. We need to get that third guy off the plane and into our custody with as little attention drawn to him as possible. Keep me informed every step of the way."

He hung up almost before Ben could reply.

Ben Mathis had impressive stature. He played middle line-backer for USC in college and still looked ready for a game. He walked down the tunnel with his men behind him and met the TSA agent guarding the plane entrance.

"I need to see your boss, Son."

"Sir, I'm sorry, but...."

Ben put on his game face. "Now!"

The agent ducked inside the plane to find his boss.

When the senior TSA agent came out, he said, "This is our jurisdiction."

"You've done your part very well," Ben said. "Now it's our turn. This is my case as of right now. I need you and your people to clear the gate area so we can get this situation under control. It's a zoo out there with gawkers hanging around.

"Please make it happen, and let's get this airport back to normal. Make sure there are no leaks. Mum's the word."

"Fine. You can have it, but the guy in there really took a beating. He might need hospitalization." He called most of the TSA team away from the scene and directed them to clear the gate area and to keep their mouths shut about what happened.

The TSA agents didn't go peacefully. There was the usual interagency grumbling to their counterparts, as they filed down the tunnel.

When Ben finally boarded the plane, he saw everything was under control. Most of the passengers were still in their seats.

The lead TSA agent told Ben what they knew so far. "This is the hijacker." He pointed at a man lying in the aisle, being tended by the rescue squad. "This is the gentleman who initiated the takedown."

He also indicated the hijacker's wounded hand. "That shoe embedded in his hand belongs to a lady in the restroom, freshening up. She got a little excited when the guy's cell phone flew at her. She thought it was a bomb."

"Thank you, Agent," Ben said. "Fine work so far. I'll make sure your work and cooperation are noted in my report. Please give my agents any other particulars on your way out."

Ben, assessing the situation, realized the hijacker was their terrorist. At least he didn't have to worry about two crazies on one flight, although it created difficulty, since word was spreading about an attempted hijacking. The press would arrive very soon. In his earbud, he already heard reports of excitement spreading throughout the airport.

"Hello, Folks," he said to the passengers. "I'm Special Agent Benjamin Mathis of the FBI. This is how we'll proceed. I beg you for your patience and cooperation. We'll get you on your way as quickly as possible.

"If all the passengers from here to the front of the plane would please follow this agent to an interview room, we can get started."

The first ten rows of passengers stood and reached for their belongings in the overhead racks.

"Your belongings will be carefully inspected before you're released," Ben added. "You still have to go through customs."

The plane was emptied of everything except Amro and the EMS attendees, who still worked to stabilize his wounded hand. His arm was immobilized to compensate for his separated shoulder.

"When you guys have him stable," Ben said, "you can take him from the plane, but that's as far as you go."

The head EMT was ready to protest. Ben glared at him as if to say, *One word, and you'll be arrested for interfering with a federal investigation.*

"Whatever you want, Man," the EMT said. "I don't know why we fixed him up, anyway, if you know what I mean."

"Yeah, I know. Can we get on with this?" Ben asked in a calmer voice.

Soon, the gate area was cleared. Ben approved of the perimeter the TSA staff set up and exited with Amro in a wheelchair, his good arm handcuffed to the chair.

Ben and his team quickly moved Amro to the security room where As'ad and Ghazi were held. Amro's eyes widened when he saw his companions.

"It seems like we all know each other," Ben said. "Good. You won't be lonely where you're going."

All three terrorists slumped in their seats. They had failed, and none knew how their plan went awry.

General Samson received word about the hijacker/terrorist and his injuries. The Miami office handled the situation well. They got a doctor to administer to Amro, and he was sedated for pain. His wound was treated, and the woman's high heel was removed.

There was just one thing left, and Samson wanted to handle it himself. Since the TSA director reported to him, he felt he could pull it off and leave no one the wiser.

He set up a press conference for later in the day. Hopefully, the glitch in the plan had been caught soon enough to keep the rest of the plan from unraveling.

"Lamar, it seems we dodged the bullet," the general said. "Wish me luck at the press conference."

"Sure thing, General. You know I do. I'm sure you know this, but you really have to watch those reporters. They can foul you up and trick you into saying something you didn't intend to say."

"Thanks for the advice, but I've been in Washington long enough to be very wary of reporters. I know most of their tricks."

"General Samson, one more question, please," *CNN News* reporter Jim Conover said.

"Fine, Jim. I can't promise an answer, but you can ask."

"That's fine, General. If I may ask, why hasn't there been any sighting of the hijacker after the FBI took him away? Why was the FBI there so fast? It seems like they were already there, as if they knew something was coming. At least, that's what my Miami source said."

That was the first mention of the FBI in the press conference. "Jim, that's two questions. Which would you prefer I answer, if I do?"

Jim smiled, thinking he had the general pinned down. "I'm not sure you can answer one and not the other. One needs the other to be truthfully answered.

"You just spent the last fifteen minutes extolling the TSA agents in Miami and telling us what a fine job they did. I have it from an impeccable and extremely reliable source, General."

"Well, now, aren't you the slick one, Jim? You think I'm hiding something. I'm not, so to answer your question, there was an operation already being conducted today by the Miami field office. The TSA agents felt since the FBI was already there and had more experience with hijackers, they should let them handle it. After all, the TSA hasn't handled a single hijacking in its existence.

"The FBI graciously accepted the opportunity to share the spotlight with a fellow agency, and they had no need to seek glory. It was good teamwork among agencies.

"As for the operation, you know I'm not the director of the FBI. Even if I was, I couldn't speak about anything like that. Your guess is as good as mine.

"As for the suspect's disappearance, I'm sure he's getting all the attention he deserves. The laws have changed a bit since the last hijacking a few years ago. I won't speculate concerning the man's whereabouts, but I'm sure he's being taken care of by those who deal with such things.

"I want to thank all of you for coming today. Hopefully, we won't need to meet again under these circumstances. Good day, Ladies and Gentlemen."

"You sure put that reporter in his place, General," Lamar said. "I thought he'd get you with that last one, but you showed quick thinking. Very impressive, Sir."

"Thanks, Lamar. To survive in the alphabet soup of the Beltway, you have to learn how to be quick on your feet. Let's get back to business. Anything come in while I was out politicking?"

"Just that all three terrorists are on their way to New Mexico, General."

Max, watching the news conference, was impressed with the general's ability to handle touchy questions and appease the ones who asked them without saying much of anything in response.

The politicians better hope he never runs for office, Max thought. *They'd be in a pickle for sure if he was on the opposite team.*

"Now all we have to do is wait out the final piece of the puzzle and wrap up this operation," he mumbled.

The operations in Houston, New Orleans, and Miami were concluded except for capturing the bad guys. Charleston, Norfolk, and Philadelphia needed to be finished, but the terrorists still hadn't armed the bombs, so the SEALs couldn't disarm them, and the FBI couldn't follow them back to their safe houses. Time was running out. September 11 was only two days away.

Max had plenty of things to watch to ensure they were done properly and on time. Events in Miami left him on edge. He hoped the terrorists weren't scared into hiding. All he could do was wait and keep his people ready to move at a moment's notice.

"Just another day at the office," he said, lying on the couch for a catnap.

Wendy spoke with her mother for over an hour that morning. She felt like a teenager again, talking about everything with her mom. Once she made her decision about her relationship with Lamar, she felt a weight lift off her shoulders.

They discussed the situation and Lamar's criminal activity that led to the national security issue Lamar and General Samson had become so involved with. Lamar was held in secrecy, not even able to contact his wife. Mostly, Wendy spoke about how she felt about the relationship with her husband.

Her mom didn't office advice based on her own feelings. Instead, like all good mothers, she led her daughter to work out her own feelings and reach a decision herself. It seemed all moms had to be part psychologist and part priest at times.

Once Wendy secretly reached her final decision, the conversation reverted to the kids and school and all the activities Wendy kept the kids involved in, trying to keep them active and out of the trouble that befell too many idle children who were left to their own resources.

Sally and Lamar, Jr. noticed their mother's change in mood when they came home from school. When they asked about Daddy and if he was coming home soon, Wendy said he was. Before that day, when they asked about him, Wendy just said, "I guess so," and looked sad before going to her bedroom.

How he was and when Lamar would ever come home again was a question Wendy couldn't answer, because neither of her parents had heard from him since the general left him at DHS headquarters. He had vanished.

Though she couldn't tell the children when Daddy would come home, she at least could say definitely that he was coming, something she hadn't said for certain before. Sally was relieved. She saw something was off about her mom's interactions with them whenever

Dad was away. Maybe the world was back on track. At least Mom smiled when she talked about Dad again.

That night, for the first time in what felt like a very long time, Wendy included Lamar in her prayers. She felt ashamed for leaving him out and asked for forgiveness for her sin, then she cried herself to sleep, half in sorrow for their predicament and half in joy for finally reaching an honest answer and committing herself to their relationship.

Charleston, South Carolina, was very active, as the FBI and SEALs finished their missions. As soon as the terrorist frogmen armed the bomb and vanished into the murky waters of Charleston Harbor, the SEALs disarmed it. The FBI picked up the tail and were ready to storm the safe house once they had word the bomb was safe and the messages were sent and received.

Agents in Norfolk prepared to do the same. Their tanker just arrived and was anchored off the Chesapeake Bay Bridge Tunnel.

Max received reports and sent messages to his agents and superiors. He hadn't slept much on the office couch and knew he wouldn't be able to any time soon. It was crunch time.

CHAPTER 33

The MV *Palm Princess* entered the Pilot Triangle, an area designated on charts where ships would receive their harbor pilots before entering confined waters where such a pilot was required by law to guide the ship safely to its final destination. The pilot boat was in sight a mile away, and the *Palm Princess* slowed to the eight-knot boarding speed as requested prior to boarding.

Karen Ann was on the bridge, which was part of her strict routine, ready to give the ship a hard turn to make a lee for the pilots to board. The seas were slight at three to four feet. It wasn't much to a big ship like her, but the fifty-foot pilot boat was bouncing and needed the lee to make boarding as safe as possible.

Her left breast pocket vibrated, tickling her left breast. She reached to cover the pocket, as the phone also flashed a light through her khaki shirt. When she pulled it out and checked the sender, a broad smile came to her face when she saw it was Larry.

It was the wrong time to lose concentration, so she pressed *Ignore* and slipped the phone back into her pocket with a little pat that sent a shiver through her loins in expectation of seeing Larry again.

Even my body knows when it's him, she thought with a slight giggle, drawing the attention of the bridge watch.

"Just a humorous thought, Gentlemen," she said. "Let's get this girl to anchor."

The *Palm Princess* already gave up two large barges of her oil on the way up from Norfolk. Once lightered enough to enter the bay, though not enough to traverse the river, she still needed to give up another two barges of oil. The pilot would take her on a very short journey to the lightering anchorage, where two tugs and their thirsty barges were waiting.

It was a breezy night, and the slight chill in the air made the crew on deck for pilot boarding and anchoring detail pull up the collars of their three-season coats to ward off the air nipping at their necks.

"Good evening, Mr. Pilot," Karen Ann said, as the senior pilot entered the bridge.

"Ah, it's a fine morning, Captain," the pilot replied, shaking her hand. "Any changes to the pilot card on file, Skipper?"

"No, nothing new about her, Mr. Pilot. How far are you taking us into the anchorage?"

"Just to the first slot, Skipper. We've been holding it special for your arrival." He chuckled.

"It's nice to be special." She chuckled with him.

Soon, the *Palm Princess* glided through the dark waters of Delaware Bay, moving at five knots, deftly guided by the pilot, as he lined up to position the ship in the exact spot he told Karen Ann.

Seeing the maneuver was going well, she let herself relax a bit, sitting in the captain's seat on the starboard side of the bridge. She was very tempted to look at the text from Larry, but she kept the urge at bay. Hopefully, he would be as excited to see her as she was to see him.

Max finalized the Charleston and Norfolk cases while waiting for the Delaware Bay case to begin. He'd been very busy in the last twenty-four hours, handling all the intricate details that were being sent in both directions, making sure everyone was up-to-date with the latest information. He was also responsible to see that the information was sent upstairs to the senior members of the operation.

General Samson, pleased with the way the operation was going, was also very interested in hearing Lamar's answer to his offer to join his team. He would understand if the man wanted to decline, but he really enjoyed the fresh perspective Lamar brought to the table. He would be a huge asset to his country if he accepted, but thoughts of that had to wait until the current operation was finished, and Lamar knew how he stood with the rest of his family. Horace hinted that the situation wasn't resolved yet when they last talked.

Ed was accustomed to getting his way. He could be very convincing, if not downright imposing, when he wanted, but he would stand back and wait. If he judged Lamar correctly, he didn't have anything to worry about, and Lamar would become his new secret weapon in the fight against terrorist and to ensure that the American way of life was kept sacred.

The radio in the pilot tower on Cape Henlopen crackled. "Eight-one-nine, this is the *Palm Princess*. Anchor down at 0310."

"Anchor down at 0310. Copy that, Captain. Eight-one-nine out."

The *Palm Princess* was just settling down from its anchoring swing and aligning with the wind and current when the pilot boat came alongside to take the pilots ashore. The first of the tugs approached on the opposite side to begin the lightering process.

As soon as the pilot boat was away, and the accommodation ladder was raised, the second tug would come alongside and begin lightering, too.

Far off in the distance toward the Delaware shore, a small boat left the Misipillion Inlet and moved toward the anchorage that held the *Palm Princess*. The occupants of the boat knew they faced a very difficult mission. Working in the dark, they had to work quickly. The ship would be rising in the water as it offloaded oil, and they would have a barge directly above them sinking deeper into the water, putting the squeeze on them.

Sitting in the radio room of the *Palm Princess*, watching the underwater monitors, Sledge Hammer waited for the terrorists to arm the dummy bomb, so he could radio the FBI boys who would start surveilling the terrorists when they returned to shore.

He previously asked the captain to have the anchor watch keep a close eye on their radar for any small vessel traffic in the area, and Karen Ann said she'd keep that vigil herself. She would notify him of any arrivals and monitor their return trip, giving him the coordinates to pass along to the FBI to make sure the terrorists didn't go to a location different from their starting point.

Karen Ann knew Carbini could run the oil transfer without thinking, so she gave all her attention to the radar. She was on the radar the moment the anchoring evolution was completed, and she soon saw a very faint blip approaching. She acquired the target using the ARPA (Automatic Radar Plotting Aide) function. Once the radar did its magic, a small box appeared around the blip on the screen.

On the side of the radar screen was another box that had all the pertinent information on the target vessel, such as its CPA (Closest Point of Approach). SOG (Speed Over Ground), true course, and TCPA (Time of Closest Point of Approach).

Sledge Hammer's sound-powered phone jingled. "Radio room, Petty Officer McCahan speaking."

"Petty Officer, this is the bridge. We have a target approaching from the northwest. Range is four miles on a true course of 165 degrees and making fifteen knots. I don't think anyone's out for a joy ride at 0330 in the morning."

"Roger that, Captain. Looks like it won't be much longer, then we can put all this mess behind us."

"Not a moment too soon for me, Petty Officer. It appears they came from Misipillion Inlet. I did a back course, and it led back to there. I'm betting that's where they're from. If you don't need anything else for now, bridge out."

Karen Ann, hanging up her handset, and watched the radar scope.

The small boat went past the *Palm Princess* and anchored due east of her by Brown Shoal, in relatively shallow water. It was a prime fishing spot, but no one put a line over the side that night.

Two of the three men in the boat slipped into the dark, warm water of the bay in wet suits and dive gear. All they carried was a small special wrench, as they motored off with their subsea scooters toward the bright deck lights of the *Palm Princess*. They planned to stay on the surface until they were within 100 meters, because they knew no security watch was checking for intruders.

"These Americans are so dumb when it comes to security," the men joked among themselves. "We could probably go in all the way on the surface, and they'd never even look over the side."

Their honor depended on their doing the job right, which was why they would submerge as planned and arm the bomb. Soon, they would rejoice with their leaders, as America was brought to its knees, ready to succumb to the Mullah's will. They couldn't wait to send their confirmation message to their leader and hear his praise for being such brave, honorable men.

Max received the message that the *Palm Princess* was entering Delaware Bay and preparing to anchor. Soon, the action would begin. He called his lead agent in Delaware.

Bill Whittington was a very good agent who divided his team to cover all the departure points the terrorists could use to make the trip out to the big ship. Delaware is a small state, and his men could converge on any area within thirty minutes. He had the Misipillion Inlet duty and witnessed the small boat heading out into the bay.

Bill gave Max all the details he had on the boat, which wasn't much, but no other agent had anything to report, so it seemed Bill's was the most pertinent. Max was satisfied that Whittington had everything under control and wished him good luck before hanging up.

He leaned back in his ergonomic chair and felt a huge yawn take over. Shaking his head to knock out the cobwebs of exhaustion, he stood and went into his small lavatory to splash cold water on his face and try to wake up.

When he looked into the mirror, he was taken aback to see his three-day growth of beard. He hadn't realized it was that long since he was home for a shower, shave, and good night's sleep.

"Well, Max old buddy, it's almost over. When it is, you'll take a well-deserved vacation to someplace quiet and sleep your cares away."

He winked at his reflection. "OK, then. Back to business. Let's get this mess cleared up all nice and tidy."

He walked back into his office.

Lamar knocked on the door to the general's office.

"Enter," the general called.

He walked in and found the general behind his desk with a mountain of paperwork laid out in front of him.

"General." Lamar sat in a chair in front of the desk. "Do you have time to talk?"

"Of course, Son. What's on your mind?"

Lamar never had a man call him "son" before with that much care in his voice, which made him feel more comfortable talking to him sitting behind such an imposing desk.

He sat back in his chair, uncertain how to begin.

The general saw something was on Lamar's mind and said, "I want you to know that I truly appreciate how you helped us in the trying times our country faces today. You were invaluable to the success of this operation."

"I appreciate your praise, General, but I don't feel I've been all that invaluable. It's my fault we were exposed to this threat in the first place."

"If it weren't for you and your operation, it could have been someone else who wasn't quite as patriotic. He might have let the whole thing happen, and where would we be? I'll tell you. We'd be in a world of hurt right now, so far behind the eight ball it would make 9/11 seem minuscule in comparison. I don't know how else to explain how valuable you've been to us and how much your intelligence would mean to the agency if you accept my offer."

"I don't feel like a very good citizen right now, General, or a very good person, either. I've been so self-righteous and belligerent in my thinking, using whatever talent I might have to aid not only the downfall of my race but the American public. I'm not so sure what I've been doing hasn't touched, in a very bad way, everyone in the United States.

"How can I ever feel good about myself again? I appreciate what you've done for me, giving me immunity from the sins I've committed up to this point, but how can I accept that and continue living my life as if nothing happened? I should have to repent for the destruction I caused to people I didn't care about except when they had money. I ruined their lives and the lives of all around them."

The general leaned back and listened to Lamar go on about his sins against humanity. It went for thirty minutes before Lamar was done, and the general didn't interrupt once, not even to acknowledge he was listening, although Lamar knew.

Finally, Lamar finished and took a breath. Somehow, it felt as fresh as if he'd been trapped underground for years and suddenly stepped into the light and fresh air above.

General Samson let him enjoy the moment and savored it with him. "Lamar, you're the product of your environment, a survivor. Drugs have been around since the time when man tromped through forests and tore off a leaf because he was hungry. As he chewed, he felt different, in a funny, euphoric way he liked. He was lifted above the troubles and fears of everyday survival that he lived with since he was born.

"Man will never eradicate drugs from human use, because humans sometimes need a separation from the real world. For some, it's alcohol. For others, it's illegal drugs. It seems some people can't live without them. There's always a market someone is willing to take advantage of in order to make a buck, then they find a way to justify it so their conscience doesn't bother them.

"You finally left that world for the real world. Now you can see the destruction you caused through the God-given intelligence that was corrupted by the environment in which you were raised. You did what you thought was necessary to survive. You were as addicted as the junkies you supplied.

"Now you've learned there's more to life than a feeling of euphoria, and you want to repent for what you did. For some people, that means prison, although it rarely works. For certain others, like you, your repentance is to use your God-given talents for the betterment of mankind.

"I can't force you to accept my offer to help keep America safe from all the threats in the world, but I believe with my entire being that anything less would be unfulfilling to the new you. That's how you can repay society for the sins you feel you committed.

"You might have enjoyed the feeling of outwitting the authorities, but that will be trumped by how you feel when you thwart attempts to destroy the ones you love and care for. I want you to think about what I've said, then make your choice. I'll honor your wishes either way and will respect the man you've become."

Lamar pondered that for a moment.

"I need to get back to the mission," the general said, "unless there's something else you need to get off your chest?"

Lamar couldn't believe such a patriotic man, someone who fought for his country since he was a teenager, could feel that way about him. "Thank you, General."

He walked back to his room. As he opened the door to the anteroom, he glanced back and saw the general hard at work with another report.

Sledge Hammer watched the terrorists on the monitors doing their best Laurel and Hardy impersonation, trying to get the limpet cover off and arm the fake bomb, while the ship kept rising, and the barge sank deeper into the water right over them. Hardy, the shorter of the two, helped his companion, then he swam up to check how much room they had between themselves and the barge, then he swam back and would stop him from working.

Laurel chastised Hardy and made him help arm the bomb, although Hardy kept watching the barge lower toward them until he couldn't stand it and swam back up to check how much space was left. Laurel showed dismay and growing frustration.

Sledge Hammer laughed, wishing he had sound to go with the video. It would be hilarious. It took those two clowns double the time necessary to arm the bomb thanks to Hardy's antics. For all his worry, the barge sank only two feet, and the ship barely rose one.

Once Laurel finished attaching the limpet cover, he looked at Hardy overhead, shook his head, and swam away using his sea scooter. Hardy realized he was being left behind and tore off in the wrong direction. Thirty seconds later, he zoomed past the camera again as he doubled back.

"Oh, my God!" Sledge Hammer laughed so hard, he fought to catch his breath. Finally, he called the bridge.

"Bridge," Captain Murphy said.

He laughed again, then said, "Sorry, Captain. It's me, PO McCahan. I just watched the underwater version of Laurel and Hardy. I'm sorry, but they were really funny. I know this is a serious situation, so I apologize."

"I understand, Petty Officer. Can I take it they finished arming the fake bomb and are on their way back to the boat?"

"That's correct, Captain. Once again, please excuse me."

Karen Ann watched the target on the radar, still in the same position, and wondered how men could be filled with such hatred that they'd risk their lives doing such things. All America stood for was freedom for people to be who they were and worship their God in the way they wanted without fear of persecution.

She walked to the bridge wing and lifted her binoculars to study the small white anchor light shining from the little boat that held enough hatred it would fill her tanker until it overflowed.

Suddenly, the light was joined by a red and green light. They were getting underway. She wanted to keep watching, but she had to keep an eye on the radar in case the ARPA lost the target.

Back at the radar screen, she saw the boat making twenty knots on a reciprocal course. She extended the vector line, and it went right to Misipillion Inlet.

Well, you don't like us, but you sure like our inventions, don't you? she thought. *You must have GPS, because you aren't wavering even a little from your course. You're also in a big hurry. I guess you need to report to your master that you armed the big, bad bomb like the good, obedient dogs you are.*

She watched the target until she was certain it would merge with the shoreline, then called Petty Officer McCahan.

"Radio Room, PO McCahan, speaking."

"This is the bridge, Petty Officer. I tracked the target. It's just entering Misipillion Inlet. I won't be able to keep on it once it merges with the shoreline."

"That's all I need. Thank you, Skipper. I'm sorry for my unprofessionalism earlier."

She chuckled. "That's nothing. I need to find out what was so funny about two guys arming a bomb the next time we meet, though."

"Will do, Captain."

CHAPTER 34

Max received the report from the *Palm Princess* that the arming operation of the fake bomb was completed, and he passed it on to Bill Whittington.

"I've already spotted them coming our way," Bill said.

"Fine, then. You know what to do, right?"

"You got it, Boss. I'll let you know when this is wrapped up."

Max ended the call and leaned back in his chair to rub his three-plus-day-old beard. "Almost home," he muttered.

Bill spaced his men out along the river as best he could to ensure the targets didn't slip past. A small boat was ready with two agents to follow the terrorists to their landing, where his team would converge on them and follow them to their point of operation and await notification from the NSA that messages had been sent and received. After that, they would proceed with the takedown.

Bill didn't expect any trouble with the takedown. All the others had gone off without a hitch.

He tried to prepare for anything. The men on the small boat would follow the terrorists, but they didn't dare come too close and let their outboard engine be overheard. The river had many turns that would temporarily hide their target, too. He tried to acquisition a boat with radar, but there wasn't time, so the best the agency could get was something with a small outboard.

He watched the target roar past him at twenty knots. "Whittington to all units. It's showtime. Be prepared for anything. Be ready to converge on their final location."

His units replied in succession. The boat unit was the first to move. When they saw their target speed past, they shoved off to follow. Both men, experienced boaters, were glad their outboard boat had a four-cycle seventy-horsepower Suzuki, one of the quietest outboard engines. It didn't have powerful torque, nor was it fast at startup, but it could easily make twenty knots pushing the eighteen-foot open center console boat they were using.

Their plan was to let the terrorists speed past them and clock them using a radar gun, then they would shove off and follow at a slightly slower speed to keep up without being overheard. It should be possible to follow the boat's wake and watch its size to tell them if the boat ahead was slowing or changing speed.

The radar gun blinked at twenty-three miles per hour. The senior agent who was acting as coxswain planned to max out their speed at the start and keep a careful eye on the other boat's wake.

Shoving the throttle forward, he swung the boat around and upriver. They slid over the three small waves of the first boat's wake without much trouble and settled into the center of the wake to follow.

Whittington got into his SUV and leapfrogged to the third checkpoint, hoping to hear from outpost two on the way. He called Max to say, "The target's keeping to the river, and our operation has begun."

Bill couldn't wait until the operation was over. Every agency in DC was on edge, working on overdrive, and he was terrified someone would make a mistake and ruin their mission.

Suddenly, he realized his brow was covered with sweat despite the car's air-conditioning. He felt like a rooky on his first big operation. Wiping his forehead with one hand, he said, "I have to get hold of myself before I screw the pooch on this one."

"Boss, Unit Two. Target has moved on. We're moving to Unit Four's position."

"Roger, Unit Two. Proceed as planned."

The two divers and their pilot cruised upriver at speed in a jubilant mood. They felt a bump, then the outboard came out of the water with the propeller screaming, as the boat suddenly stopped. All three were thrown forward. One struck the steering wheel, while the other two sprawled on the deck and console in a surprised heap.

The sound of the terrorists' screaming engine was clearly audible to the FBI agents in the trailing boat, who immediately chopped the throttle to idle neutral and shut down the engine, hoping they hadn't been overheard.

Since their boat was still moving forward, the two agents agreed to back down a ways to avoid drifting into view. The coxswain restarted the engine and reversed until they began moving astern just as the lights of the terrorists' boat came into view ahead. He didn't dare rev the engine any higher for fear of announcing their presence.

The terrorists in the grounded boat shouted back and forth in Arabic. It was clear the two divers were haranguing the coxswain for running them aground.

Chaos reigned in the terrorists' boat. Their engine stalled when it flew up out of the water, automatically releasing itself to avoid damaging the prop.

The one McCahan labeled Laurel screamed at the coxswain for being so stupid he ran them aground. The coxswain retorted with a tirade of his own curses. Hardy joined the fracas. In all the bedlam, they never noticed the FBI boat.

Their own boat listed, having been driven up onto a sandbar and partially out of the water. Laurel made Hardy and the coxswain get out and try to push them free. Their first attempts did little except make Hardy lose his grip on the bow and fall into the water, splashing the coxswain and drawing more curses, as he almost fell, too.

"Rock the boat as you push, you idiots!" Laurel screamed.

After several attempts, they moved the boat back far enough that the engine lowered into the water. Laurel started it.

"Get in the damn boat," he told his fellow conspirators. "We need to report to the Mullah that the bomb is armed, and our mission is completed."

The two FBI men in the other boat had to keep from laughing aloud at the freak show playing out in the darkness ahead. They were far enough back not to be seen. They told Whittington the situation via cell phone, because they didn't want to use radios, which were louder and might be overheard.

Once the other engine started, and the shouting calmed down, they moved upriver slowly and listened for the moment when the terrorists sped up to normal speed.

Laurel, taking over as coxswain, told the other two to shut up and sit down until they were back at the dock. He slid the throttle forward, and the boat picked up speed. He got them back into the channel, muttering about how their mission wasn't complete until they reported in. He also planned to ask why he'd been saddled with such idiots for Allah's work.

Whittington arrived at Unit Three's position just as the terrorists' boat came into view. It appeared to be slowing, which he told his agents on the radio.

Four vehicles were waiting to do the landside tail. They could leapfrog at intervals to avoid alerting the terrorists they were being followed.

The target boat slowed, as it approached a small marina, more like two piers jutting into the open river, while a longer pier paralleled the river just beyond the overpass for Route 1. Bill watched through night-vision goggles, as the three terrorists prepared to dock.

"Chase boat," he said into his radio, "they're preparing to dock. Lay back until I give you the all-clear. I'll pick you up once the targets have left the marina, so you can join the tailing operation.

"Our tail begins when the terrorists' car pulls out onto Brown Street. Unit Three, you circle back from your spot on the overpass and begin the tail as they leave the marina road."

In Mecca, Ari Bohanni paced the floor, concerned about the complicated plan and hoping it worked. He had little choice but to continue with it, because it was already in play when he came to power. He went to the Mullah's desk, where the folder holding all the details of the operation lay, and snatched it up in a disgusted motion, cursing the soul of the recently departed Mullah for being so arrogant and trying to plan the whole thing himself.

"What were you thinking, you arrogant bastard?" he muttered.

For the tenth time, he read through the plan and shook his head before tossing it back onto the desk. *I need more information from the operatives,* he thought. *How can I know what's going on, if no one gives me any information?*

He reached for the receiver of the desk phone and pressed the intercom. "Get me the communications room." He slammed the receiver down into its cradle.

A moment later, the phone chirped, and he answered. "Speak."

"My great Mullah, this is communications. How can I be of service?" the duty cryptographer asked.

"Why aren't we receiving more information from the operatives?"

"Mullah Modula's orders were that communications were to be kept to a minimum for this operation. Everything must be sent encrypted. The operatives have only a basic knowledge of such things, so it takes them a long time to decrypt incoming messages and then encrypt their reply, Sir."

"What kind of one-eyed buffoons did he select for such a harebrained operation, anyway?"

"Great Mullah, these men are our finest trained operatives. Mullah Modula selected them personally."

Ari composed himself. He had to show respect for the departed Mullah, because he was surrounded by the man's handpicked men. He needed to cement his reign until he could replace them with his own loyalists.

"Please keep me informed as soon as you know anything. I know it's not your fault there's no new information to relay. Thank you." He hung up without waiting for a reply.

Karen Ann finished her rounds. As usual, Chief Mate Carbini had the lightering operation well in hand, so she went to her statement to try to rest before the upcoming river transit in a few hours. The clock on the bulkhead read *0430*, and she rubbed her face in relief before sprawling on the bed.

She had forgot about Larry's text and was quickly asleep, giving her body and mind the rest they deserved and needed.

So much happened in the last two weeks, her subconscious mind raced to process it. Her sleep was filled with snippets of dreams that ran the gauntlet from her daring sea rescue of the Coast Guard helicopter and crew of the *Natural High,* the peril of her ship suffering a split hull and overheated shaft bearing, to her romantic interlude with her old teenage crush.

The last dream made her eyes suddenly snap open, as she remembered his text. Digging for her personal cell phone, she fumbled through the menu until she found it.

So glad to hear from you! Can't wait to see you. Let me know how much time you have, so I can ask for time off work. Be safe on the big blue, Honey.

Thinking of you and our time in Norfolk. Can't wait for Philly.

Larry

He added a kiss emoji after his name.

She sighed. *I'll text him after I get my wakeup call.* She lay down with Larry on her mind, her fingers creeping toward her erogenous zone without conscious thought. She fell asleep with thoughts of Larry on her mind, a smile on her face, and lust in her loins.

Wendy woke from the first good night's sleep she had since Lamar confessed his sins on the beach in Puerto Rico with a smile on her face and renewed strength and conviction for her family in her heart.

She roused the children from their slumber and asked what they wanted her to make for their breakfast. The kids were shocked. On school mornings, breakfast was usually cereal or Aunt Jemima frozen pancakes or French toast. It was never a personal choice. When they asked her for such things, she always told them, "This isn't a restaurant."

Lamar, Jr. asked hesitantly, "Can I have eggies in a cup?" He loved soft-boiled eggs, which his grandmother taught them about during a sleepover at her house once. It was the only thing Grandpa wanted for breakfast each day.

"Sure thing, Honey," Wendy said, not caring it would take longer than usual to get them off to school.

Sally wasn't so adventurous. "I'll have my cereal and milk." She didn't want to tempt fate.

As Wendy walked down the hall toward the kitchen, the children looked at each other with the expression kids used when something weird just happened. They didn't want to jinx themselves by saying it out loud, so they began dressing for school.

Detectives Sharper and Hobnobski arrived for work. Warren was going over some leftover paperwork, because the Labor Day rush of stabbings, muggings, a bank robbery, and two homicides had mostly been cleaned up or gone cold when he came to the case file the Feds took over, when he and Gavin helped FBI Special Agent Max Gordon track down the burner cell phone used in the drug ring.

"Hey, Gavin. You think we'll ever hear back from that Fed Gordon about the case where those two drug pushers ended up in the C&D with their eyes superglued open?"

"Nah. We're too low on the food chain for them to care about filling us in on the details of something that had national security concerns. I don't see us ever finding out how or why that case involved national security."

"I guess you're right. I should file this with the unsolved cases in the basement. Who knows? Maybe the cold case division will be bored enough someday to try to solve it.

"When I get back from the basement, you want to get a doughnut at that new shop where the girls serve them in bikinis?"

"Man, Warren, you just had breakfast. You're already thinking about food and break time? Don't you ever get full?" He sighed. "I could use the distraction, and a pretty girl in a bikini sounds like just the thing. You got me hungry, so don't dillydally, Detective Sharper."

"Got you loud and clear." Sharper gathered his unsolved cases and walked toward the elevator and the basement.

Detective Sharper was eating a jelly-filled sugar doughnut, barely noticing the bikini-clad vixen who was pouring his second cup of coffee, when Gavin looked over at him.

"Remind me to never get my hand between your mouth and some food. How can you be so interested in that jelly doughnut that you don't notice all these lovely girls dressed for the French Riviera?"

"Huh?"

"Never mind." Gavin's attention was diverted by a long-legged redhead with 38Cs spilling out of her skimpy bikini top, as she walked past in four-inch spiked heels that clicked on the tile floor.

Warren never even looked up.

"Damn. Mmmm-mmm good," Gavin said, as she moved away.

Warren kept munching.

A few minutes later, after Gavin called to Warren three times just to get his attention, he finally replied with, "What?" around another doughnut he was eating.

"I've been thinking. Maybe we could run the MO of those two drug pushers through the national database and see if there are any similar cases in the U.S."

Warren chewed slowly. "That might be worth a shot, but you can get the file from the basement. You know I don't like going down there, and once a day is my limit." He finished his last doughnut and coffee.

"Jeez," Gavin complained. "No 'brilliant idea, Gavin?' Just a 'might be worth a shot?'"

He ogled another bikini-clad lady while thinking, *We might as well be married, we've been partners for too long,* as he waited for his partner to finish eating.

CHAPTER 35

The car pulled out and turned right onto Cedar Beach Road. Unit Three started the tail at a reasonable distance. Traffic was light on those country roads at that time of night, and they didn't want to spook the terrorists.

A call went out to all units advising them which road and direction of travel they were taking. Unit Two replied they were south of Cedar Beach Road at the intersection with North Rehoboth Boulevard and would wait to see if the suspect vehicle stayed on Cedar Beach or turned and would take over the tail.

Whittington retrieved the tail boat crew when the report came in. "My team and I will circle around to secure the next intersection," he said over the radio. "Unit Four can join the tail coming from the north on North Rehoboth."

He hung up and thought, *So far, so good. This should be fairly routine from here on out.*

If there was one thing the FBI knew how to get right the first time, it was setting up a tail. He planned to contact Max after they had a location and wait for verification that the signals were sent and a reply received. Once all the terrorists were in bed, the FBI would break through the doors and take them down.

He finally was calm enough to listen to the boat tail tell their story of the terrorists' antics. For a minute they were wondering if they had to act as Good Samaritans and tow them off the sandbar, which got a good laugh.

"Unit Two, this is Unit Three. Subject vehicle has its right turn signal on to go north on North Rehoboth Boulevard. We'll turn left. You pick up the tail."

"Unit Two, copy. Out."

"Unit Two, this is Unit One coming south on North Rehoboth. We'll take it slow. If they turn off Rehoboth, we'll follow. If not, we'll circle back, and you can turn off and leapfrog ahead."

"Unit Two, copy. We have the tail. Unit One, it looks like they're taking the first right toward a small housing development. Can you follow?"

"Unit Two, this is One. We see them turning and will follow. All units, prepare to converge on the development on my command."

All units, replied in the affirmative and parked near various entrances to the housing community to be ready if the subject vehicle left. It was possible the terrorists were checking to see if they were being followed. Otherwise, the units were prepared to move in and commence their takedown of the subjects, if that turned out to be their base of operations.

Special Agent Bill Whittington was ready for the assignment to be over.

After five minutes, Bill couldn't take the suspense any longer and said, "I'll walk through the development and see where they stopped. You keep a lookout to make sure they don't double back out. If they do, don't wait for me. I'll get another team to pick me up."

He slipped out the driver's door, and the man who'd been the coxswain on the surveillance boat took his place.

Bill walked toward the development. As he turned down the street where the suspect vehicle entered, he saw a house three lots down with its lights on. It was the only one on the block lit up like that, and a vehicle similar to the perps' was in the driveway.

Looks like you guys are having a toast to celebrate the shenanigans you think you did tonight, he thought, quietly moving closer to the vehicle until he could touch the hood. It was still warm.

He crossed to the opposite side of the street to observe the premises and stay away from the streetlight on the far edge of the suspects' property line.

As he arrived on the other side of the street, he heard a door close. A figure left the terrorists' back door into the backyard. He noticed a large shed standing there, and the figure walked in, allowing a few rays of light to escape from the doorway.

That's where they must have their radio equipment set up, he thought. *We should hear they've sent a signal soon, and we can finally finish this op.*

Whittington radioed the rest of the stakeout crew what he found, adding he would remain on foot to watch the perpetrators until the takedown was ordered. Through his earbud, he heard their quick replies.

He found a small hedge for cover that allowed him to see most of the property unseen. With his night-vision goggles, he was all set for the next few hours before sunrise.

In Washington, Max paced his office, wishing the operation was over. He checked his phone and computer screen every two minutes, but nothing came in so far. He wished there was something he could do to make time pass faster. Of all the operations he'd been on as a field agent, none had been so stressful or so vital to the national security of the United States.

How can anyone despise the U.S. so much he would risk the balance in the world to try to take us down like this? he wondered.

He answered his own question. *They're jealous that America built itself up from a lorded-over collection of ragtag colonies into the most-prosperous, mightiest nation the world has ever seen—or ever will. Its citizens have the freedoms other people in the world can barely dream of, and we still live in relative harmony with each other.*

He knew in his heart the attack wouldn't take down the U.S., just serve to ensconce in its people the conviction they had to eradicate the vile scum who perpetrated such grievous acts against their beloved nation, just as Japanese Admiral Isoroku Yamamoto once did when he attacked Pearl Harbor. After the attack, he said, "I fear all we have done is to awaken a sleeping giant and fill him with a terrible resolve."

Once again, he recalled the adage that people who didn't understand history were doomed to repeat it. He also knew it was his job to ensure these acts of terror were thwarted before they happened. The peace-loving people of the United Sates would never know how close they came to a radiological nightmare. If they ever found out about the attack or the many others that had been stopped, they wouldn't be so peace-loving anymore.

It was early in the morning at General Washington's home outside the nation's capital. Lillian Washington was cleaning up the breakfast dishes while the general prepared to mow the lawn. It was a chore all his neighbors had long since stopped doing themselves, hiring landscapers to take care of menial chores, but Horace loved it. There were many times earlier in his career when he couldn't do such things, leaving them shamefully to fall on his wife's shoulders in his absence. Since his retirement from his first love, the U.S. Army, he refused to let anyone mow his lawn.

In the kitchen, the phone rang, much to Lillian's dismay. She was doing dishes, and her hands were wet and soapy. After quickly drying her hands on a dish towel, she answered, "General Washington's residence."

"Mom, it's me, Wendy. Do you have time to talk?"

"Oh, Honey, I always have time for you. Has anything changed from yesterday that I should be concerned about?" She smiled, glad to hear from her daughter.

"I've reached a decision. I want your and Dad's blessing, or maybe your reasons why I might be wrong."

"Honey, slow down. Do you want your father on the extension? It seems it might be something he would need to hear if you're asking his opinion."

"Sure, Mom, if he isn't busy."

"Hold on. I'll take the extension to him. He was just getting the mower ready to cut the lawn."

Wendy heard her mother place the receiver on the kitchen counter. She smiled, knowing they still had an old-fashioned wall-mounted phone, a princess model. Her stomach attempted to tie itself in knots, as she waited for the discussion to begin.

"We're here, Honey," Lillian said. "What's on your mind?"

"Mom and Dad, I want you to hear me out before you say anything. Is that OK?"

"Wendy," her father said, "we'll do our best to let you speak your say, but you know us. If we interrupt, we'll apologize now. Go ahead, my little soldier."

"I haven't had a restful night's sleep since the night before Lamar told me about what he did, back on the beach in Puerto Rico." She hesitated and swallowed, expecting her father to interject, but he didn't

"That is, until last night. I had a really restful night. I slept all the way through without any nightmares or sleepless fidgeting, with my mind running at a thousand miles an hour.

"It's because I finally came to a decision. That's what I want your blessing and support with. I...I'm going to let Lamar back into my life. I still love him. He's a great father to our children, and he wants to be a good husband to me. I finally felt that if the government could forgive his transgressions, and if I was raised to believe God could forgive even the most-grievous sins of a repentant man, how could I not do the same and let him back into our lives, so we can be a family again?

"I guess I'd like to know if you feel I'm making a big mistake, or that you might treat Lamar differently and make him feel unwelcome in our family."

She waited anxiously for their answer.

General Samson looked as alert and refreshed as the day Lamar first met him, sitting behind his desk on the top floor of the DHS building, smiling at a picture of his old friend. He was a young Captain, dressed in jungle green pants sporting an M16 propped on his leg with bandoliers crisscrossing his bare chest in Viet Nam, Horace Washington. Lamar knew the stress of the operation was intense, as he checked and rechecked his agents' progress.

Lamar gave the general's offer a lot of thought. He felt he had a viable alternative to offer, but he was waiting for the general to get off the phone. He was currently listening to an update on the operation from the lead FBI Special Agent, Max Gordon. He was the one that wanted to continue hunting the leader of the drug-smuggling operation that delivered the materials and carried the bombs put on the ships, the one General Samson had to ring in to just concentrate on the operation.

As soon as the crisis ended, Lamar knew Gordon would resume the hunt. He wouldn't let such a thing go until he knew who masterminded the plot and had the man arrested. SA Max Gordon had the tenacity of a world-class bloodhound. Once it had the trail of its prey, it wouldn't stop until the prey was taken down or it was called off the hunt. Even then, there would be the urge to break ranks and return to the hunt. Lamar kept hoping the general would come through and end the hunt for good.

He sat across the desk from the general, watching and listening to what he said about the operation. It was clear most of the ships were cleared of their deadly limpet mines. *Real mines,* he thought. The last part of the operation was happening even as the general spoke on the phone. The situation made Lamar wonder if it was the wrong time to approach the general with his idea.

General Samson finally hung up and looked at Lamar in consternation. Lamar didn't know if it was the operation or if was that it hadn't even been an hour since he and the general talked, letting Lamar spill everything in his heart before he calmly wiped away his sins and offered him almost-saintly status.

"Well, Lamar, the operation is a little behind schedule, but so far, so good. What brings you to me so soon?"

"It's your offer, General. I've gone over it since we talked. It's all I've been able to think about. I know I'm in no position to negotiate, but it seems that's part of my DNA. I have to be true to my character if I ever hope to move forward from my past. It's just that I can't see being a full-time employee of the DHS."

Much to Lamar's surprise, the general's expression didn't change one bit. Lamar gulped and pitied anyone stupid enough to play poker with that man.

"I make a pretty good living doing my financial advisory work, as I'm sure you know from checking my background. You probably know more about me than I do. You know, then, that I make a good living.

"My counteroffer is that I'm willing to be at your beck and call if you need a different perspective. I'll remain on the job until my assistance is no longer needed. I'll give you information on anything I can offer by doing research and giving you a different perspective on possible ways terrorism can be brought into the country.

"I don't want to be paid, though. I owe you and my country so much, I don't want to profit from that work. I'd call it *pro bono*. That's my counteroffer."

He watched the general's face for a reaction. The man had an uncanny ability to hide his emotions, and Lamar felt he was staring into a vast abyss of neutrality.

The sound-powered phone beside Karen Ann's bunk rang, bringing her out of a blissful sleep, back into the reality of responsibility and command. "Captain."

"Captain, Watch Officer Hanratty here, with the wakeup call you requested."

"Thank you, Mr. Hanratty. Where are we with the lightering operation?"

"Just about complete, Skipper. One tug has already shut down, and the other is topping off as we speak. I've spoken with the agent, and they have the pilots scheduled for 1000 hours. We'll arrive at our pier shortly after 1600 to begin the final offload. Do you want breakfast brought to your cabin, Skipper?"

"Thank you, Mr. Hanratty, but no. I'll head to the officer's mess when I'm ready. When the last tug is safely away, let's get the engines fired up and the crew ready to bring on the Pilots and weigh anchor. I don't want to miss our docking time. I'll see you once I finish breakfast."

She hung up and walked toward the head to wash up for the coming day's work.

Showered and refreshed, she dressed in her khakis. As she slid her phone into her breast pocket, she realized she hadn't answered Larry's text. She sat on her bunk and read it over.

So glad to hear from you. Can't wait to see you! Let me know how much time you'll have, so I can get off work. Be safe on the big blue, Honey. Thinking of you and our time in Norfolk. Can't wait for Philly.

Larry

He added a kiss emoji after his name. She smiled, thinking back to Norfolk and how much she enjoyed being with him. She felt young again, almost like being a teenager who was with her teenage crush. She realized Larry was the reason she never got serious with another man.

Time is ticking. If I want him to get to Philly for a couple of days, I'd better let him know.

She typed a text to tell him where she'd be and when to meet her. With her fingers crossed and a quick knock on the wooden paneling of her stateroom's bulkhead for good luck, she pressed *Send*.

The phone went into her breast pocket, and she walked toward the officer's mess and a well-deserved breakfast.

"We've got one in the backyard shed," Whittington whispered into the radio to the team. "I see two moving in the house."

He heard them count off in acknowledgement. All were poised to go the moment they received the OK.

Ari Bohanni lifted the receiver of his desk phone. *"Na'am?"* he said, meaning yes in Arabic.

"My Great Mullah, we have received confirmation that the final unit has been armed. Do you wish to have these agents return home, as the others were ordered to do?" the communications officer asked.

"Na'am." He slammed down the receiver to end the call, cursing the air his predecessor breathed while conceiving such a half-baked plan and exposing their organization to the world instead of letting Hamas or Al Qaeda or any of the other well-known terrorist organizations they had on the payroll handle such a high-risk-low-reward scheme.

In the palace's communication room, the watch officers coded the outgoing message and sent it quickly, hoping the agents would send a reply quickly, so they'd be through working with their new Mullah for the day.

Bill Whittington used his night-vision goggles to stare at the backyard across the street, watching the shed to ensure he knew where all the terrorists were. Something nudged his back, and he froze, mind racing, wondering if one of the terrorists had escaped surveillance and spotted him, or maybe the owners of the house whose lawn he trespassed on had gotten up early and seen him, coming out to investigate.

He slowly lowered his goggles and raised his free hand, whispering, "I can explain my actions, Sir," while trying to reach his service weapon without being seen.

There was no reply. Bill thought it was time to act. He grabbed his weapon and spun around, aiming it at the tomcat that brushed against him. It screeched once and batted at the gun with a paw before walking away slowly, as if to say, *No one comes into my territory without being checked out.*

He sighed in relief, then chuckled and realized he'd just been busted by a cat. He returned to a sitting position and saw that the small rays of light coming from the shed door were gone.

Damn! I missed his exit. I don't know where he is. I have to find him to make sure all are accounted for.

He scanned the darkness with his NVGs, looking for the missing perpetrator, when a light came on in the house, almost blinding him and making him quickly lower the goggles. After blinking a few times to regain his vision, he focused on the window where a light shone and saw a shadow moving inside.

That must be him. What the hell is he doing?

He knew the other two terrorists were already in bed. Each went to a separate room. After a few minutes, he saw their lights go out, and no one moved in those areas ever since. He kept his main attention on the third man, the only awake terrorist.

The terrorist occupying his attention was Sledge Hammer's "Laurel," but the FBI boat crew dubbed him "Moe," with his accomplices named "Larry" and "Curly." Curly was the coxswain of the boat until he ran them aground. The team was waiting for Moe to give Curly a two-finger poke in the eye, while Curly would split the fingers with his hand and do the Curly Shuffle.

Whittington didn't care much about what the trio did on the water. His only identifying clue with the boat team was that Moe was the tallest, and Curly was heavier, so he called them by the team's Three Stooges monikers.

"Lead to all units," he said softly. "Larry and Curly appear to have turned in. Moe is still up, working on something in the house. Out."

He heard them call off their numbers in reply.

A glance to the east showed him the sky was beginning to lighten from the deep blackness of true night. Shaking his head, he realized something had to happen soon. He was badly exposed, and people would be getting up.

Overhead came the whine of four large engines, and he looked up to see a C-17 cargo plane with two bright landing lights shining into the darkness, descending toward Dover Air Force Base. That was the country's receiving unit for all the servicemen and women killed overseas. Their bodies were brought home in such planes, and seeing one brought a chill to his bones and repurposed his commitment to the mission.

Whittington never thought of himself as religious, but he silently prayed to his Maker that if there were any coffins aboard that flight, the occupants hadn't died in vain.

CHAPTER 36

Larry rolled out of bed and let Harry, his faithful Cocker Spaniel, into the backyard to do his morning business. After starting the coffee, he went to his bedroom to start his morning routine. He was pretty regimented in how he did things, but that just assured he accomplished everything he felt he needed to do to begin his day. He always started out feeling he accomplished something that day, even if it was no more than checking and cleaning up his email account. It felt good to start the day with something accomplished, which would hopefully set the tone for the day.

As he said to anyone who commented on how regimented he was about his routine, "Success leads to more success. I'm one up on the next guy before I even step out the door."

After he walked into his bedroom, his cell phone growled like a Harley Davidson motorcycle, which meant he received a text. He disconnected the phone from its overnight charger and looked at the screen.

Much to his delight, it was from Karen Ann, and he smiled, as he read her words. Her ship would be tying up at the Fort Mifflin Terminal south of the Walt Whitman Bridge. She would remain in port for forty-eight hours.

It was his first day off of the two per week he usually had. If he wanted to spend the night with Karen Ann on the night before she set sail again, he had to ask for the following day off, too.

First thing, he had to run to work and put in for leave for the day he was supposed to return to work. It would be tight, and he hoped he could get off on such short notice, but he had a personal day he could use if it came to that. He'd have to check the book to make sure a relief was available before he put in his A/L request or switch it to P/L. He didn't want to miss any time with Karen Ann.

His morning routine would be rearranged, but he didn't mind at all. With a smile, he walked to the bathroom to shower and shave.

The terrorist labeled Moe went back into the house and found his cohorts asleep. They'd be little help in decoding the reply, and, if an answer needed to be sent, he would have to code it and send it to Mecca himself.

He wasn't very happy with the other members of his team, adding the item to the evening's earlier fiasco in the boat. The work had to be done, though, since Bohanni was their new Mullah, and he didn't want to make him upset.

He got to work decoding the message. After thirty laborious minutes, he read the completed message in surprise. They were being pulled back, without even a "well done" or "Allah be praised for your work fighting the devil." There was no praise for everything they did to meld into a foreign society and remain unnoticed and unsuspected. It was all for nothing.

There would be many other opportunities if they remained in place, though. He slammed down the message, cursing and raising his fists. Finally, he felt so disheartened, he covered his face with his hands and screamed a curse on the new Mullah.

"Seven years! For seven years, we've lived with these infidels and acted like we wanted to be like them, and for what?"

Still, he was a good soldier, so he would obey the orders from his new commanding officer. He went back to work, formulating and coding the reply to be sent to Mecca.

"Wendy," Horace said, "I don't want to speak for your mother, so I'll just say my piece and let her say hers."

Wendy's mind went through a tumult of heart-wrenching emotions, and she immediately began preparing a defense of her decision.

"I've always thought a lot of Lamar. I was truly dismayed to find out all the things he did. Bringing drugs into the country to sell to those who are weak is bad enough, but it affected his own kind, young African Americans who need our support and encouragement. Then they can rise from the squalor in our inner cities.

"He betrayed you, his children, and his country. I'm concerned about all that, but he hurt my little girl with his deception. That's an ultimate sin in my eyes.

"I must add, with all the things he did, there's a good man inside. When faced with two ways out when his house of cards began to crumble, he first got his family to safety, then he confessed his crimes to you, and then to us. I chose to try to make the most of the situation by offering to take him to someone who'd be able to use it and who would also treat Lamar fairly.

"I didn't take Lamar to see General Samson to get preferential treatment, just fair treatment. I had no idea how the situation would turn out, but it seems Lamar came through with the best outcome I could have imagined. His decision to confess and provide as much help as he could to prevent any more damage being done to our country saved him from a multitude of very bad outcomes.

"This isn't over yet. There's still real danger for you and the children from the people he's trying to bring down, not to mention the drug cartel, which will be looking for another transport system for their drugs. They won't be happy about this, either.

"Wendy, you're my only child and have been the light of my life, second only to your mother. I've always been proud of the way you've led your life. Your decisions have been sound and carefully thought out. Based on that knowledge, I will support you any way I can. I'll do my best to base my treatment of Lamar on the decision he made to face whatever the law might have in store for him. I give you my full blessing. I won't hold any ill will toward him or treat him any differently, although I'll pay more attention to the details I should have seen earlier.

"I hope I've given you what you need from me, so you can move on with your life. I don't want to see my baby sad anymore. If this is what you want, I won't stand in your way."

Wendy felt herself breathing easily again. "Thank you, Daddy. I weighed the facts of this, and I tried to keep my heart out of the equation, but I realized it's just as much part of the answer as my rational mind. Mom, I haven't heard your answer yet, so I'll let you have your say, too. Please be frank. If you don't agree with Daddy, that's OK. I want to know what you feel about my decision."

There was a pregnant pause in the conversation. Time stretched for Wendy.

Finally, Lillian cleared her throat. "Wendy, yesterday when you called me and said you were battling with your feelings over this decision, I didn't offer an opinion either way. I let you bounce your emotions off me so you could get a better handle on what you were feeling and what your choices were. You didn't ask for advice or opinions, so I didn't give any.

"Today, you seem to want your father's and my opinions, or maybe a mutual acceptance of your decision. I've always liked Lamar and appreciated how well he provided for you and the kids. I'm a little confused how he went about it. Was it the fruits of his ill-gotten gains that gave you your lifestyle?"

"Mom, I can only tell you what he told me when I asked him the same thing. I've never known him to outright lie to me, so I believed his answer. He said he never used any of the monies he acquired through his illegal activities for his home or business life. He banked every penny from that after his mother died. He admitted he used some of that money to get her and his brother out of the city and into better surroundings. The rest is in an offshore bank account he started when he first got paid for transporting drugs in and money out of the country.

"He said he plans to use his ill-gotten gains to create inner-city rehab centers to try to heal some of the victims of drug addiction he created or were created by others like him. I believe him on that. We're well off and live very well, but we still have a budget, and, when the market goes bad, it hits us as well as everyone else. There are times when we get a little overextended. If he was using drug money, we wouldn't need to tighten our belts and rework the budget to make ends meet."

"Very well, then, Wendy. I guess I can formulate an answer for you."

Moe finished coding the reply requested from Mecca and was walking out the back door to send it when he saw it was morning, and the sky was slowly lightning. He smiled, knowing how the world would be forever changed in four hours, once those timers clicked down, and the charges on the infidels' ships went off. They were set to coordinate with the other bombs up and down the East Coast and throughout the Gulf of Mexico the other cells armed earlier.

"Allah be praised," he whispered, closing the door and walking toward the shed.

Whittington looked up at the lightning sky, too, when he heard the door slam shut behind Moe. He turned and saw Moe walking toward the backyard shed. He also saw the hedge being lit from the house behind him, with his shadow visible against it. Turning, he saw movement in the house and realized the occupants were up, beginning their day. He had to move and still keep surveillance on the terrorists.

"I have to move," he told his teams. "The neighbors are waking up, and Moe's back in the shed. The rest of you sit tight and acknowledge."

He quickly heard acknowledgements from the teams.

The MV *Palm Princess* just finished its transit of Delaware Bay and the river and approached its assigned pier at Fort Mifflin. The docking pilot arrived with the tugboats and positioned the tugs alongside the ship to nudge the behemoth to the dock. The two river pilots departed after the docking pilot was aboard, after they successfully guided the ship up the bay and river. Their job done, they moved to a downbound vessel back to Lewes and home.

The final portion of the arriving evolution was, for Karen Ann, the most nerve-wracking of any. Her vessel was in the hands of others. Although she knew they were professionals who were good at their jobs, it was still her responsibility to see the ship safely to its dock.

She was on the outboard bridge wing, studying the tug arrangement and ensuring all lines were in order. Her deck crew was good at its job, and she knew it, but she believed in the motto, *Trust but verify*. She always checked to make sure. On those rare times when she had to point out something, she knew she probably saved someone from injury or death.

Seeing all was in order, she went back to the bridge to observe the docking pilot and ensure her crew responded as needed to bring the vessel to its pier.

They moved very slowly toward the pier. Karen Ann took the handheld radio to the inboard bridge wing to supervise tying up to the pier. As she looked up and down the length of her ship, preparing to order the first line sent ashore, she saw Larry standing on the dock, waiting for her. Her heart skipped a beat in anticipation of being in his arms again, but her professionalism and pride in her abilities took hold. Wanting to do a good job for her new observer, she immediately focused on getting the ship secured. Feelings in her loins, however, reacted to her innermost thoughts.

She sneaked a brief glance at Larry, and he returned her look with a suave salute, paying tribute to her status as Any Waters Unlimited Tonnage Master, a feat held by very few men, let alone women. He was proud of the little galley girl who set her heart on going to sea and was willing to disobey and estrange her parents to follow her dreams. He was also proud of himself for recognizing the sparkle in her eye and knowing she wouldn't be denied. That was why he offered a compromise to Karen Ann and her parents years earlier, something they could live with and be happy about.

His loins twitched in anticipation, too. Smiling, he backed away, so the line handlers could get the big ship secured to the pier.

A short time later, the accommodation ladder was positioned and secured so people on the ship could disembark, and personnel waiting to board could get on. Ship arrivals were a busy time, with plenty of comings and goings of officials visiting the ship to conduct business, including customs officials. The ship arrived from a foreign port and was back in the U.S., so DEA officials had to sweep the ship for illegal drugs or contraband someone might be attempting to smuggle in to the States. Port workers needed to prepare to offload the ship's cargo.

The list went on to include union officials, shipping agents, and company representatives, with an occasional visitor to someone in the ship's company. In the cacophony of all the people coming and going, the captain had to pay off the crewmen who would be leaving on vacation or going back to the union hall to seek employment on another vessel.

A newly arrived vessel was a busy place, and all of it had to be done in a hurry. A ship that sat still wasn't making money, which was bad for business. No company executive wanted to see a ship remain idle any longer than it must to discharge its cargo or take on new cargo. The science of all those moves was figured down to the minute to ensure no ship remained in port any longer than necessary.

Karen Ann brought Larry onboard and asked him to wait in her stateroom until she finished with the ship's business. She knew she wouldn't be able to focus on necessary tasks if he was within view. Larry obliged her, because she was the captain, and he knew how a guest should act aboard a ship. A captain's requests were just polite orders. As a captain himself, even if only on a small ship traversing a bay, he understood her job.

The seaman assigned to escort Larry to the captain's stateroom was polite and efficient, although he added it was highly irregular.

The captain usually didn't allow even the steward into her stateroom, let alone someone unattended.

"The captain and I go way back," Larry assured the man, "to when both of us were very young. I guess she doesn't think of me as just anyone."

"That's good enough for me," the seaman muttered, closing the door behind him.

Larry wasn't a nosy person who rooted through someone's personal belongings when left alone, so he was ready to sit down when he saw a picture tucked into the desk blotter. It came from the time when Karen Ann worked in the galley on the ferry boat.

He picked it up and saw how well-worn it was, with curled corners and the look of something handled a lot. "Wow. That was a long time ago."

He couldn't believe how young he looked, wearing his khaki uniform and standing near the ship's ensign, the American flag. The sun set behind him, and tankers were at anchor on the horizon.

As he went to set it back in place, he naturally turned it over to see if anything was written on the back, and immediately blushed. He hadn't known he could still do that, but he did, like a schoolboy caught with a copy of *Playboy* by his mother.

On the back was a carefully drawn heart with an arrow through it, with the words *Larry + Karen Ann* written inside the heart. Below were the words, *Ah, but he's married. This will never be,* followed by a small heart broken by a jagged line down the middle.

He knew that was something schoolgirls put in their schoolbooks when they had their first love. Some of them wrote, *Mr. and Mrs. So-and-so,* imaging life with that person.

He slowly put the picture back and sat down to contemplate the meaning. His mind spinning, he decided to put thoughts of the picture aside and wait for Karen Ann to finish her business so they could go out to dinner and head back to the hotel he booked for the two nights he hoped to spend with her.

CHAPTER 37

Lamar sat across from General Samson, feeling like a schoolboy in the principal's office waiting for punishment to be rendered. His knees shook slightly, and he fidgeted with his hands. He couldn't believe how nervous he felt. He had mingled with governors, senators, congressmen, and other well-known public figures when he handled their financial needs, and he never felt that way before. What did that man have that made him want to be accepted and found worthy so badly, to the point his body began shaking?

Five minutes passed, but Lamar felt it was more like five hours. His stomach churned, and acid gnawed at his stomach lining.

Finally, the general shifted in his chair and cleared his throat. "Well, now, Lamar. That's a very interesting proposal. I need to do some research to see if it's even possible. There are many security issues involved, which would have to be worked around if you just want to be on call for consultation. That includes setting up secure data lines and voice communications, to name a couple. There is also the fact that the government doesn't know how to work with someone off the books.

"I'll delve into this once we're secured from the present operation."

"I understand, General. Those are aspects I didn't think of, and I can see their importance. I'll wait to see what you come up with, and we can move on from there."

"All right. I need to get back to work on this operation. If you come up with any more thoughts about this, be sure to bring them to me." He opened a folder on his desk, signaling the end of the meeting and hinting that Lamar needed to return to the anteroom and do the same.

"Thank you for your time, General." Lamar retired to his work space, leaving the general to carry the burden of national security on his shoulders alone.

Bill Whittington felt anxious to move. His attention was diverted from watching the shed, looking for Moe to monitor his movements, and to check the house behind him to make sure his cover wasn't blown.

He remembered how the tomcat busted him, and that gave him an idea where he could hide in plain sight. First, he needed to contact Max in Washington. They hadn't spoken in a while, so he knew Max was probably pacing his office, wondering what was going on.

"All teams, I'm leaving channel to check in with the boss," he whispered into his earbud mike.

Hearing their replies, he switched over to the secure line to call Max.

"Special Agent Gordon," Max said immediately.

"It's Bill, Max. Just checking in to keep you abreast of the situation. It appears the lead perp is sending a reply to his headquarters. I'm on foot but will have to move soon, as the neighborhood is waking up."

"OK. Sounds good, Bill. Thanks for the update. I should hear from NSA soon to confirm the signal. Then hopefully, we can put this whole nasty business to bed."

"Roger that, Max. I'm getting too old for this shit anymore," Bill said tiredly.

The call ended, and Bill changed channels to say, "Lead back on channel." The teams replied briefly, then all was silent again.

The sun edged closer to the horizon. The clear sky became lighter, and only the brightest stars were still showing. Bill had to move or risk being compromised, so he put his plan into action.

He had to remove his FBI body armor and place it somewhere accessible but hidden for quick donning in case the situation went sideways. Glancing around, he saw a low blue spruce tree that could hide his vest. He slipped it off and stood, not wanting to run, just move with purpose to avoid drawing attention if anyone saw him before he could slip the vest under the tree.

His plan was to pretend to be a pet owner looking for his runaway, but he couldn't go into character until there was open activity in the neighborhood, so he would walk slowly up and down the street while keeping the shed in view and maintaining his watch of Moe.

Lillian Washington had a mind of her own she developed through years of being an army wife and, by default, a single parent for most of Wendy's early years. Lillian had to deal with extended periods of separation from her husband, not knowing if he would return from deployment or if she would become single permanently. She also grew up in the "ban the bra" and "civil rights" eras and was well-versed in speaking her mind.

"Wendy, I raised you to be an independent woman. We sent you to the best schools we could afford and hoped you would take advantage of the opportunities you faced to learn and grow. Your father and I gave you as good a life as we could. It was tough in the lean years, and it was harsh on you to move as often as we did during your formative years. You bounced from school to school, always having to make new friends and say good-bye to them a couple years later.

"All that formed you as you are today, and I believe you're a wonderful, kind, loving woman who's generous to a fault at times, but you're also strong and have the ability to make tough decisions. I've seen you do it.

"You'll always be my little girl. If you are hurt physically or in the heart, I'm ready to fight to protect you. That's my right as your mother. I can only agree with your father on continuing your relationship with Lamar. We will keep an eye out for any sign something is going on, though, and I will speak my mind. I'm sickened by what he did to you, his children, our family, and the poor people whose lives he helped ruin with drugs.

"He did the proper thing when necessary, though, and he stood up for his country by coming forward to help, and, hopefully, defeat those seeking to harm this great land of ours. I respect him and admire his fortitude to do the right thing in the end.

"I'll allow Lamar back into our lives to begin building a new relationship with us if that's your desire. That's the best I can offer, Honey. It's not a free pass. Our love and trust need to be earned again. I'm happy that you reached a decision that feels right for you and your family, and I will always support you."

The connection was silent again, as Wendy fought back tears of gratitude. "Thank you. I love both of you, too. I'll be more vigilant, too. Although I love him with my whole heart, he has to earn my trust again. That will be a large part of our conversation once he's finished in DC."

Wendy ended the call with, "I love you, Mom and Dad."

"I love you," they replied.

Horace, bringing the extension back into the house, found Lillian in the kitchen. When she turned toward him, he saw tears running down her cheeks.

"No, no, no, Honey," she said, seeing his concern. "It's all right. These are tears of relief. I was so worried about her and her well-being after our conversation yesterday. Now it seems she has a handle on her situation and can keep things in perspective.

"Yesterday, when she called me, she sounded like a giddy teenager. I was worried she'd fallen into a dream world. I didn't get a wink of sleep last night. Thank God she called this morning with her feet back on the ground."

Horace, wrapping his arms around her, looked down at her tear-stained face. "That's why I love you so much, my precious little flower." He leaned over and kissed her forehead.

Karen Ann wrapped up her official duties very quickly and gathered an overnight bag so she could spend the night with Larry at the hotel down the street near the Philadelphia International Airport where Larry made reservations.

"Can we stop by the hotel room, so I can freshen up and change clothes before dinner?"

"Sure."

Over dinner, she regaled him with the events of her latest voyage and informed him how the SEALs received confirmation that the bomb was attached to the ship, how they met the sub and the SEALs who removed the bomb, then the long wait for the terrorists to come out to arm the dummy bomb.

Larry was a good listener. Neither of them realized it was almost ten o'clock until their waiter appeared to say it was last call for drinks, because the bar was closing.

They apologized profusely for hogging their table and left him a large tip to make amends for their bad manners.

Once outside, though, they broke into uncontrollable laughter over the whole episode. They held hands as they laughed and walked, not watching where they were going, bumping into strangers, apologizing, and starting over once they were a short distance away. They felt like they were in their teens and couldn't help themselves.

Once back at the hotel, they rode a crowded elevator and tried to behave themselves. After they got off and the doors closed behind them, they laughed all the way to their room, each trying to hush the other for being too loud, which triggered more laughter. If they'd been drinking a lot, they might've had an excuse, but neither had more than three drinks that evening, and they were sober. Their intoxication came from their lust for each other.

As they opened the door to their room, he swept her off her feet and carried her across the threshold.

"Well, aren't you the gallant one?" she asked. "Is this the honeymoon night I never had?"

They laughed again.

He carried her to the bed and said, "No, my sweet. I just want you to know how much you mean to me." He set her down and lay in the space beside her, rolling her on top in one motion.

It was the start of the most-intimate love-making session Karen Ann ever experienced in her forty-odd years. It wasn't just the sexual encounter of a schoolgirl fantasy. It was something she never felt before, and she enjoyed it more because of that.

When Larry woke the next morning, he reached over and found empty space in the bed, which surprised and worried him until he heard water running in the shower. With a grin, he joined her, startling her pleasantly. He stood behind her and wrapped his arms around her, bringing his erection against her perfectly rounded bottom.

"You seem happy to see me," she said, rubbing her ass against his erection. "Didn't you get enough last night?"

"I don't think I'll ever get enough of you, Karen Ann." He held her tighter, massaging her erect nipples and firm, round breasts. She liked being pinched slightly and responded with moans of pleasure.

She slid her hands behind him, grabbing his butt and pulling him closer. Warm shower water cascaded over them, increasing the effect, heightening their sensitive nerve endings, and bringing their desires to a climax.

He guided her to bend over and entered her. His stamina from the previous night was restored, and her vaginal muscles contracted in spasms, signaling the onset of an orgasm. He increased his thrusting, and her moans grew louder, her breath in short gasps.

He had to concentrate to hear her words, but he slowly understood them.

"Fuck me harder! Deeper! Don't stop! Fuck me, please! Don't ever stop!"

Larry obliged as much as he could on weakening legs that started to shake, as he built to his own orgasm. They were two animals in the full throes of rut, and nothing would stop them from completing their lustful act of sharing while also being selfish about its desired conclusion.

Arching her back and thrusting her head back, Karen Ann let out her deepest, most-aggressive moan, bringing her to a rewarding orgasm, to which Larry responded by thrusting even harder, as her vaginal muscles contracted around him and created a tug of war with his spasming member that sent him into his own orgasm.

They held onto each other, feeling like two spasming masses of jelly, trying to catch their breath. They felt as if their bones had melted, leaving behind nothing but limp cartilage to keep the form of their bodies.

She laboriously asked, "See what you did? Now I'll be late for work."

That only served to bring back the laughter of the previous evening and a giddy atmosphere.

The shed door opened. Moe left, closing and locking the door behind him, then went inside the house without glancing at Whittington even once.

"Moe's back in the roost," Bill told his team. "Shouldn't be long now. Make final preparations and stand by for the go command. Remember, no sirens or lights. Absolutely no speeding in this neighborhood. There are toys in every yard, so there will be kids going to school soon. I want this quiet and smooth. Over."

All four teams acknowledged.

Max sat at his desk, rubbing his four-day stubble and wondering why anyone wanted to grow a beard. He tried it several times in his life, but he couldn't get past the seven-day mark before the itching drove him crazy, so he shaved it off.

His phone rang.

"Special Agent Gordon," he said quickly.

"This is Section Chief Pickles of the NSA. We have the final confirmation sent from Delaware. They're calling all cells home, and this last one isn't very happy. They feel they can do more, because they think their cover is secure."

As Pickles spoke, he hoped his name would be remembered, not those of the two nerds, when promotions and gratitude for a job well done was given.

"Thank you, Section Chief. Please extend my thanks for a job well done to your two employees." He hung up, leaving Pickles cursing.

Max immediately punched a number into his cell.

The neighborhood was starting to wake up. The first workers were leaving, and a teen stood on a corner, waiting for a school bus. Bill used his ruse to create a viable reason for being on the street. No one challenged him or paid him any notice.

It was a great relief, though, when his cell phone buzzed in his ear. "Whittington."

"Go, go, go!"

"Go, go, go," Bill repeated, before hanging up. Switching back to his radio, he said, "All teams, go. I repeat, go."

He walked back to the house where he hid in the yard all night to pick up his vest and take his position for the raid.

A few minutes later, he was ready and saw the SUVs approaching the house. He saw Moe in the kitchen, preparing what looked like tea, but he wasn't sure. He also looked like he had his prayer rug under one arm. It wasn't clear if he just finished his sunrise prayer or was ready to begin.

He radioed his teams about where to set up the breach of the premises, and all acknowledged. He would remain outside as backup, in case one of the suspects evaded capture and ran. He refused to contemplate any scenario in which the takedown didn't go as planned. It was just a basic house breach and capture of three unknown suspects who also happened to be jihad terrorists.

Once they were ready, he said, "Breach."

Team One fired a flash grenade through the living room window. One second after the glass broke, Team Two battered down the front door and entered, while Team Three did the same through the kitchen door. Team Four was dispersed below each bedroom window in case anyone tried to escape. Bill stood near the tree where he hid his body armor ready to backup any of his teams.

He saw Moe's reaction to the flash-bang grenade. His cup flew from his hand, spilling hot liquid on him and scalding him. The other two perps were so startled, they ran from their bedrooms and were met with M-16s aimed at their faces. Each tried to retreat to his room, but another man in full body armor and gas mask was outside each window, aiming his weapon through the glass he just broke.

The time lapse was three minutes before all three terrorists were handcuffed and walked toward the waiting SUVs, one for each of them. They would be alone from that point forward and wouldn't see their compatriots for a very long time.

Larry and Curly jabbered all the way to their vehicle. Bill assumed they'd continue on the ride to DC. His heart went out to the four agents who were assigned to transport them. He'd seen suspects with diarrhea of the mouth before. He wanted to gag them before they were fully into custody, but he didn't.

Each SUV was rigged with a digital recorder to capture what each suspect said for later analysis. Moe was different, defiant yet stoic, walking erect and proud and not speaking a word. He turned to look at Bill, as one leader to another, and smiled. It gave Bill a chill down his spine, because it was a victory smile, not defeat, as if to say, *We will never be defeated. More are coming.*

Whittington gave orders to the remaining agents to put up police tape and go through the property to see what goodies were left behind. He also passed out personal NBC (nuclear, biological, and chemical) sniffers to each agent. None of them wanted to be surprised by any remnants of bomb material left behind, or even worse, any prep work toward their next attack. He hoped it was just a precaution, and no one needed a sniffer alarm.

That would be a good way to end this operation, he thought.

He called SA Gordon.

It's over, Max."

"Give me the details."

"The takedown went like a dry run. No shots were fired except the flash bang. We caught them with their pants down. All three perps are on their way to DC. We're tearing the place apart now to look for anything useful."

"Good job, Bill. Let me know when you wrap it up. Do you have the locals involved yet?"

"I think someone called them. I hear sirens in the distance. I was going to do that after I called you."

"OK. Glad everyone is good. I'll let you deal with the LEOs (Law Enforcement Officers). Good luck. See you soon."

Max hung up and called the Director of Homeland Security.

The message light on the bedside phone blinked, and Larry lifted the receiver to punch in the code. He received a short message that his package was ready for pickup at the front desk.

Karen Ann and he shared two wonderful nights in Philly, seeing the sights and enjoying the city. Since she was preparing for work, he slipped from the room and went to the lobby for his package. Opening it in the tiny Internet room, he saw the four-by-six-inch picture they posed for at the restaurant the night before and nodded.

He took the picture from the frame and drew on the back a large heart with an arrow through it. Inside the heart, he wrote *Larry and Karen Ann.* Below it he added the words, *Never say never.*

He slid it into its frame with a sticky note attached that read, *Read the back,* then he rewrapped it before taking it to their room to hustle her along.

Arriving at the Fort Mifflin Terminal gate, they showed their credentials. The guard told him to pull his Corvette into the parking area behind the gate. A golf cart would be brought around for Captain Murphy.

"Thanks for your time and the golf cart," Larry said, pulling into the parking area.

Karen Ann reached for the door handle to open it, and Larry stopped her.

"Larry, the cart is coming around the corner."

"Just a kiss good-bye until I get you back." He slid his little package into her overnight bag. The tag on it read, *Don't open until underway.*

She giggled, leaned in, and kissed him, then exited the car and walked to her ride to the ship. He watched her from behind, loving what he saw.

CPSIA information can be obtained
at www.ICGtesting.com
Printed in the USA
BVHW040026211121
622157BV00002B/3